PRAISE FOR

The Surrogate

"*The Surrogate* is a fearless thriller that tackles uncharted territory with uncompromised skill and ease. It's a terrific and exciting read."

— Bill Myers,
best-selling author of *Eli* and
The Face of God

"Kathy Mackel is one of my favorite writers. Her stuff is always tightly woven and sharp, cutting to the marrow. *The Surrogate* is a prime example of her best work. You'll savor every page."

— Jerry Jenkins,
best-selling author of the *Left
Behind* series and the *Soon* trilogy

"With a deft touch, Kathryn Mackel weaves contemporary ethical issues into an extraordinary pulse-pounding thriller that will keep readers up at night. *The Surrogate* rides like a roller-coaster and reads like a dream!"

— Angela Hunt,
author of *The Debt*

"Kathy's writing is always engaging, drawing me into the drama and conflict. *The Surrogate* drives to the heart issues immediately and doesn't let go. I can't wait to see what is next!"

— Ralph Winter,
Producer X-Men, X2: X-Men
United, and *Planet of the Apes*
Executive Producer *Star Trek V:
Final Frontier*

the Surrogate

by

#3009

KATHRYN MACKEL

WestBow
PRESS

A Division of Thomas Nelson Publishers
Since 1798

visit us at www.westbowpress.com

Published in Nashville, Tennessee, by WestBow Press, a division of Thomas Nelson, Inc.

Publisher's Note: This novel is a work of fiction. Names, characters, places, and incidents are either products of the author's imagination or used fictitiously. All characters are fictional, and any similarity to people living or dead is purely coincidental.

All Scripture quotations are taken from the HOLY BIBLE: NEW INTERNATIONAL VERSION®. Copyright © 1973, 1978, 1984 by International Bible Society. Used by permission of Zondervan Publishing House. All rights reserved.

Library of Congress Cataloging in Publication Data

Mackel, Kathryn, 1950–
    The surrogate / by Kathryn Mackel.
      p. cm.
    ISBN 0-7852-6228-8 (tp)
    I. Title.
PS3613. A2734S87 2004
813'.54—dc22   2004001937

Printed in the United States of America
04 05 06 07 08 — 5 4 3 2 1

To Steve,
for whom there is simply
no replacement

PROLOGUE

he pain cut through her like a knife.

Bethany gripped the podium with one hand, keeping the beat with the other. *It's nothing*, she promised herself. *Just keep the music going.*

Unto us a child is born, she mouthed with her singers.

For unto us a son is given, they answered. The Forge Hill Chorale was forty strong. Kids of many colors, they all had voices of angels—the kids' salvation, the community organizers had hoped when they put together the music program for the charter school.

And his name shall be called—

Michael, Bethany thought, trying to ignore the spasm in her side. They had already decided to name him after her father, the renowned Michael Testamarta. If only he could have lived to see his first grandchild. Bethany leaned her hips into the podium, willing the ache away.

—*Wonderful*, the kids sang.

—*Counselor*, Bethany sang with them, her voice no more than a whisper. The kids' voices were the ones that should be heard. She was there simply to call out their talent.

—*the Mighty God*. Her side cramped. She took quick, shallow breaths.

For unto us a child is born—

Kyle would be so disappointed if something . . . no, she couldn't think that way. The pain was nothing, just a touch of food poisoning or even constipation from the prenatal vitamins. Things were different this time—not even a hint of morning sickness. It was just Murphy's

Law that she would catch a stomach bug the night of the Christmas concert.

Her face flooded with perspiration. Maybe she should sit down, just for a moment. No. She couldn't stop, not now. She had worked too hard, invested long months of cajoling and inspiring to bring these kids from hip-hop to Handel.

The soloists were about to begin. Anthony Martinez stood stiffly, his eyes fixed on Bethany, his fingers white on his folder. You will not crack on the A, she had promised him, though he had at every rehearsal. She smiled as she cued his entrance.

Rejoice greatly, O daughter of Zion, Anthony sang, his tenor vibrant and at perfect pitch.

She brought in the rest of the tenors. *He shall speak peace unto the heathen.* She saw Tyler turn his head to catch Charissa's eye. Rumor was that it was his daughter that Charissa carried. These children bore children as easily as they breathed, it seemed.

He shall gather in the lambs with His arm, and carry them in His bosom.
She let their music fill her.
And gently lead those that are with young.

Bethany relaxed as she led them through the end of the piece, then grinned as she signaled the cutoff. The music stopped. "We'll count three," she had told the accompanist. Any longer and the audience would applaud. She raised her baton–two-three-NOW!

Hallelujah! The kids sang it out joyously, some celebrating the end of their ordeal, others celebrating their own talent. All soared far beyond any height they had imagined.

For the Lord God omnipotent reigneth. The air rippled as the audience members rose from their seats.

Hallelujah! They were in the staggered sections now, the basses leading off in sure, strong tones. The tenors were crisp, the altos shy as always, but perfectly on pitch. The sopranos came in, flying high, then higher.

She loved them with a fire, these kids who had at last surrendered to the touch of the divine that is music. Bethany sang with them, now in full voice.

And He shall reign—

She was flooded with sudden heat. Before she could tighten her grip, the baton flew out of her hand. She kept on conducting—until the pain pierced her from front to back, making her collapse against the podium.

— forever—

Then the blood came, a cruel gush.

—and ever, she sang hopelessly, sinking to her knees.

My frame was not hidden from you

When I was made in the secret place.

When I was woven together in the depths of the earth,

Your eyes saw my unformed body.

(Psalm 139:15–16)

I

Kyle Dolan was convinced that his wife was trying to kill him. Forty degrees with a chill wind, but he was sweating like a prize-fighter.

Fifty feet ahead of him, Bethany poked her stick along the trail, bracing against slick rocks. Headphones on, she conducted an unseen orchestra that long ago had laid down its instruments.

"Bethany!" If Kyle's lungs didn't explode, his heart would. He was an avid racquetball player, but his wife set a killer pace. Was this what she had been doing for the last month—racing up and over mountain trails as if they were highways? He never should have let her go to the New Hampshire farmhouse without him.

"I need the time away. Time to be alone," she had said. Too much consolation from friends and colleagues was choking her in Boston.

She had gone north at the end of March. In the last week of April, spring was in full force in the Mount Washington Valley. The grass was lush and green, the Saco River swollen from snow and running hard. Strawberry plants were already full with foliage, their fruit blossoms just short weeks away.

Beautiful, yes, but Kyle knew that spring in the White Mountains was the most dangerous time of the year. Ice still choked the upper slopes. Snowstorms could spin out of the clouds without warning, stranding hikers who had left the valley in shorts and T-shirts. Even vigorous, experienced climbers weren't immune to the avalanches in the ravines.

And his wife had been climbing there for weeks, all by herself. Anything could have happened. "Bethany!" Kyle bellowed.

She slid the headphones down and scrambled to him. "You look like you're having a heart attack, Southie."

"You won't be laughing when you have to drag my body off this mountain."

She grabbed his side. "Especially with this extra twenty pounds you brought with you." She half-pinched, half-tickled his ribs.

"Looking for love handles?"

Bethany put her lips to his ear. "Looking for love."

He pulled her close, sliding his hands under her backpack. She was hot under her pack but cool against his chest.

"Some heart rate you got going there," she said. "This little stroll too much for you?"

"You. You're too much woman for this Southie kid to handle."

"That's blarney, Dolan. I know you. Deli lunches, stack the ham high. Chinese takeout, extra noodles and double chicken wings. And cookies for dessert. Though I maintain that no one needs dessert after breakfast."

"You sent them to me!" he protested.

"To share with your staff! Not to eat in front of the television every night."

"I was just being a good husband. Doing my duty by eating every single one."

She kissed the tip of his nose. "You are the best husband. I missed you, Kyle."

"I missed you. Oh, how I missed you." He could feel it now, that slight tremble in the small of her back—the crushing fear that this pain would last forever. What he would give to lift that from her, or for her to at least let him help carry it.

He laced his fingers into her hair. Her father had gone gray early, but Bethany didn't even have a hint of silver. Just that rich brown, so dark it was almost black, and glossy, like an elegant cat. And like a cat, she loved having her head rubbed, his fingertips deep in her scalp.

"Beenie, I shouldn't have left you up here so long by yourself."

"I needed the time. But I'm glad you're here now." Her smile was convincing. "So what do you say, old man? We have to summit by noon so we can get down before dark."

"Get down?" He faked a dying gasp. "You mean, there's not a car service up there, waiting for us?"

"There ain't even portapotties up there, sweetie!"

"I've been holding it all morning! And now you're telling me—"

"There's a nice tree, right over there. And there, and there, and there—" Laughing, she started up the trail.

"Hey! You never answered my question," he called after her.

"What question?"

"Pick one."

"Why is the sky blue?" The standard question that always began the *why* game. The *who* game began with *Who's on first?* The *what's up* game began with *What's up, Doc?*

"Why do men sweat and women glow?" Lame choice—Kyle was never as sharp at this as she was. Bethany insisted that he could never win because he wasn't a question kind of guy; he had all the answers. He only wished he did.

"Why do people water their lawns in the rain?" she parried.

"Why do people climb mountains for fun?"

"Oh. So we're getting personal, are we?" Bethany scrambled up a boulder and assumed a prophet's stance. "Answer me this, son of the mountain."

He bowed at the waist, his face grave and attentive. "Speak, daughter of the skies."

She bit her lip, trying to wipe the grin off her face. "Why— WHY—do the Red Sox blow it every year?"

He grabbed his heart, staggering backwards. "Why do I root for them anyway?"

"Why are you such a sweet fool?" Bethany looked sixteen in that moment, her skin clear and unlined, her eyes dancing with mischief. He ran up the trail. Too fast—he slipped, scraping his hand. When he reached her, she took his hand and kissed the scrape.

"Why do I love you so much?" he asked, knowing the answers were endless.

She was silent.

"Beenie. It's your turn," he prompted.

"Why—" She buried herself in his chest.

"Why what?"

"Just why," she whispered to his heart.

The breeze swelled, now cold and raw, sweeping down from the north side of the ridge, the shadowed side where the sun never shone. Kyle held his wife as tightly as he could.

It was not much of an answer, but it was all he had.

———— ∞ ————

Bethany savored this time, the smooth rock under her back, the sun on her face. Her husband beside her, snoring lightly as he slept. She stretched from toes to fingertips, enjoying the warmth in her body, the new strength. Kyle had called her *chiseled* last night, exploring her with love but also care, wanting to make sure she wasn't too thin. He was the athlete, she the artist, but the constant hiking, from dawn to sunset, had made her body hard.

Her heart was proving more difficult to conquer.

"Beenie?" Kyle's eyes were blurry with sleep, his hair flat on one side. Those lines around his eyes were new. But they were inevitable, weren't they? He was forty-one; she was thirty-nine. Still young by many measures, they had lived a lifetime in the past few years.

She kissed his cheek. "It's almost two. We need to get going."

"Not yet," he said, pulling her to him.

"You do realize the whole world can see us up here."

"Let them look." He kissed her, sweet and deep. And then, despite all they had been through, despite how she had failed him, she knew he loved her still.

He sat up and leaned against the boulder, drew her into him, her back against his chest. There was no sign of civilization, only miles of sky, trees, and mountains. "Bethany. There are things we could be doing now."

Bethany pushed away from him. "Like starting down this mountain before the sun goes down and the night wind turns us into giant Popsicles."

"Every day we don't talk, we're a day older. A day further away from what we want."

"There is nothing to discuss." Without thinking, Bethany moved her hand to her abdomen.

"We still have one embryo. It would still be our baby if we used a surrogate."

"It's not that simple, Kyle."

"Maybe not simple—but it has become very routine. Remember that thing on the news last night, about a sixty-year-old woman carrying a baby for her daughter? Easy."

She nodded, watching a redtail hawk cruise in the wind. It was always so easy for Kyle. Something either worked your way or it didn't. Their marriage was a tremendous success. The acclaimed pianist, Bethany Testamarta, and the dashing entrepreneur, Kyle Dolan, were an attractive, exciting couple. Even in private they were a good match. His temperament soothed her; her passion inspired him. Their faith rooted them.

"Won't you at least consider it?"

"I can't." She shouldered her pack, then pulled her cap down on her forehead to hide her face.

He turned her around and pulled her into him. "Hey, it's okay," he whispered. "We'll talk about this later. You'll come around when you have time to think it through."

Bethany hugged him, then turned for the trail. She would never come around. It had taken all her courage to survive the death of her baby and the hysterectomy. She had nothing left to hope with. God had lifted His hand and let nature take its course.

It had been a cruel one.

2

$\mathcal{S}$able Lynde ran for her life.

Fool. There's nothing to be afraid of, she told herself.

Fool. There's plenty to be afraid of.

A wet street, slick with rain and motor oil. A bad neighborhood, teeming with lowlifes, pushers, and prostitutes. A late hour, when respectable people were barricaded behind window bars and deadbolts.

The darkness. Always the darkness. Lurking in alleys, stairwells, doorways. Lingering between the yellow pools cast by streetlights. She knew what foul thing crouched in that darkness, waiting for her to slip. Expecting her to fall.

Sable needed to get back to the apartment. She had installed window bars, deadbolts, and a sophisticated alarm system. But none of it could keep her safe if she wasn't there. She had high-speed cable in her apartment, but today's business required leaving an untraceable trail. She had intended to stay at the Internet Connection for only an hour, but six hours later she pushed back from the workstation, startled to see that night had fallen.

Sable had hopped the bus, gotten off at Ninth Street, and begun walking home. As the rain came down and the darkness closed in, it suddenly seemed better to run. The wind was raw even though it was late April. Her lungs felt like cut glass. As she passed a narrow alley, something shuffled, then grunted. She knew better than to look.

Her building was only three streetlights away. Sable slowed to a walk, focusing on the pap-pap-pap of the rain. Then a slap-slap disturbed the rhythm. Footsteps. *Don't look back; don't show fear,* she knew, though adrenaline raced through her, making her quiver.

6

Sable slid the safety off her pepper spray, but she was still too far away. Use it there and he'd have time to catch up to her, punish her double. Besides, there were things in the darkness that pepper spray wouldn't stop. No, she couldn't think like that. The medication and her own willpower had banished *him*. This was simply someone out for a walk.

Only a few feet away now, coming up even with the edge of her building. Sable broke for the front door. She was inside, then up the stairs. Almost to the top when she tripped, feeling more shock than pain as her chest hit the floor.

She tumbled through the fire door and knew in an instant that this darkness had been prepared for her, that the lightbulb was crushed in its socket. She felt the doors with her fingers as she raced down the hall. When she got to the fifth door, she felt for the key-pad and pressed in her code. The light flashed red.

The fire door opened behind her. She keyed in the numbers again. Finally, green. She unlocked the door one bolt at a time while she aimed the pepper spray toward the stairs. "Stop!" she shouted with every ounce of fierceness she could muster. "I am armed."

The follower stopped walking, started laughing. Then she heard other footsteps. Behind her, trapping her in the darkness.

Oh, God, if You're there, let it be anyone but him.

———

Sand in a sock. Bernard was a professional; he knew how to get the message across without leaving a mark. Sable could ignore the pain that washed over her in hot waves, but no, *I beg you*, she wanted to cry, *don't put me in there*. Before more than a cry could escape her swollen lips, Bernard had duct-taped them shut.

After he bound her wrists and ankles, he threw her into the closet. He slammed the door, leaving her in a musty darkness. The only sounds were her gasps, pinched out through her nose. She smelled *him* first, that odor of decay that was as wet as the blood it had sprung from. The shadows shifted, and she felt him rising from whatever foul place he lay.

Despair gripped her like an icy vise—she had fought and worked and programmed and medicated and put up alarm systems and dead-bolts, but *he* found her anyway. *I will not fear you*, she wanted to cry as a cold finger traced her cheek. But he was over her now, casting a shadow blacker than the darkness.

Welcome back, sweetness.

———

Strong hands pulled Sable out of the darkness. "What are you doing in the closet, Sab—omigosh! Who did this to you?"

Her stomach seized. Bernard had beat her and left her. That she could understand—business was business, and she had defaulted on the payment. But to leave her where *he* could find her, that had been cruel beyond understanding.

"Come on, girl. Get with it!" Cade Parker stood over her, tall, muscular, sandy haired, clean featured. Looking every bit the white knight, though Sable knew better.

As soon as Cade ripped the tape from her mouth, she spoke. "Go away."

"Think maybe I should untie you first?" He ripped the tape off her wrists. "You okay?"

She batted away his hand, then pulled her knees to her chest, blocking him. "I'm fine. Now go away. I can take care of myself."

"Oh, yeah, you look like you're taking great care here."

"What's it to you?"

"What? You think I don't care? No one's going to do this to you and get away—"

"Bernard DuBois gets away with whatever he wants." Just as she thought—that shut up Cade's threats.

"Here. At least let me help you up," he said, boosting her.

Sable shook him off. The nicer Cade was, the more it would cost her. She pushed up, then stumbled down the hall and into the bathroom.

Cade followed her in. "You look like you're going to go face first into the bowl."

"Just give me a minute to myself. Can you do that for me?"

He made a theatrical bow. "I'll just have a look around while you're doing your business. Make sure nothing was taken."

"Nothing was," she yelled, reaching out to slam the door shut. *Not yet, at least.*

Sable had to have a scam going, Cade knew. She always did. But never on this level before, involving a big-time player like Bernard DuBois. She should be grateful she had ended up in the closet, and not in some stinking dumpster somewhere.

Had to be the computers. The Internet was her Vegas, Sable liked to say. The only place she could make the odds pay for her.

She sat across from him at the kitchen table, her head in her hands. Cade popped open a beer, then slid a bottle of pills across the table. "I could make that pain go away." As Sable grabbed for it, he covered it with his hand. "You gonna tell me what's up here?"

"Do I have a choice?"

"Sure. You can sit there and suffer."

She sighed, stretched out her hand. "It was the perfect plan, Cade."

"It's *always* the perfect plan." He gave her the bottle.

Sable popped three pills, then gulped Cade's beer. "Voice mail."

"Voice mail?" Cade shook out a cigarette and lit it, letting the smoke curl out of his lips. He knew she loved his smile, loved him in her own peculiar way.

"Some voice-mail providers allow users to make calls from anywhere and charge it to their corporate accounts," Sable said.

"Kinda like a phone card?"

"Yeah."

"So you hack into people's voice-mail accounts. That gives you—?"

"Long-distance dialing from anywhere."

Cade liked what he was hearing. "Then you sell the accounts."

"For a hundred-dollar flat fee, you get unlimited calls for a year. You give me your credit card number, and I assign you a phone number to dial through."

"So where does Bernard DuBois come in?"

"I needed 10K in start-up money. Had to get a powerful server to handle the transactions. Plus some switchers, routers, monitoring and control programs—"

"Yeah, yeah. Give me the bottom line."

"Twelve thousand so far."

"Twelve thousand bucks?"

"Twelve thousand accounts."

"At a buck per—that's how much?"

Sable grinned. "That's $1.2 million."

Cade was dizzy, thinking of Sable with that much cash. "And you're taking a beating from Bernard? Just pay the sucker, then go live happily ever after somewhere."

"I can't. I can't get at the money."

"Why not?"

"I searched a long time for a bank with sloppy reporting policies to handle my credit-card transfers. Finally found this dump in southern Florida. Set up my accounts, programmed the transfers. Money flowed in."

"So what's the problem?"

"The little bank under the radar that I found? The state found it too. The banking commission slapped a two-month restraining order on everything while they do an audit."

"So the number boys will find out your account is a scam," Cade said.

"Maybe, maybe not. I am legitimate—until some corporate geek finds out I'm playing in their ballpark and blows the whistle on me. I've got time. Just don't know how much."

"You can't get Bernard to just wait it out?"

"If he knew how much I've pulled in, he'd want a bigger cut. Might even find a way to take me out so he can grab all of it. It's a time bomb, auditors on one side, Bernard on the other."

"So what are you going to do?"

"Find a place to lie low and wait out the audit. And hope and pray that for once something goes my way."

Cade grinned. *Oh yeah, he'd be hoping and praying too. Hoping and praying that some of that money would be coming his way.*

3

S he's beautiful," Bethany said. "How old is she?"

"Three months." Charissa boosted the baby higher in her arms, as if Bethany's approval had lightened her burden. "And look! She's already got her first tooth. That's early, right? Maybe that means she'll be really smart or something. Check it out, Mrs. Dolan."

Bethany dutifully pushed her finger into baby Tawndra's mouth. The baby began to suck.

"Look, she likes you!"

"I like her too." Bethany focused on holding her smile.

It was good that the sponsors of the charter school provided day care, counseling, legal services, social referrals, and whatever else they could muster to keep the kids going to classes. Kyle and Bethany had supported the school wholeheartedly. The chorale had been Bethany's idea, a way to discover talent and encourage discipline and study.

"You should go back to conducting," Kyle had said that morning. "The kids miss you."

"Geoffrey does a wonderful job," she had said. "They don't even know I'm gone."

Charissa was holding the baby out. "Want to hold her?"

"I'm in a bit of a rush," Bethany said. "I'm looking for Anthony Martinez."

"He didn't come to school today."

"You sure? There was no answer at his house. I called his mom at work, and she said—"

Charissa leaned close and whispered, "So Mr. Perfect is ditching, huh?"

"Not Anthony. He wouldn't skip school."

Anthony Martinez loved singing with a passion, threw himself into the whole grind of studying, practicing, and performing.

"His mama thought he was here? I hope he's okay."

"I'm sure he is. Listen, I've got to run to a doctor's appointment. Maybe I'll catch up with Anthony another time." Bethany gave Charissa a quick hug.

"You okay, Mrs. Dolan? We were so worried, so bummed out when—"

"Just a checkup, that's all. Nice seeing you, and meeting Tawndra."

Bethany was almost out the door when Charissa called her back. "Mrs. Dolan, wait." The girl's lip trembled. "I'm scared."

"For Anthony? I'm sure he's fine. You're probably right. He's just skipping school."

Charissa shook her head. "Not Anthony. For me."

"What about you?"

"Nothing. That's the thing. There's nothing about me. Except I got this baby girl now. What do I do? I got nothing to give her, nothing to do for her."

Bethany drew Charissa close. The girl's tears were hot on her shoulder, the baby soft and sweet between them.

"Love her," Bethany said.

"What?" Charissa asked.

"Love your baby, and you'll be just fine. I promise."

⸎

"I don't want to be like this, Patrick. Hating the sight of babies. Dreading the thought of never giving Kyle what he deserves."

"I know Kyle. He thinks your marriage has already given him far more than he deserves." The Reverend Doctor Patrick Drinas slumped in his chair, long legs sprawled out. He looked like a college kid, with wiry curls, ripped jeans, and hiking boots. But he was wise, even beyond his fifty years, and godly—a man Bethany could trust.

Bethany got up and went to the window. She loved Patrick's office, housed in the old stone church that was a cool, green sanctuary in the middle of Boston. She loved the ancient cemetery, fenced in with granite posts and iron chains, bordered by ancient oak trees. Some of the gravestones went back to the American Revolution.

Blessed are those who mourn, for they will receive comfort.

"I can't find my faith, Patrick. I'm trying, but . . ." She couldn't breathe, choked by her tears. "I can't find God anywhere."

Patrick went and stood with her. "When we can't find our faith, when we can't find God, there's only one thing we can do."

"What's that?"

"Let God find us."

∞∞∞

Crowds of people thronged Boston Common—walking, roller-blading, biking, pushing baby carriages. The sky was crystal blue, the trees bursting with leaves. Not that the beauty of the day mattered. Dr. Nora Hemlow knew they could be in the middle of a howling blizzard and Kyle wouldn't notice. Nothing would distract him from the course he had chosen.

"Why isn't Bethany here?" she said.

Kyle looked down at his feet. "She said she didn't want to know the nuts and bolts—or, as she put it, the 'sharps and flats'—until we found the right woman. She wants me to go ahead, set everything up. So here I am."

Nothing would stop Kyle, Nora knew, now that he had his wife's grudging permission. "Okay, then. What can I do to help?"

"How do I find a surrogate?"

"I'll say it one more time. An agency—"

"I've researched the agencies. We relinquish control if we go through one."

"That's life, Kyle. We can't control every detail."

"But I have to. There's too much at stake. Our last embryo. And Bethany's privacy."

"The agencies have strict confidentiality standards."

Kyle laughed bitterly. "Tell the tabloids that. You saw what happened last December. 'Famous Pianist Loses Baby During Concert.' And those pictures . . . "

Two days after the surgery, Bethany had finally managed to put words to her anguish. "To have it happen in front of everyone, Nora. To fail at motherhood so spectacularly."

Nora had shared her friend's grief and would do anything to heal her pain. But was this the best way?

"Most agencies recommend using a woman who has already birthed a baby. But if you want this surrogate to live with you during the pregnancy, you'll have a hard sell convincing a woman to leave her own children."

"The surrogate has to stay with us for the duration. It's an absolute criterion. Maybe I'm being overprotective—"

"Honestly, Kyle? You're being a jerk. If you try to micromanage every aspect of life, what does that say about your faith?"

"My faith is in doing my duty as a husband. God expects me to provide for my wife's welfare the best I can. It certainly won't be a hardship for the surrogate to give us nine months. I will compensate her for every moment. This is it, Nora. Our last chance. Our last little one." His voice trailed off.

"Okay. But you'll have to forgive me if I'm not wildly enthusiastic about your finding the surrogate yourself, without at least consulting an agency."

"Your objections are duly noted. So tell me—what would you do? You and David?"

How could Nora answer that? Jenny was born while Nora and David were in medical school, and four more children followed like clockwork. Even on her worst day, trapped between toddler and teen tantrums, she would move heaven and earth for her kids.

"I guess I'd look for a recent college graduate," she finally said. "A young woman with impeccable credentials. Someone who has the time and incentive to give up nine months, but a bright future so she'll move on willingly when it's all over. The trick is finding such a woman."

"I will make that happen. Whatever it takes."

Dear God, that's what I'm afraid of, Nora prayed. *Please bring Kyle and Bethany the woman You would choose.*

4

orge Hill was one of the toughest neighborhoods in Boston. Only a ragged chain-link fence and a strip of dirt separated Anthony's street from the expressway. The triple-decker that Anthony lived in hadn't been painted in years. Broken toys, a tire, and trash littered the hard-packed dirt of the front yard.

Bethany knocked on the front door. It swung open under her hand, its bolt ripped out of the door frame. The foyer smelled of sour milk and cooking fat. A scrap of paper taped to the door on the right read *Martinez*. Bethany knocked, then waited, but there were no footsteps, no sounds of television or radio from inside.

She should just catch up with Anthony some other time. But she had waited too long as it was. He had been so faithful, sending cards decorated with hand-drawn clefs and notes.

Sorry, Mrs. D., about your baby. It really stinks . . . the kids are all saying hi. So hi, Mrs. Dolan . . . we'll even sing more of that Bach stuff if you'll just come back . . . we're praying, just like you asked . . .

How she had missed his crooked smile and wide, innocent eyes. He was always tripping over something, a real klutz—except when he sang. Then all the awkwardness fell away, and Anthony soared. Bethany just couldn't leave without seeing him.

She dug her notebook and pen out of her purse, sat down on the step, and began to write.

Skree . . .

A chill ran up her arms. What an odd noise. Bethany walked partway down the driveway, stepping over ruts and a bent tire rim. "Hello? Is someone there?"

Skree . . .

Two men in hooded sweatshirts burst out of the backyard. Before she could say anything, they ran into her, knocking her over. She went down, caught in that moment of shock—*What do I do? What will happen to me? This was so stupid. Will anyone even know?*—before she felt the pain. One man ripped the purse off her arm while the other just stared with dead eyes. Then they were gone, strolling toward the street as though nothing had happened.

Bethany held her breath, praying they wouldn't come back. She could hear the cars on the highway, then a squeal of tires as her Lexus pulled away. Was it safe to go out in the street and flag someone down? What if they were just joyriding and were coming around the block? It might be safer to go around back.

Bethany got up and limped into the backyard, looking for a way to the street behind the house. The backyard was cluttered with broken lawn chairs, a mangled bicycle, a toddler's shredded swimming pool. In the corner of the yard there was another wreck of a car. Near the wreck, a pile of rags.

Oh, dear God, no! Not rags! Anthony was slumped against the wreck, his hands tied over his head, his mouth gagged. Bethany ran to him and pulled the gag out of his mouth.

Then she wished she hadn't.

Sable wanted to rip Cade's eyeballs out. "Five hundred dollars?" she yelled. "That server had a top-of-the-line processor, multiple gigabyte drives with fault-protection—"

"My boy don't give a rat's hoot about your giga-stuff. You're lucky to get the five."

"Really. And how much went into your pocket?"

"A few bucks, just to cover transportation." Cade shrugged, earnest as a Boy Scout.

More like four or five hundred dollars, Sable knew. Cade's help always came with a price. But what choice did she have? If she went out on the street to fence the equipment herself, word would get back to Bernard.

"Where you heading?" Cade asked.

"None of your business." Sable stuffed the cash into her jeans pocket.

"You could stay with us. Rent free. Ain't that right, Hailey?"

Hailey Slonik glanced up from her paperback. "Whatever."

Why did Cade keep that slug around? Sable wondered. It certainly wasn't for her looks. The woman had a face like a hyena and an appetite to match. But she was long on street sense—Sable had to admit that. Good in the gutter.

"You oughta think about hooking up with us," Cade was saying.

"No. No way," Sable said.

"Then at least tell us where you're going. What if something happened to me? You'd want to know, wouldn't you?" Cade pulled her close. He smelled of smoke and musk.

"Fine. I'm heading for Buffalo. I'll call you when I get settled."

"Whatcha gonna do there?" Hailey had moved in on Sable's other side, hemming her in.

Sable grabbed her bag and headed for the door. "Get a job."

"Oh, that is rich." Cade laughed, with Hailey joining him.

Let them laugh. Sable would show them. She'd show everyone.

The hospital waiting room was packed with kids. They had left school when they heard about Anthony. Bethany had gone with him in the ambulance, staying with him until the ER doctors began working in earnest.

Too much blood loss . . . the splintered bone ripped into the artery . . . we can't go to surgery unless we stabilize him . . . can't promise we'll save the foot . . . no more than animals . . . using a baseball bat . . . pounding his ankle like a piece of meat . . .

Maria huddled against Bethany. The girl's eyes were raw from crying. "They're sayin' his mama dimed out the corner."

"I don't understand." Bethany kept her voice to a whisper.

"Drugs. Mrs. Martinez saw something big go down, called the cops. So these guys made an example. It's how they hold their turf, Mrs. Dolan. The last fool who crossed 'em? Talk is they burned out the whole family. A couple years back, it was all over TV. Remember?"

Bethany put her hand to her throat. Three children, burned in their beds.

The kids gathered around her. Charissa and Tyler, their baby still in the school's day care. Antwone, Shyla, Evie, Juan. She knew every note in their octaves, every shade to their voices. And yet what good had she done them? Exposing them to fine music, training their talents, conducting their voices—was it just an empty gesture? Her teaching hadn't protected Anthony from those thugs.

"What do we do, Mrs. Dolan?" Maria asked.

Only one thing to do.

"We can pray," Bethany said.

Charissa bowed her head right away. Maria crossed herself. The others looked to Bethany, unsure how this worked. She met their eyes, each one of them, then bowed her head.

No words came—only music. Bethany started, and her kids followed.

Amazing grace, how sweet the sound . . .

5

able expected Worcester, thirty miles west of Boston, to be the frontier of high-tech heaven. Instead, it was a graveyard of dot-coms and biotech start-ups.

This motel was typical of the whole rat-trap city. Sable would have loved an upscale hotel with high-speed cable, but if she had to wait for data exchange over dial-up, well, she had plenty of time, didn't she?

Hocking the server had really stunk. If she had kept the Web site open another week, she would have billed another half mil. But why be greedy? She had over a million now. Once the money freed up, she could buy a small house, top-of-the-line computer equipment, maybe a sensible car. It could happen. If her account could slide under the audit. If she could duck Bernard. If Cade and Hailey didn't suck the life out of her.

If *he* didn't get too close. When she least expected him, he was there. A face in a window. A figure in the back of the bus. A mist oozing out of the shadows. She could block him during the day by calculating sums and creating algorithms. But when she was alone in the dark, she felt his icy fingers trickle down her spine.

No. Not now, not ever again. She would make this new life happen. Her plan was solid. Wait for her account to come out from under the audit. Stay out of New York, get a small job, make enough to keep off Bernard's radar.

But who knew the economy was this tight, especially in Massachusetts? She had scanned the online job listings for hours. There was nothing available under Programming or MIS. Maybe she should check the universities. Boston and Worcester were both big college towns. Even with the economy out to lunch, the universities stayed in business.

Why not start at the top? Sable typed in *Harvard.edu*. Harvard's home page came up. She clicked on EMPLOYMENT OPPORTUNITIES. *General cook. Parking attendant. French tutor. HVAC specialists. Offensive line coach. Electrician. Senior researcher, neuropsychology.* Oh, wouldn't they just love to see inside her head?

On to the personal HELP WANTED section. *Nanny for twins, must speak French. Dog walker. Russian tutor.* Then it caught her eye. *Wanted: Nine months of your life.*

Maybe it was a house-sitting opportunity. How perfect would that be? Sable double-clicked on the NINE MONTHS. As she read the ad, she laughed. *Never* was her first thought. *Maybe* was her second. *It's crazy* was her next.

And finally, *It's perfect. Absolutely perfect.*

It had been three weeks since the attack on Anthony. Bethany had stayed in Boston until the previous Monday. She was relieved to be back in New Hampshire, staring up at a sapphire sky coming alive with stars. The White Mountains loomed on every horizon, never changing. If only she could be like that, take what life threw at her and not flinch.

She should go inside, practice, pack—whatever. She shouldn't be out there, collapsed on a lounge chair, gazing into the night. But she was so exhausted, it felt as if her bones had melted inside her. It had been a long week.

On Tuesday she had helped the Martinez family move into an old Victorian in Conway Village. Joan would have been happy just to move across the river to Cambridge, but Kyle had been adamant about taking them to New Hampshire. "You need distance between you and those thugs." He had made some phone calls, set Joan up with job interviews, and found a safe place for them to live.

On Wednesday Bethany had taken Anthony to audition at Cornish Academy. Even though he was almost eighteen, he looked forlorn in the wheelchair, wearing a cast to midthigh. And yet, the expanding of his range and the vigor in his voice showed his soaring talent. The admissions committee offered him a full scholarship for September. They had even found a family for him to carpool with back and forth to school.

On Thursday Bethany had taken Anthony's younger brother hiking. At twelve years old, Jacob already had mastered a slang that she never could have understood had it not been for her time spent with the chorale. Even though Jacob muttered about being dragged into what he called "cow country," Bethany knew Jacob would be better off away from his precious street.

But what about the kids she had left behind in Forge Hill? Would Shyla and Antwone and Maria still be singing when school opened in the fall? Was Charissa and Tyler's baby okay? Children raising children—it just didn't make sense.

The bitter thought came again, unbidden and unrelenting. *Why everyone else but us?*

She and Kyle had prayed about *in vitro* fertilization, even consulted a Christian ethicist. They decided it would be okay if they committed to implant all the embryos. They had joked about being the parents of five kids. Three years ago, it had seemed like a glorious dream. That was before their four attempts at a child, resulting in four losses. Now only one embryo remained. Cryopreserved in its own purgatory, the tiny soul was complete in its potential, though it had never drawn a single breath.

Would it have the quick hands of a musician or the quick mind of an inventor? Was it destined to be Italian-dark or Irish-fair? Would she play the saxophone? Would he play for the Boston Red Sox? Would he cuddle or squirm? Would she sing softly or speak boldly? Would a child ever call Bethany *Mama?*

She stared into the night, where the stars were endless and the answers hidden.

<hr>

Bethany jolted awake. The sky was inky black, the stars brilliant over the mountains. Her skin was wet with dew, her legs covered with goose bumps. She'd go have a hot bath, wash off the bug spray. She pushed up from the chair, shaking out stiff muscles.

Something wailed in the darkness.

She had to be dreaming. But no, there it was again, a high, frantic squeal, coming from the west side of the house. Had there been a horrible accident? Bethany ran around the side of the farmhouse and down the driveway.

The road was quiet. Maybe she had just imagined it. She walked around the yard, letting the crisp night air awaken her. Had it been a coyote, deep in the woods? Or a remnant of a dream?

She went into the house, comforted by the familiar smell of lemon oil and home cooking. There—that long, high wail. She stood in the front hall, a hard chill driving deep into her. The shadows under the stairs were so deep, they seemed endless.

Anything could be hiding there.

Bethany flicked on the light. There was nothing in the hall except the cherry table, the pewter lamp, and the hand-carved coat tree. Décor that had gone unchanged for forty years.

Aunt Mary used to tell ghost stories about this house. Bethany's favorite—and most feared—was the one about the farmer who murdered his wife, then plowed her body into the back meadow. *The farmer's wife would walk through the house, crying for someone to wake up and come find her bones.* None of it true, of course. But each time Aunt Mary told the story, Bethany had slept under her quilt, blocking her ears with her pillow so she wouldn't hear the wailing. Just the wind in the old willow, her father would say. Nothing to be afraid of.

Kyle had cut the willow down years ago.

There it was again, not as clear in the living room. Bethany ran upstairs and checked all the bedrooms, turning on lights as she went. Nothing. And a good thing, Bethany realized. She would be no match for either a crazed burglar or a bitter ghost.

She should just grab her car keys and drive over to the Hemlows'. But no—hadn't she run away enough? She crept up the stairs to the attic. Deep into the darkness at the top of the stairs, she yanked a string. The lightbulb flashed, then popped.

Bethany gasped, clutching the railing. *It's only a sound*, she told herself. She stepped into the attic, fingering the wall until she found the light switch. The wailing was more distant up there. Where could it possibly be coming from? She had checked the whole house—except for one room.

She left the attic and paused outside the nursery door. That hungry keening that sounded every bit like a—

No. It just couldn't possibly be true. But why not? What if the past three years had been a horrible dream? What if she were waking up from a long night's sleep? Bethany slowly opened the door and peered inside. The cry was perfectly clear in the nursery.

It had all been a bad dream, and now she was awake.

Now her baby needed her. She would pick him up and—

The crib was empty.

Bethany sank to the floor, hands over her ears. "STOP! Stop, stop, stop—"

And it did, just like that. Silence flowed over her, an icy stream of nothing.

Bethany curled up, knees to her chest in a tight ball, and stayed there for a long time.

6

*T*he *rip* was so sharp, it was almost painful. Bethany had begun tearing the wallpaper from the wall, hoping to uncover the source of that crying. She had kept it up through the night, finding the dismantling of the nursery strangely satisfying.

When they had hung this paper last fall, she had been five months pregnant. The World Series was under way, and Kyle had joked about what it would be like in twenty-five years. Michael Dolan would go to bat for the Boston Red Sox. "Boston's own," the broadcasters would call him. Bethany laughingly had agreed that her son could be a homegrown superstar as long as he was also an accomplished classical musician.

Rip. That was in the past.

She had made every bargain with God she could think of—serving more, giving more, praying more, studying more, believing more. She had repented of every sin she could remember and some that she had only imagined. If it was God's will that she and Kyle not be parents, then why—

Rip. No more whys.

The room was filled with the summer sun, flickering through the lush maple tree outside the windows. When had December turned into June? Surely God didn't intend Bethany to cower in her own shadow while the world went on.

Almost twenty years ago, she had joined her life with Kyle Dolan's. So things hadn't turned out as they had planned, or prayed. They were still together—at least, when she wasn't running away.

She had to get home to him, right now. Where her love was, God's love had to be.

Bethany left the last piece of wallpaper still hanging on the wall and walked out of the nursery without another look.

⸻ ∞ ⸻

Pilgrim Road reeked of money and class. BMWs and Infinitis lined the granite curbs. Well-dressed people walked dogs, kids, and each other. Sable strolled through there as though she had been born to privilege.

Assuming the role of Laurel Bergin had been effortless. Enunciate clearly, mix amusing slang with serious discussion, throw in blond and breezy, and a psych-ward runaway was now a Southwick grad. It had taken her a day to hack into Southwick's administrative files. Once she was there, she had full access to transcripts, recommendations, and medical records. She replaced Laurel Bergin's scanned picture with her own in the alumni directory, then printed herself an official Southwick ID badge.

She had breezed through the prescreening, the physical, and even the psychological exam. No problem—she had been fooling these suckers for most of her life.

The hard part had been getting clean. She could live without the weed and the painkillers, but going off the Xanax, Ritalin, and the other fun stuff—well, that was one bad trip. Ten days of cramping and diarrhea, but what choice did she have? No one was going to hire a surrogate on the kind of medication doctors gave to a head case.

It would be worth it. This was one scam that wasn't going to go bad. Because it really wasn't a scam. She would have the Dolans' little brat, turn the kid over, take their money, and get out of their lives. That's all they wanted and all she wanted. Something in it for everyone.

⸻ ∞ ⸻

Bethany parked in the carport behind the townhouse. Kyle wasn't expecting her home until the next day. She hoped he hadn't ordered that greasy chow mein he loved to chomp on when she was gone. Seventeen years of marriage, and she still hadn't tamed his appetite for junk food.

She walked across the little patch of grass and flowers they called their backyard. Nora teased them about country living in the heart of Back Bay. She and Kyle loved the culture of Boston, the elegance of Pilgrim Road. Years ago, they had begged Nora and David to buy the place next to theirs.

"We need a real backyard for the kids," Nora had insisted. She and David always enjoyed spending time at the farmhouse and finally settled up in North Conway. Kyle and Bethany had bought a swing set for Jenny and Kate as a housewarming gift. In the years that followed, the Hemlows added Benton, Melissa, and Dorothy to fill their "real backyard."

It had been as easy as the wind blowing for Nora and David to make a family. *Why*—no. No more whys. It was all forward from today.

Thank You, Lord, for this day. For this home, for this husband. For my music and . . .

Kyle was in the kitchen, brewing some tea. He looked around, startled, as she came in the back door.

She paused there, feeling like a stranger in her own home. "I'm early."

"Which gives me just an extra day to do this," Kyle said. His arms were around her, warm and sure and strong. "Bethany, I'm afraid I've scheduled a meeting—"

"No problem. I'll get the sauce going, maybe practice a little."

"Not a Dol-Pak thing. I'm meeting with a candidate for surrogacy."

Bethany had expected this. But not today, and certainly not the moment she walked in the door. She held tighter to him, letting this possibility settle in.

"If you're uncomfortable, you can wait upstairs while I talk to her," he said.

"No. I was wrong to expect you to do this without me. Go ahead; tell me everything."

Kyle told her how Nora had examined each of the candidates,

about the psychologist they had hired, the background checks, and how this candidate seemed simply perfect. He showed Bethany the girl's references, her school transcripts, her acceptance to medical school, even her picture. She was a pretty girl, with sun-streaked hair and a sweet smile.

A tiny spark kindled deep inside Bethany. She wanted to dash it to pieces before it took hold. But with each heartbeat, it drew more life. As much as she wished to will it away, she couldn't. It was here again and she let it take her over, surrendering to it one last time.

Hope.

What do you say to the stranger who might carry your baby?

"Do you like sports?" Kyle asked.

Laurel Bergin's eyes lit up. "That's why I'm going to U.Conn.— so I can listen to the Sox games."

"You're kidding me, right?"

"Only a masochist would *fake* being a Red Sox fan. Guilty as charged," Laurel said.

"Aren't you from the West Coast?" Bethany said.

"Yeah. But my grandfather was from Worcester, and raised on Williams and Pesky. He brought me up on Roger Clemens—that Yankee turncoat."

Kyle laughed. Nora had warned him to be tough, ask hard questions. But Laurel's face was so open, her manner so relaxed, she couldn't be hiding anything.

Laurel looked around with open admiration. "So I'd be living here?"

"Not here," Kyle said. "We have a farmhouse in the Mount Washington Valley of New Hampshire. A four-season paradise with rolling fields, farms, forests."

"You sound like a brochure."

"I know. I can't help it. Bethany inherited the place from her aunt. We love it there. In the spring, with the snow runoff, the Saco River powers over the rocks, all white water. The mountains are on all sides, with sunrises and sunsets that blow you away."

"Is this a problem, Laurel?" Bethany said. She sat stiffly.

"I suppose it might be a nice change, living out in the country like that."

"Don't worry, we've got flush toilets and satellite television," Kyle said. They all laughed.

"Has Dr. Hemlow made the conditions perfectly clear?" Bethany said. "Nine months—more, including the prep and recovery time— that's a long time to put your life on hold."

"I've taken that all into consideration."

"We will compensate you generously, but even so . . . " Kyle's words trailed off as he looked at Bethany. She had gone pale. A child of theirs making it through the nine months had been a given three years ago. Now it was a step of faith for her. He took her hand.

"You've been through a rough time, haven't you?" Laurel's voice was soft.

Bethany's hand tightened on Kyle's. "Rough time" didn't even begin to describe it, Kyle knew. He had to hope and pray that this girl would finally help them achieve what they couldn't on their own.

Lord, let this girl make us a family. And please, help us welcome her into our home.

"Who's on first?" Kyle whispered.

Bethany pulled the quilt up to her face. She was in no mood for that game, but she was in no mood to talk about anything else either. Too much thinking to do. Thinking and praying. She shivered, remembering the cry up at the farmhouse, that impossible wail. Was that just last night? It must have been a delusion. Or a stupid dream. Either way, she had to forget it. She had needed to be home with Kyle. It was that simple.

"I don't know," she whispered. "Who's on first?"

"Every player in the Sox lineup. Trouble is, most of them got stuck there. Those idiots had twelve hits but lost the game. Fifteen runners left stranded. It's almost a record."

"It's always almost a record with them," Bethany said, smiling.

Kyle snuggled next to her but stayed on top of the quilt. He'd sleep that way, comfortable in his Boston College T-shirt and mesh soccer shorts. He hated to wear long sleeves and socks, even in the winter. "So who's on first, Beenie?"

"Jenny Hemlow. Nora took her to Brown yesterday—apparently she blew them away in her interview."

"Makes me feel old, little Jenny applying to colleges."

"Ancient. It's a wonder that I haven't mummified you yet."

"Ha ha. Like you're just out of high school?"

"No matter how old I am, you'll always be older."

"You got a point there," he said, tickling her.

She batted his hands away, laughing. "So who's on first, Methuselah?"

Kyle groaned. "Don't know who's on first, but the Yankees are pushing *into* first. What did I expect? It's almost July—time for the Sox to start their slide. Who's on first, Beethoven?"

Bethany put her lips to his ear. "Laurel Bergin. I think . . . "

He pulled her closer. "I know."

"Do you, Kyle?" she whispered.

"Shush," he said. "Game over. Go to sleep."

The last thing Bethany remembered was Kyle's warmth, seeping through her skin and into her heart.

―⊗⊗⊗―

For you created my inmost being;

You knit me together in my mother's womb.

I praise you because I am fearfully and wonderfully made;

Your works are wonderful, I know that full well.

(PSALM 139:13–14)

―⊗⊗⊗―

7

o this is what family life is like, Kyle thought. *Kids shouting, parents chasing, balls flying. Noisy. Chaotic. Crazy. Wonderful.*

He was glad that Bethany had suggested the picnic for Labor Day weekend. "We'll have Nora, David, and their gang, and the Martinez family. Maybe then Laurel won't feel so isolated up at the farmhouse."

As soon as Laurel had tested positive for pregnancy, they had gone north to redecorate the apartment over the barn. Laurel stayed in the Boston townhouse until the renovation was complete. Kyle had ordered a huge entertainment center with a flat-screen TV, DVD/CD player with stereo. Bethany had wallpapered, painted, curtained, and bought all new furniture.

This weekend was a gem. The only hint of autumn was in the wetlands, where the brush was edged with gold. Major attractions like Thor's Falls were jammed with people. Kyle had promised to take the younger Hemlow kids and Anthony's brother up right before sunset, when the crowds would be gone.

He stretched in the lawn chair, tuning in the radio. It was too nice a day to go inside to watch the Sox, especially since the bums had blown their five-game lead in the division. They were up by four runs. But it was only the second inning—anything could happen.

Now, there's a fun analogy, Kyle thought. *Nine innings, nine months.* He'd have to tell Laurel she was in the bottom of her second inning of pregnancy. She'd tease that she'd have to pretend to be a Yankee so they could count on a championship season.

Their surrogate had stepped right into their lives as if she belonged.

Sable thought the Labor Day picnic would be stupid. But this was almost fun, especially after having a hit of weed. She was respecting the pregnancy, only smoked half the joint. Plus, she had to conserve; the stock she had scored in Boston was almost gone.

She was up in the apartment, sitting on the deck where she could catch the breeze. Below, in the backyard, Bethany fussed over the picnic tables, while Nora's husband baby-sat the fire. David Hemlow was one of those professor types, with beard, spectacles, and sandals. Kyle dozed in the lawn chair. He looked like a kid, with that straw-berry blond hair and sunburned nose.

The older Hemlow girls talked Anthony's ear off. Poor kid couldn't get away, not with that cast on his foot. The younger kids ran around, screaming. That Jacob Martinez was a stitch. Sable thought she'd split her gut when he called Benton Hemlow a little *mother-whatsit*—without skimping on the *whatsit*. The youngest Hemlow girl was dressed like something out of Prep Central. Sable would never do that to her kids. She hoped Bethany and Kyle wouldn't do it to their baby either.

Baby. What would it be like to have a baby filling her up, mov-ing inside her? Didn't matter—for the money Kyle was paying, she'd grow a poodle. Ten thousand for just going through the implanta-tion, and six thousand for every month she remained pregnant.

Sable thought it would be a big drag, living with the Dolans, but it had been cool. Bethany hovered too much, but she could cook up a storm. And Sable enjoyed Kyle, with his easy charm and end-less jokes. Last night she had asked him: "Why are you so happy all the time?"

He didn't have to think about it, just smiled and said, "Because God is good." Okay, so maybe Kyle Dolan was a deluded idiot. But if Sable made him even more deliriously happy than he already was, well, then she'd be doing a good deed too.

Someone knocked on the door. Sable got up, found Nora stand-ing on the porch.

"Sorry to bother you, Laurel. I need a specimen." She pressed a plastic container into Sable's hand.

"You said the blood test came back fine. Nice and pregnant, all those hormones."

"Your contract calls for random drug screenings, at my discretion. You understood this, right? Kyle said you consulted your lawyer about it."

Sable had pocketed the thousand bucks Kyle had given her for a lawyer and instead took a crash course in contract law from the Internet. She never expected anyone to actually pull a pop urine test on her. Was the marijuana absorbed into Sable's blood yet? It was definitely in her brain—she wasn't thinking at her usual light speed.

Urgent screams sailed in through the sliding glass door to the deck. Down in the yard, Jacob had Benton in a half nelson. Sable smiled.

"Why don't you break up the wrestling match? I'll grab a soda, then be ready to give a sample in about half an hour. And maybe you could leave the cup here, so we don't gross everyone out?"

"Oh. Sure."

Gotcha, Sable thought.

⌘

That Laurel was hot. The *sizzle*. So when she came looking for Jacob, he thought, *All right*.

Minutes later he was up in Laurel's apartment, playing video games on her PlayBox and her thirty-four-inch television. He was lost in a laser battle, keeping it so real that he could smell the sewer breath of the dragon and feel the whiz of the Annihilator's sword. Laurel had told him to play alone for a while. "It won't be a fair fight until you get some time on the game." He was about to lop off the Gorgonetta's four heads when she came in and hit pause.

"Whassup?" he said, kicking back.

"You know that Dr. Hemlow lady?"

"She be riding me all day 'cuz her loser kids can't keep up with me. What does she expect? You name a kid Benton and you gotta figure he's gonna get his backside whipped."

Laurel laughed. "Here's the deal, J. She wants me to pee in a cup for her. Some medical test or something. But I can't get it going. Must be nerves or something. So I'm thinking—would you mind making a donation? I'll pay you five bucks, and it'll be just our secret."

Jacob laughed. It was too sweet, Laurel thinking he just rolled off the kindergarten bus. "Nah, I'll do it for free. If I get to play your games whenever I want."

"Deal," she said. "Now hurry up. Doctor FrankenSlime is heading this way."

After Jacob did his good deed, Laurel capped the bottle and they washed their hands together. She smelled really nice, and when he brushed against her arm, she felt nice too. All those grown-ups at the picnic, but she'd been the only one to see that he hated all the trees and mountains, hated this place that was so uncool he might melt away from breathing its fresh air.

But suddenly Jacob thought that living up in New Hampshire might not be so bad after all. Between him and Laurel, they'd have things shaking in ways that cow town had never seen.

8

*S*he's getting bored," Kyle argued on the phone. "She needs to get out."

"If you get her a car, she might . . . I don't know . . . get reckless," Bethany shot back. "We already had a frost, Kyle. The sanders were out this morning—"

"And they'll be out again anytime the roads are icy. We can't keep her a prisoner. I don't see why we can't buy her a car."

"Because I will drive her wherever she needs to go. That's why," Bethany said.

After another minute of sparring they hung up, issue unresolved. Kyle wished he could be up north, but he was needed at work. Dol-Pak was about to become the packager for TradeWinds, one of the world's biggest catalog retailers. He shouldn't have had to baby-sit the details, but with Ron's broken leg and Bev on maternity leave, he had to shepherd the deal.

Kyle had built Dol-Pak from the ground up, developing a product line of biodegradable packing materials that were now industry standards. He loved designing and enjoyed working with employees and customers, but he hated all the legal mumbo jumbo.

Even more, he hated being in Boston without Bethany. Kyle missed everything about her. The flowing music that he never took for granted. The gourmet stews and elegant treats. Holding her at night, especially now that they had so much to celebrate.

Laurel was just a few days from the twelve-week point in the pregnancy, that critical time when odds shifted in their favor that the baby would make it. Kyle could hardly wait to close the TradeWinds deal and get to North Conway. He wanted to be with Bethany to watch Laurel and their baby grow.

The doorbell rang. Kyle checked his watch. Nine-thirty. Who was coming by now? He hustled down the stairs, looked through the peephole. A cop stood on the front stoop. Kyle unbolted the door and swung it open. "Can I help—"

The cop pressed his nightstick against his neck. Kyle instinctively struck out, but the cop whacked the stick against his ribs. He went down hard, pain exploding through him, followed by a rush of panic.

The cop slapped handcuffs on him. Before Kyle could kick or roll, the man used another handcuff to lock him to the radiator.

"What do you want?" Kyle gasped. "Are you arresting me?"

"Oh yeah. You have the right to remain silent, sucker." The man—no cop, Kyle realized—kicked him in the ribs, then disappeared into the house.

He struggled to get free, then gave up. He had taken a few punches and thrown a few growing up in South Boston, but he had no chance against a professional thug.

The man was back in a minute, holding the diamond necklace that Kyle had given Bethany on their tenth anniversary and wearing Kyle's Rolex.

"What do you think you're—" Kyle protested.

"What did I tell you about making demands?" The cop-thug rapped the nightstick against Kyle's temple. "Now listen, and listen good. I want you to deliver a message."

Kyle struggled to focus through the pain. "Who's the message for?"

"Let's say, anyone who wants to know."

"What is it?"

"Bernard."

"Bernard? What does that mean?"

The man bent close to Kyle's face. "It means you don't want me coming back. It means if I do, it won't be pretty."

She should bolt right out of there. *Don't panic—just think*, Sable told herself as she paced through the apartment. But it was so hard. Why was her head so muddy lately?

Bernard obviously had resources she hadn't counted on, tracking her to Pilgrim Road. Even so, the Dolans didn't have a clue that this had anything to do with her. Bethany had freaked, thinking it was those guys who had beat up the Martinez boy. Kyle had lucked out, only gotten bruised ribs and a bad headache. The police predicted that the guy wouldn't be back, that the home invasion was all a case of mistaken identity.

Sable knew better. Kyle had relayed the message unwittingly, never dreaming it was for her. *Next time it won't be pretty.*

If Bernard could track her to Boston, what was to stop him from finding her in North Conway? The smart thing would be to put a lot of space between herself and the Dolans. Sable had twenty-two thousand dollars already—two months' pay plus the implantation bonus. That could set her up for some time while she waited out the audit of the Florida bank. The liens were off all accounts, but Sable didn't dare to move large amounts of cash, not while the auditors were still monitoring all transfers.

Twenty-two thousand dollars was enough to sit and wait in comfort somewhere. But what about the baby? She couldn't feel it inside her yet, but she knew it was there. Already her stomach was puffy and she couldn't button her jeans.

Maybe she should sneak off to Concord, have a quick abortion, then tell Bethany and Kyle she'd had a miscarriage. That woman expected the worst anyway—Sable could tell from the haunted look in her eyes. They could pray all they wanted, but this wasn't going to work, that was becoming clear. Sable's life was one horror show after another.

But wait—she wasn't Sable anymore. How would Laurel approach this?

Of course. If her thinking weren't so confused, she would have seen that right away. Why not pay off Bernard and just make him go away? Then Sable—and Laurel—could live happily ever after. And if the Dolans did, too, well, hooray for them.

Troy, New York, wasn't as rough as Forge Hill, but it was no prize, Bethany thought. Sajewski's Funeral Home was hemmed in by Lou's Tattoo Emporium and the Nite-Delite Exotic Dance Club. She was relieved to see that the parking lot was bordered by chain-link fencing and supervised by a security cop.

This whole week had been a nightmare. First, Kyle's beating. The next day, Laurel had come to her in tears. "My college roommate died. I need to go to New York."

"I'm so sorry. What can I do?" Bethany had said.

"Could you take me to a bus station? I need to get out to Albany for the wake."

"I'll drive you."

Laurel argued against it for almost an hour, but Bethany was glad she had insisted, especially now that she had seen the place. The thought of Laurel walking around that nightmare of a neighborhood—with their baby inside her—was chilling.

"I'll walk you in," Bethany said, turning off the car.

"That's all right."

"It's no trouble."

"Please, Bethany. My friends don't know about the surrogacy. If they see us together, they'll be asking all sorts of questions. I want to keep this private, and I'm sure you do too. Just pick me up in three hours, if you could."

Bethany watched Laurel until she disappeared into the funeral home. So sad, at her age, to be attending the wake of a friend. She pushed her seat back, intent on taking a nap or reading, when a flash of color on the far horizon caught her eye.

Troy was close to the Adirondack foothills. In mid-October, the foliage was at its peak, the day crisp and clear. Perfect for hiking. All spring Bethany had climbed to escape her emptiness. Now she could climb and thank God for using Laurel Bergin to fill her up.

———— ∞ ————

A woman approached Sable as she stood frozen in the door. "I'm the daughter. Samantha. Thank you for coming."

Sable shook her hand. "I worked with—" What did Cade say her name was? "with Sally."

"We'll miss her so much," Samantha said.

"Oh, I know. I'm sorry for your loss." Sable hadn't meant to arrive at the casket, but there it was. She was about to slip away when an older woman stepped to her side. "Samantha said you worked with my sister. What did you do at Centorr?"

Sable glanced at the corpse, really seeing it for the first time. Words froze in her throat. "I want to . . . um . . . excuse me." She dropped to the kneeler, folding her hands. How could Cade do this? Was this some kind of sick joke? This dead woman—this Sally— looked just like Sable's mother.

Sable couldn't bear looking at the dead woman but couldn't tear her gaze away. The cheeks were fuller on the corpse, the nose more turned up. But the cotton hair, destroyed by constant bleaching, and the strong chin were identical. She even was painted with the same shade of lipstick and was dressed in peach—Angela Lynde's favorite color.

Her mother hadn't been beautiful, but she was warm and kind. "Where did I get a doll like you?" she used to ask Sable. Angela Lynde's life had been hard, her choices foolish. But she had loved Sable the best she could. Loved her to the very end.

Sable covered her face with her hands. Where was her mama now? Had God shown her more mercy in death than He had in life? Why even bother asking? If God had any mercy, He would have shown up long ago.

———— ∞ ————

Mama's latest fellow smelled like beer cans and old pizza. He had come every night for a week now. His teeth were crooked and stuck out over his lower lip when he smiled.

Nights they stayed in were closet nights for Sable. It was quieter out there in the back hall. She loved Mama but hated that smacking sound the men made when they kissed her. Like they would swallow her whole. Mama knew the closet was a good thing. Sable had her books and her blanket and a flashlight—all she needed to keep her happy.

Crooked Teeth had come in that night with a bag from Ling Pao's. He and Mama settled in front of the television. "Hey, kid. Want some?" he had asked. Sable shook her head. She had had cornflakes for supper, with orange juice because there wasn't any milk.

Sable whispered something about going out back for a while. Mama knew that meant the closet, didn't even blink when she headed out through the kitchen. Sable had her hand to the back door when it banged open. She almost jumped out of her shoes.

A big man stormed in, bigger even than that gorilla guy who ran the gas station. Big Man didn't even look her way, just stormed into the living room as if he owned the place. Sable smelled him as he went past. Sweat, liquor, lots of cigarettes. The scent of her whole life, it seemed.

She hated it.

<hr/>

"Are you okay, miss?" Someone touched her shoulder.

"Uh . . . yes. Just sad." She struggled to stand. How long had she been kneeling?

The stranger was a white-haired man with soft eyes. "Sad, because we'll miss her. But happy because we know Sally has gone home to be with Jesus."

"Well, . . . yes." *Whatever you say,* she thought. *Just leave me out of it.*

"You sure you're okay?"

She spotted Cade, coming in with the latest batch of mourners. "Fine. Thanks." Sable pulled away from the old man and pushed through the crowd.

"You put on a good show," Cade said, hugging her.

She pushed him away. "Shut up. Did you call Bernard?"

"Sure did."

"I called him too. So there's no . . . *mistake* in what you'll be delivering."

Cade frowned. "You don't trust me?"

"I know you too well to trust you. So when do you meet him?"

"He's picking up the money here, at the evening showing. Right in this room."

"Are you insane? Why didn't you arrange some other place?"

"What's safer than this? Bernard won't pull anything here. Besides, you'll be long gone before he gets here." He grinned, pulled her close. "I know how to take care of you, kid."

"Some caring," she snapped.

She had told Bethany to pick her up after three hours. If Bethany was just half an hour late, it would be a nightmare—Bernard and Bethany, with Sable caught in the middle.

9

ethany's hands flew over the keys in mindless etudes that she had known since childhood. Her thoughts were on Laurel— three months pregnant and thriving.

"My kid's age is minus six months," Kyle said that morning, overflowing with confidence. Bethany wanted to show the same sunny optimism, but every day she fought the impulse toward fear and regret. How could she tell Kyle how hard this was to bear, the reality of her child's heart beating in the body of another woman? Even the age of the baby was a puzzle—thirteen weeks past implantation. But the embryo had been created over three years before, so in one sense, the baby had existed since then.

And what of the baby's soul, that precious gift of God? Had it sat in cryopreservation for all those years? Or did God quicken the soul after the baby's heart beat for the first time? Was the manipulation of conception offensive to God? God knew the desire of Bethany's heart, and God was merciful—she knew that with every fiber of her being.

Bethany's fingers picked out a melody that had somehow shortcut around her mind and gone straight to her hands. She let the music go, playing on, her gaze turning to the window. She loved that time of year—the bleakness of late autumn that wasn't bleak at all, but a time of rest until spring burst onto New Hampshire in a haze of sunlight and birdsong.

She could do this. She could believe that she would hold her child when spring came back to this valley. She could wait for God's mercy. Words were coming for the tune now.

When the birds of spring
Come alive to sing
in their golden wonderland

More melody and more images, hope dawning from her music, from the place where she first knew the glory and grace of her loving Father.

I will dance for you
Under skies of blue
'Cause I will love you forever
And I'll be here with you,
For always.

Bethany had never written a lullaby before. But it was time—she was going to be a mother. Time to believe in what would come, in what would be for always.

———— ∞ ————

"You really think she's pregnant?" Cade said.

"I know she's pregnant. The real question is—how?"

Cade pulled Hailey onto his lap. "Want me to show you?"

"I've got something to show *you*. The afternoon sitting in that strip club across from the funeral home wasn't wasted." She handed him some photos.

Hailey had gotten a clear shot of Sable getting into a big, shiny Volvo. Another of a dark-haired woman hugging her.

"That chick is mighty happy to see Sable," Cade said.

"We'll figure out Sable's love life later," Hailey said. "First things first. I need a thousand bucks for that guy at Rensselaer Polytech."

"You already cost me three hundred bucks on that deal."

Hailey had persuaded Cade to keep the server, see if they could track down the bank account where Sable had stashed all that money. He had had to lift a monitor and keyboard so they could see what was on the hard drive. It gave them one simple message: *No files found.*

"Someone formatted the drive," the kid from the college had told Hailey. "That wipes out all the info that had been on it. But I might be able to retrieve some of the files anyway."

"We've got to go for it. It'll be worth it," Hailey promised Cade. "If we can track down those account numbers, maybe we can grab a piece of the pie for ourselves."

"I'd love to see Sable's face when she goes for her million bucks and it ain't there."

"Hey, maybe she won't even care," Hailey said.

"Huh?"

"She'll have her baby to keep her warm."

⟡

So this is what it's all about. Until that moment, Sable hadn't gotten it—the fixation Kyle had, the devotion Nora showed, the attention everyone seemed to pay to Bethany.

It was all about the music. Sable sat outside in the gazebo, but she could hear Bethany playing the piano and singing, as she had so many times before. And yet, that day there was something different. Something that seemed to make Sable's mind clear and her heart swell.

It was all about the music, and it was all about the beauty.

Not physical beauty, though Sable had to admit Bethany had plenty of that. Somehow, the woman knew how to call the best out of everything she did. Certainly in the music. But also in the way her home was decorated, the variety and taste of everything she cooked. She made Anthony stand taller, Kyle laugh louder, and Nora relax.

And now, Bethany's music made Sable want to just sit in that patch of sunlight forever.

For always.

Words were coming on the breeze now. Sable strained to listen.

I will bring a light to your darkest night. Because I will love you forever and I'll be here, with you, for always.

Sudden, almost unbearable pain gripped Sable. Her mama had promised her, "I'll stay here with you, Sable. I swear I won't leave."

And she hadn't.

Anthony found Laurel collapsed in tears in the gazebo.

"What's wrong?" he said, wanting to give her a hug but not knowing how.

Where he came from, you weren't gentle with women; you just took what you wanted. Unless you were a music geek like Anthony. He just wasn't like that, would never be like that. So he went without.

Suddenly Laurel was in his arms anyway, burying her face in his jacket. He patted her back, smoothed her hair, tried to figure out what to say to stop the tears. She smelled like lilacs, and she felt like velvet. There was no way he could think straight now.

Then, just as suddenly, she pulled away, smiling. "Hi, there."

"What's wro—"

Laurel stopped his words by pressing her hand to his lips. Even with her wet cheeks and red eyes, she was beautiful. Her hair was a soft honey, her eyes as blue as a summer morning. "Is your leg good enough so you can go for a walk, Anthony?"

The truth was, his leg ached all the time, and he still wore a brace. But the bigger truth was, none of that mattered. From the first time he had seen her on Labor Day, Anthony had wanted an excuse to be alone with Laurel Bergin. Jacob said she was pregnant, but so what? Back in Forge Hill, half the girls he knew were either pregnant or already mothers.

"The leg's coming along. The therapist wants me to start pushing it." Anthony would walk to the moon and back, if he had to. Anything to be alone with Laurel Bergin.

Anthony Martinez had it for her, that much was sure. Men got off on all sorts of things. Why not pregnancy? Sable had to admit she was looking pretty good. Must have been all the vegetables Bethany was forcing on her. Or maybe those walks. She hadn't ever been much for exercise, but she was starting to enjoy getting out every afternoon. Stretching her muscles, breathing some real air, looking at something besides a computer screen.

He had caught her in a bad moment, there in the gazebo. Bethany's music had unnerved her. Sable knew better than to let down her guard, knew she couldn't let anything touch her. If Anthony hadn't come upon her and held her, well, who knows what might have happened?

He might have come. He loved tears, thrived on any show of weakness. Was that him now, moving through the brush? No, just the wind whipping down the hillside.

Sable couldn't think about him. That was like an open invitation. She needed to focus on Anthony and the crisp day. They were hiking up to Thor's Falls, less than a half mile from the farmhouse. It was beautiful among the pines and birches, with squirrels scurrying in the leaves, birds flying overhead. Now that the tourists were gone, Sable loved going up there, drowsing in the afternoon sun while the water rushed over the boulders.

"So where are you from, Laurel?"

"Washington State. The Spokane area. A small town called Gantry."

"What brings you up here?"

Sable stopped. "You really don't know?"

Anthony shook his head.

Sable laughed. "You're lying, fool. You know very well why I'm here."

"They're adopting your baby, aren't they?" he asked.

"What makes you think that?"

"I was there the night Mrs. Dolan lost her baby." He closed his eyes, turned away.

"Anthony. Tell me." She took his hand.

"It was awful, Laurel. We were finishing up our concert, singing the 'Hallelujah Chorus' from the *Messiah*. Mrs. Dolan was conducting, and then BAM! She just disappeared behind the podium. I jumped off the riser, got to her first."

"What happened?"

"There was blood down her legs, so bright red it almost hurt to look at it. They called an ambulance, but Mr. Dolan didn't wait, just picked her up and carried her away. Afterwards, they told us she had lost the baby, then had to have an operation or she would have bled to death. She can never have babies, not after that."

"How awful." Sable had heard enough, wanted Anthony to stop. But he couldn't.

"There was so much blood, Laurel. Everywhere . . . "

A chill ran through Sable as Anthony continued to describe the scene. *All that blood . . .*

"So I was guessing that was it, that you were giving them your baby," Anthony said.

"Not my baby," Sable said. She could barely get the words out, because she was seeing the blood now. *So bright red, it almost hurt . . .*

"Sorry," he said. "I didn't mean to be a jerk."

Sable took a long breath, trying to steady herself. "It's their baby, through and through. Bethany's egg and Kyle's sperm. I'm what they call a surrogate. Carrying the baby for Bethany because she can't do it."

"Wow! You are so cool, doing something that special for them." Anthony's eyes went to her belly, then up to her face, gazing at her as though she was as beautiful as the sky above.

Being with Anthony was almost as good as sleeping in the sunshine, Sable thought. *If only he would shut up about that blood.*

10

*T*hanksgiving Day. So much to be thankful for that Bethany couldn't help singing as she cleared the dishes.

Let all things now living—a song of thanksgiving—

The Hemlow and Martinez families had joined them and Laurel for dinner, filling the dining room to capacity. The turkey had been splendid. Even Jacob had wolfed down the wild rice stuffing, though he swore it looked like birdseed.

To God the Creator, triumphantly raised—

The day was sterling—chilly but clear, the mountains already dressed in winter white.

God's banners are o'er us, His light goes before us—

Kyle was up at the farmhouse at least half of the time. He claimed Dol-Pak was running itself, though he spent long days on the phone. Joan Martinez enjoyed her job, working the overnight shift at the hospital. Jacob was moody and quiet, except with Laurel. Joan was patient, praying for him to adjust to a life away from the street.

Till shadows have vanished and darkness is banished—

Anthony was filling out like an oak tree, his shoulders broad, his voice vibrant, his range expanding. He was studying Italian and German to prepare for opera.

As forward we travel from light into light.

Laurel was eighteen weeks pregnant. Her abdomen was full, rising into her waistline. The baby was healthy and thriving. Kyle and Bethany would have a daughter in April.

Bethany smiled as she stacked the dishes. Everyone except Jacob had tried to volunteer to clean up for her, but she had shooed them all away. She wanted the time alone. She poured herself a cup of tea, then sat and bowed her head to give a quiet moment of thanks. She could smell the apple pie baking, the hot chocolate simmering, the spiced cider in the Crock-Pot.

Bethany opened her eyes, the music already rising in her.

Till all things now living unite in thanksgiving—

She got up again, working at the sink. Were her mother alive, she'd have shuddered to see Bethany washing dishes. Claire Testamarta had grown up having servants and had raised her daughter the same way. It was Kyle's mother who had taught Bethany how to make a home. A blessed saint, Hannah Dolan. Her name had fit her, with its earthiness and simple beauty.

Hannah. The very sound of the name was gracious. Bethany prayed her daughter would be like the grandmother she would never know—cheerful, affectionate, and wise.

Hannah. Yes, that would be her name.

Next year at this time, she'd be putting Hannah down for a nap. Bethany could see her—a rosy-cheeked baby with dark hair, blue eyes, and her father's rascal grin. Kyle would tease her and she'd tease back, smearing apple pie on her face just to make him laugh.

Laurel would be in medical school, but she'd be able to join them for Thanksgiving. Their agreement specified that she was never to contact them after the baby's birth, but now that Bethany and Kyle knew her—and were growing to love her—who cared about that?

Lord, bless this young woman as she is blessing us, Bethany prayed, as she had prayed every morning since Laurel had come into their lives.

She grabbed her jacket and went outside to find Kyle, singing as she went.

The sun was low on the horizon even though it was midafternoon. The grass had faded to brown, the flower beds were tucked under mulch until spring. Bethany wouldn't see green again until April. When Hannah would be born.

Kyle was out in the meadow, playing with the kids. He pounced on a football, then jumped up before Benton could grab him.

"Give it right here!" Laurel called out.

Kyle wound up to throw the ball. Little Dorothy grabbed his arm. He spun around, swinging her in a full circle before he brought her in for a landing.

"Come on, man. I'm open!" Laurel waved her arms.

Bethany's stomach turned sour. Surely Kyle wasn't so foolish as to allow—

He whipped the football at Laurel. She knocked it down, then fell on it. Jacob was on her in a flash, followed by Melissa.

Jacob locked his arms around Laurel's waist. "Come on! Give it up, girl."

"Bite me, mutt," Laurel said, laughing.

"Stop it! Get off her!" Bethany yanked Jacob off Laurel.

He twisted out of her grip. "We're only playing."

Kyle was at Bethany's side now. "What're you doing? The kids are just playing."

"Me? What are *you* doing? Allowing Laurel to be tackled!"

"No one is tackling me." Laurel rolled onto her back and tossed the football to Kyle.

"We're just playing keep-away," Kyle said. "It's good exercise."

"You're playing football with a pregnant woman!" Bethany had to get Laurel off the cold ground—that couldn't be good for the baby. She tried to grab her arm. "Are you okay?"

Laurel pushed her heels into the ground and scooted backwards. "Just cool it, okay?"

"Cool it? You're the one who needs to cool it!" Bethany heard her voice go shrill but couldn't stop herself. "What if something happened—"

"Nothing was going to happen," Kyle said.

"No? What if someone kicked her in the stomach? Or pushed her down? Or she could have just fallen, fallen too hard. If anything happened, how could I forgive—"

Kyle grasped Bethany's arm. "Bethany, calm down. Please. You're overreacting."

"Don't you think I'm entitled?" She tossed in a river of anger now, a torrent rushing her where she knew she shouldn't go; yet she was powerless to resist.

Kyle tried to take her into his arms, and she hit him. And kept hitting him, not knowing why except to punish him for putting her through this again—this hideous fear that life was so fragile that the flight of a football or the play of a child could dash her hope to a million pieces.

Hitting Kyle because she couldn't hit God.

Kyle held Bethany while she cried it out. The sun was sinking behind the mountains when she was ready to go back inside. "The pie. It's got to be burnt to cinders," she said.

"David took it out," Kyle said.

"How do you know that?" They walked together, arms around each other's waists.

"He was on the back porch, munching a big piece. Hope he left some for the rest of us."

"I need to apologize to Laurel. And the kids."

"She understands. We all do."

"I still need to tell her how sorry I am."

Moments later, they were at the apartment.

"I'm sorry—" Bethany and Laurel said at the same time.

"No. Nothing to be sorry about," Laurel said.

"I was just—" Bethany's words died as she saw Laurel clutch her stomach.

"What's wrong?" She pulled away from Kyle.

"Are you sick?" Kyle asked.

"No. I feel—" Laurel's face blossomed into a smile. "No way! Oh, no way!"

Laurel pressed Bethany's hand to her stomach, and Bethany felt a tiny tap. She reached for Kyle, but Laurel was already guiding his hand to her stomach.

Kyle focused intensely, then burst into laughter. "That is so cool!"

"Isn't it?" Laurel asked, laughing with him now. "She's kicking."

Bethany laughed through her tears. *Not cool*, she thought. *A miracle*.

11

$\mathcal{S}$able Lynde couldn't believe what she was seeing. "The Department of the Treasury is pleased to inform you that—"

"Yes!" she yelped. December 13 would be a day she remembered for the rest of her life. Her account had survived, and she was a millionaire!

Sable typed furiously. There was so much work ahead. She had already begun opening online accounts throughout New England—quasi-commercial accounts with Sable Lynde or Laurel Bergin as the financial officer. Now, without the eye of the government on her, she could slowly transfer money to these fictitious businesses. It would take months, but eventually, neither the IRS nor anyone else would be able to follow her trail.

Her computer *pinged*. This e-mail was from an address she didn't recognize. GUNGHO@smartsend.com. She double-clicked and read:

Hey Kid, What's happening? Where are you? Hailey and me are worried about you. Write back. Tell me you're okay. Love and kisses, Cade.

Btw, Hailey thinks you're having a kid. I think she's whacked.

Oh yeah. Who's the lady in the Volvo?

It hit Sable like a hammer. She would never be safe. She slipped to the floor and curled up as tightly as her pregnant belly would allow.

He would come for her. Piling up money and running to North Conway, even growing a baby in her belly couldn't keep him away. Some people thought they had guardian angels at their sides, but they were fools. Sable had seen the truth. *He* was on standby, tucked in the corners of your room or under the tread of your foot. Waiting to come.

Waiting to feed. He had sucked her dry. So what more could he want?

The baby.

No, she cried, but the word was smothered into herself.

Such sweetness.

Mama, she tried to cry, but that gasp tangled in her throat. The baby moved inside her, curling into itself just as she was curled. She had to get away before he reached right into her and ripped away the only innocence she had left. The innocence that she would give birth to.

His fingers brushed the back of her neck, turning her nerves into icicles. Numbness spread into her skull, then her mind. Down her arms, into her fingers.

That's right, sweetness. Don't feel. It's better this way. Remember?

Mama, she remembered. Mama had stood between her baby and him.

Sable pushed herself up and bolted for the door. Down the stairs, into the winter mist, but she didn't care. Crying, longing for some- one to save her. "Mama. Please. Where are you?"

—✸—

Bethany sat at her desk in the upstairs office, looking at the calen- dar. December 13. A year ago, her placenta ripped, her baby, Michael, died, and her uterus was taken.

Bethany went to the window. The morning was hazy and cold. It would rain or sleet later this afternoon. A dreary day, but even so, she had to make a new start of it, transform this day into something lovely, in honor of Michael and in anticipation of Hannah.

Maybe she'd do more composing. She had recorded the lullaby and given Laurel a cassette tape player. Bethany had felt foolish, ask- ing Laurel to play it often for her "stomach." It seemed silly, and yet it seemed right too. A baby needed to hear her mother's voice.

Bethany went to the cupboard, looking for a composition book. It was good to be occupied, to be useful. That's what it was all about, wasn't it? People had grand schemes for changing the world, but in the end, it was good simply to be useful to someone else.

Mmm . . . What was that? Sounded like a voice.

Momm . . . Bethany went out to the hall. "Who's there?"

Mama Mama . . . Bethany ran downstairs. "Who's there? What do you want?"

No answer. Back upstairs, looking now through all the rooms. This house was too big sometimes. The crying wasn't as clear in the master suite. Bethany checked the bathrooms, the linen closet, the other bedrooms. Not very clear in there either.

Mama Mama . . .

Her heart twisted. That cry she had heard last summer, that surely had to have been a dream. What—or who—was this?

She ran through the front hall, checking the guest rooms and Kyle's office. Around to the back of the house, going down the stairs, through the kitchen. Even checking the back porch. Nothing there.

Inside again, where the plaintive plea floated from far away. *Mama, are you still here with me?*

Bethany flung open the front door. Cold air poured in, and the whoosh of a car, then another, sped past on the road. She took deep breaths, filling her lungs with winter air. More blessed quiet. It had to be a television or radio playing somewhere inside.

She went back down to the cellar and shut off the electricity to the whole house. She hadn't noticed the background noise until it was gone—the hum of the refrigerator, the distant rumble of the furnace, the whir of the humidifier. Nothing now.

That must have been it—some stray signal, maybe, from the research station high on Mount Washington. An inversion of air, and somehow, the signal had skipped into the farmhouse. Bethany stretched her arms over her head, willing her hands to stop trembling.

She went upstairs and sat at the piano, flexing her fingers.

Mama! Please! Don't leave me here!

Bethany slammed her fingers onto the keys, pounding out heavy chords, dark music. Drowning out every sound except her own music.

12

*I*f Laurel held him like this forever, Jacob would be in a better heaven than the one Mrs. Dolan was always yakking about.

"Thank you," she whispered, letting him out of the hug. "I knew you'd help me out."

"It was Switch that did it. The man is connected." That hunk of hair and tattoos was one scary dude, though no way he'd tell Laurel that.

"How much was the stuff?"

"Ten. Hold on; I got your change." She had given Jacob a twenty. Neither of them had been able to guess North Conway street price. He dug into his pocket for the cash.

"Keep it. Finder's fee."

"You don't need to—"

"Just shut up and keep it."

"Thanks."

She handed him a soda, then sat down across the table from him. "You know I'm no big-time user, right? A little weed now and then, just to take the edge off."

He'd seen plenty of hard-timers in Forge Hill. The women looked like old paper bags, used up and torn. The men were skinny and mean. "Sure. You're what they call a recreational user."

She laughed. "You got it. But that's it. Nothing more. It pays to keep the mind clear. And you gotta be keeping a clear head on you all the time. So even though you're moving the stuff between Switch and me, don't be digging in until you're older. Anthony's age or so."

He nodded again, trying to look like the choirboy his mama

wished he were. Laurel was his friend—maybe his best ever—but his business was his business.

"To you, Jacob. The coolest dude I know." As Laurel raised her glass of O.J. and clinked it against his can of soda, her hand shook.

She really needs a hit, Jacob thought. *Glad I could help her out.*

Sable sucked deeply on the joint. She needed it to settle her nerves. She'd blacked out earlier today, then woke up blabbering under the lilac bushes. Good thing Bethany hadn't found her. It was that blasted Cade's fault, breathing down her neck again, chasing her wherever she went.

Maybe Sable had panicked over nothing. Cade didn't have a street address or a phone number—if he did, he'd already have been at her door, looking for a handout. Then again, Bernard had tracked her to Boston. She kicked herself for having her security deposit forwarded to Pilgrim Road. At least the trail ended there. Bethany had told her how they kept the farmhouse in her aunt's name so she could have privacy from her fans. Apparently even classical music groupies could be obnoxious.

Fame, fortune, and fans—as if those were the worst things in the world. Bethany Dolan had no clue how life could rip a person apart, leave her tattered and bleeding. Leave her lying there where *he* could

Stop it, Sable told herself. *Stop and think.* What else did Cade know, besides the e-mail address? *The lady in the Volvo.* He must have seen Bethany pick her up at the funeral home. That woman clung to her like wallpaper.

Like that tape and tape player thing. Bethany had made a recording of some lullaby she had written. She insisted that Sable play it at least twice a day, pressed against her stomach. Every once in a while she'd sing the lullaby to Sable's stomach directly, mumbling some garbage about the baby getting to know her mother's voice.

Well, it was Sable's voice the baby knew. Sable was the mama now, though both Kyle and Bethany chose to ignore that fact. There were times when Bethany couldn't get enough of Sable's stomach—feeling the baby move, measuring how big the belly was. And times when Bethany was in one of those dark moods, when the woman couldn't even bear to look at her. That was understandable. Sable, as Laurel Bergin, was doing something Bethany couldn't.

Stop it, she told herself again. None of that would matter in four months anyway. *Get back on Cade.* But she couldn't focus, not with her head feeling like glass on the outside, mush on the inside. Maybe she should just sleep.

And pray that *he* would stay away.

———— ✺ ————

Anthony did not like what he was seeing, and he sure did not like what he was feeling. Laurel was stretched out on her bed, her mouth hanging open. A half-burned joint smoldered in a dish on the night table.

"Leave her be," Jacob said, trying to shove him toward the door.

"I can't leave her be, fool. She's all drugged up!" Anthony snapped.

"She's just a little high. A little pot never hurt no one."

"That so? What do you know about a little pot?"

Jacob grinned. "Who's the real man here? The man who delivers!"

"You get out before I kill you. Or tell Mama. You think North Conway is off the planet? She'll send you to Siberia."

Jacob swore, then ran out of the bedroom. Moments later, the outside door slammed.

Anthony rubbed the inside of Laurel's wrist. "Laurel. Come on! Wake up. Please!"

This was nuts—he should just call an ambulance. But if he did that, they might arrest her. He should go get Mrs. Dolan. No, scratch that. She might send Laurel away somewhere. Anthony couldn't bear the thought of that.

Laurel's eyes fluttered open. "Hey. Anthony. What're you doing here?"

"Nothing. Just making sure you're okay." He got up from the bed, thinking he'd better flush that joint before Mrs. Dolan came up. Laurel grasped his hand, pulled him down to her.

"Don't go," she said, pressing her lips to his.

Leave, he told himself. But his arms had their own mind, wrapping around Laurel, holding her close. Then her lips moved down his neck, sending a shock through his body so powerful that all he could think of was her.

And then he couldn't even think.

13

*S*able had choked when the Dolans asked about what her family did for Christmas. "I wasn't exactly raised in a spiritual home," she said. No lie there.

Kyle explained again about how the baby Jesus would return someday as a king for His people. Sable smiled and nodded, all the time thinking that Jesus better not come before she got all her money.

Christmas Eve started first thing in the morning. Kyle, Bethany, and Sable hiked into the backwoods until they found the perfect spruce for the living room. As Kyle hacked it down, Bethany teased him. "You swing an ax better than most of your Red Sox swing a bat."

The tree was so tall Kyle had to use a stepladder to string the lights. Bethany had brought down the ornaments from the attic— glass balls, angels, shepherds, stars, and bells.

"Family heirlooms and keepsakes," she said. "And now that you're part of the family, we've got one for you." She gave Sable a box wrapped in red foil and tied with a gold ribbon.

Inside was a silver bell, with the engraving: *May God bless you, Laurel, for bringing us great joy. Kyle and Bethany*

Sable was surprised to feel tears trickle down her cheeks.

For Christmas Eve dinner, Bethany served beef tenderloin stuffed with baby spinach and mushrooms, and baked potatoes topped with goat cheese. Kyle raved as if the brownies that Sable had made from a box were the most amazing dessert ever.

Then Bethany was at the piano, playing carols. Sable leaned back on the sofa, filled with supper and baby. Kyle lay on the floor under the Christmas tree and stared up through the lights.

"I used to do this when I was a kid," he said.

"You're still a kid," Bethany said without missing a note.

"Does that mean Santa is coming tonight?"

"Only with a bag of coal, Southie."

"Come on, I've been good. Did you see how I cleaned my plate at supper?"

"Yeah, you cleaned your plate and the brownie plate. Maybe Santa needs to bring you a treadmill."

Kyle rolled out from under the tree and went to the piano. He lifted Bethany's hair and kissed the back of her neck. "Come on, Santa's fatter than I am."

"Well, you'll have the opportunity to catch up to Kris Kringle tomorrow. We're having ravioli with the ham." Bethany turned, kissed Kyle on the lips without missing a note. Then she caught Sable staring at her. "Whoops. Sorry."

"No, that's fine," Sable said. "I'm just glad there's someone in this house that's got a bigger belly than me."

"Hey!" Kyle protested.

"If the shoe fits . . . " Sable said.

"You mean . . . if nothing fits . . . " Bethany said, laughing and still playing.

Kyle rolled back under the tree and closed his eyes.

Is that what a content man looks like? Sable wondered. Cade was the only man she had ever known well, and he was never satisfied, didn't matter what he got. This was the world she wanted to live in. If only it were as easy as sending Santa a letter, then Sable might have asked for that night to last forever.

A fire roared in the fireplace, the crackling of the wood a perfect accompaniment to the music. The mantel was decorated with forest greens and gold ribbons. Scarlet candles in brass holders blazed in all the windows. Sable put her feet up, letting the night settle over her—Bethany's elegant music, the scent of Christmas pine and burning wood, the sparkling lights and festive decorations.

"When are we opening presents?" Kyle asked.

"Oh? Are you getting gifts this year?" Bethany teased.

"You are."

"Well, in that case, let's get to it. Oh, wait. Santa left stuff for someone else—someone far better behaved than you, Kyle Dolan." Bethany grinned at Sable.

"Oh, you mean Hannah?" Sable said. "She hasn't caused any trouble. Not yet, at least."

Bethany took Sable's hand. "I mean you, Laurel." She led Sable to a small stool near the tree. Kyle dragged a huge sack out of the den, humming as he arranged brightly wrapped presents around her feet.

Sable's heart hammered—she had expected something, of course, but not all this. No one had ever done that for her. Her mama had tried, but there was so little money. "These aren't all for me, I hope."

"Almost all," Bethany said. "There might be one or two for the number-one Red Sox fan in the universe."

"A pennant for next year?" Kyle asked, eyes wide in mock innocence.

"Sorry. Santa doesn't do miracles." Bethany tossed a bow at him.

He put it on top of his head, grinning like a clown. "Go ahead, Laurel. Dig in."

"I don't know where to start." Her hands shook as she took the first gift from Bethany.

Bethany clutched her hands. "Are you all right, Laurel?"

"Why did you do all this?" Sable whispered.

Bethany kissed her cheek. "Because we love you. Now, open your presents so you don't upset Santa."

Sable opened boxes until her fingers ached. Most were maternity clothes—flannel nightgowns, soft woolen slacks with elastic waists, corduroy overalls, hand-knit sweaters, silk blouses, cotton T-shirts. Even long underwear and maternity tights.

There were other gifts. A gold bracelet. A navy blazer, cashmere sweater, and gray wool slacks, all in her prepregnancy size. A portable television. A gold chain with a delicate cross.

Bethany gave Kyle a photograph of an elaborate satellite dish. "I may regret this, but I'm giving you two full sports packages—one for here, one for Pilgrim Road—so you can watch any game of any sport at any time. Rumor is you can even watch curling from Canada and boccie from Europe."

Kyle faked a swoon. "I've died and gone to heaven!"

He gave Bethany a diamond bracelet and necklace. "I know I can't replace the one that was stolen," he said. "But I hope you'll enjoy these."

A chill ran through Sable. Bernard had ripped off Bethany's jewelry when he invaded the Boston townhouse. That seemed like two lifetimes ago. She pushed it out of her mind.

"Now it's my turn," she said. "I have something for you both."

"Oh, no, you didn't need to," Bethany said.

Sable grabbed her backpack. "I wanted to." It wasn't totally a lie—Anthony had thought of it, but now she was glad she hadn't gone to Christmas Eve empty-handed. She pulled the box out of her backpack and passed it to Bethany. "I hope you like this."

"I'm sure we will. You have such—" Bethany's words died abruptly as she opened it.

"What is it?" Kyle asked, bouncing up from the floor.

"A christening gown. Oh, Laurel, it's . . . " Bethany choked up.

"Anthony's mother helped me make it," Sable said. The truth was, Joan Martinez had made almost all of it, teaching Sable how to attach the lace and do the buttons. She had insisted that Sable take full credit.

"I love it," Bethany said. "It's so beautiful."

"Thank you. And merry Christmas." Kyle hugged her.

"Merry Christmas." Sable hugged him back, then hugged Bethany. "Everything will work out. It's going to be wonderful."

It was going to be wonderful, wasn't it? After all, what was 'joy to the world' about, Sable thought, if not getting everything you wanted?

14

*K*yle drove down Route 93, heading for Boston. He had a mound of papers to sign off on to complete the partnership with TradeWinds. If all went well, he'd be able to retire from an active role with Dol-Pak and spend his time with his family.

His family. The thought of it filled his heart. This was no way to spend Valentine's Day, not for a guy who was married to the most beautiful, talented, delightful wife in the world. He had ordered roses for Bethany and lilies for Laurel, to be delivered later in the day.

He had tried to persuade them to come to Boston with him. "The change of scenery will be good for you. Take in some plays, a concert."

Laurel had declined. "I'm a bear, hibernating until spring."

And wherever Laurel was, Bethany would stay. At least she had agreed to go to Bridgton that day and perform for the arts center benefit. That would give Laurel some time on her own.

Kyle would miss the lazy pace of life at the farmhouse. Watching the snow fall on the mountains. Tromping the trails in snowshoes. Snowboarding. Skiing. Sitting with Bethany by the fire.

Laurel was seven months pregnant now. It had seemed like seven eons since the implantation last July.

"You think this is slow?" Joan Martinez had teased the last Sunday at church. "Wait 'til that baby of yours is bawling all night. You're gonna miss these days when she didn't say a peep. Just sat there in her mama's belly."

But the baby wasn't in her *mama's* belly. She was in Laurel's. Bethany never said a word, but he knew it hurt her to be denied the privilege of carrying her child.

Kyle's cell buzzed. He checked caller ID, then picked up. "Nora. What's the matter? Is the baby—"

"The baby is fine. It's Laurel. She's got a slight rise in her blood sugar."

"Diabetes?"

"Prediabetes for now. We'll want to adjust her diet and check her sugar every few days. Something to watch, nothing to be alarmed over."

"There's a *but* in there somewhere," Kyle said.

"But her urinalysis didn't show any sugar. Which means the blood test was wrong or the urine test was. We retested them both, got the same results. So I asked the lab to run a pregnancy test on Laurel's urine. It was negative."

"Hold on a minute." A dump truck was on his tail, flashing its lights. Kyle pulled into the breakdown lane and stopped. "Okay. So you're telling me that there was a mix-up at the lab."

"I had the lab check the original sample bottle. My initials were on the container, so I know it was Laurel's. Or at least, it was the urine she gave me."

"What are you saying, Nora?"

"This isn't Laurel Bergin's urine."

"But I saw her go into the bathroom, come out with the sample. So how—?"

"She must have had someone else's urine, ready to put into the sample bottle."

"Why would she do that?"

"Don't be naïve, Kyle."

He gripped the steering wheel with his free hand. "If she's been doing drugs—what about the baby?"

"The sonograms have been fine. Of course, there are things we can't know until Hannah is born. We'll just have to hope for the best."

"Bethany will melt down over this."

"No, she won't. Not if we get a handle on it right away. I want you to talk to Laurel, find out exactly what she's been taking. And get me a specimen from her today, even if you have to stand and watch her go into the bottle."

"I want the truth, Nora. How dangerous is this for Hannah?"

"If Laurel was into something big-time, Bethany would have spotted it. She's with her all the time. Just talk to Laurel; get her to tell you what she's been using."

Kyle closed the phone. That familiar sensation—dread—settled over him. He would move heaven and earth for Bethany, if only God would let him. He pulled the car off the freeway, then got back on, heading north.

Anthony stood on the step, holding a bouquet of roses.

"I didn't get you anything," Sable said.

"You're all I want." Anthony kissed her as she led him to the bedroom.

How sweet he talked! Sable knew better than to believe him, of course. She was working hard to keep this thing with Anthony real. To convince herself that he was just a moment in nine months of boredom. After all, wasn't that all love really was? A spark in an otherwise dreary day?

Two hours later, the sky had turned the color of dull lead. Sable snuggled with Anthony on the sofa, feeling safe and warm. He had turned eighteen in December and was becoming more man than boy. The irony was just too fine—this high-school kid was closer in age to Sable than any other lover she had had. Not that the others were lovers, not by any definition of the word.

A car backfired, right outside the window. Sable sat up, startled. Bethany had nagged Kyle the previous night about getting the muffler fixed when he got to Boston.

Why had he come back? Maybe he'd forgotten some papers or something. A quick in and out at the farmhouse, and he'd be gone. But no, she heard footsteps storming up the stairs, followed by knocking at the door to the kitchen.

Kyle could not find her with Anthony, not entwined on the sofa like this, half his clothes still on the floor of her bedroom. She could forfeit half her bonus if she violated the contract with any sort of sexual contact.

No time to think it out—Kyle was in the kitchen already. "Laurel? Where are you?"

Anthony, exhausted from school and work, didn't even stir. Even if she could get him quickly awake, he'd never get out in time.

Sable had to protect herself, no matter what. She had to act smart and act fast. She just hoped Anthony would forgive her. If he didn't, well—that was life, wasn't it?

She got on the floor and pulled Anthony on top of her. Then she screamed as if her world were ending.

———∞———

Kyle was shocked to his core by what he saw—Anthony Martinez, half-naked and sprawled on top of Laurel.

"Don't, please don't! Get off me!" she cried.

Kyle yanked Anthony up, spun him around, and punched him. Anthony went down on one knee, his nose gushing blood.

Laurel got up and tried to pull Kyle away. "Don't! You'll kill him!"

"That's right. I'll kill the son of a—"

"Stop! Stop it!" Bethany's voice cut through the chaos. "What is going on here?"

Where had she come from? Kyle wondered in the only corner of his mind that was still rational.

"Your little pet was trying to rape Laurel."

Bethany's face drained of color. "No."

"No," Anthony echoed. He had backed into the corner like a wounded animal. "Mr. Dolan, I didn't. I wouldn't—"

"You did, you little puke. I caught your filthy—"

"Kyle, slow down. Please." Bethany pressed her hands against his chest. Behind her, Laurel stood white-faced and shaking.

"Laurel, tell them," Anthony pleaded. "I wouldn't do that."

"He misunderstood," Laurel said. "I told him how much I loved his music. He thought I was saying something else. I shouldn't have hugged him, but I didn't realize he wanted to take it further—" She broke off, gasping for air.

Bethany drew her close. "Are you hurt?"

"No!" Anthony said. "I wouldn't hurt her. How can you even ask that?"

"I'm okay," Laurel said.

Every sound was magnified to maddening proportions for Kyle— Anthony's breathing, Laurel's weeping, his own heart pounding. Anthony mumbled explanations, but one look at Laurel's face, her body trembling, her belly full with his child, made Kyle want to tear Anthony to shreds. He opened his cell phone instead, his hands shaking.

"What are you doing?" Bethany asked.

"Calling the cops."

"Laurel!" Anthony gasped. "Tell them—"

"Kyle, don't!" Laurel said.

"We need to calm down and think this through," Bethany said.

"He attacked Laurel!"

"We were just being together. Tell them, Laurel," Anthony cried. "I swear, Mrs. Dolan. I swear that's the truth. Laurel, why aren't you telling them what really happened? What we've been doing, and how we feel about each other?"

"Blame me," Laurel sobbed. "Not Anthony. He misunderstood. I must have led him on without realizing . . . "

Kyle pressed his hands to his head. His skull was splitting. "Was this the first time he tried anything?"

Laurel's gaze was steady now, her breathing calmer. "Yes. Just let him go home."

"Let him go," Bethany whispered.

Kyle pulled Anthony to him so they were eye to eye. "I never want to see your filthy face around here again. You understand?"

"Oh, I understand all right." Anthony walked out, grabbing his shirt and jacket as he went.

No one said anything until the door slammed.

"I'm so sorry," Laurel said, crying.

"Should we call Nora?" Kyle asked. "Have her come over, check Laurel out?"

"No. Really, you have to believe me. I'm all right."

"Kyle, go make her something to eat while I clean her up," Bethany said.

Kyle went into the kitchen, grateful for something to do. He was looking for a pan to heat some soup in when he spotted the roses. They were stuck in a glass of water in the window. *Dumb florist—the roses were for Bethany. Laurel was supposed to get lilies.* Then he saw the card: *Sweet Laurel—you are music to my ears—harmony to my heart. Love always, Anthony*

He opened the back door and flung the roses into the snow.

What a fool Sable had been, messing around with Anthony. Fortunately, the Dolans were bigger fools than she was. To think a harmless dope like Anthony Martinez could be a rapist! Then again, that's all men really wanted, when you got down to it. Sable was willing to bet that even Kyle had some action going on the side. All those weeks alone in Boston—did Bethany really believe Kyle would cool his jets while she was up at the farmhouse playing mother hen?

There was a knock at the door. Kyle stood on the porch. She mustered a wounded smile. "I'm glad you came back up. I wanted to say again how sorry—"

"We have to talk." He sat at the kitchen table and motioned her to join him.

"You want a diet soda or something?"

"No." Kyle looked everywhere but at her.

She sat across from him, willing herself to keep her face open and unassuming.

"Your blood sugar is elevated." Kyle went on to explain about the gestational diabetes. The bottom line was that she'd have to follow a strict diet, keep away from sugar and refined flour. "No more of Bethany's cookies, I'm afraid."

"Now, that is a bummer," she said, laughing. Why wasn't he laughing with her?

"This isn't a joke."

"I'm sorry, Kyle. I'm a little buzzed, after—you know."

"I do know. I know more than I care to, I'm afraid."

"What do you mean?"

"I know that you've been switching your urine on us."

"What? What makes you think that?" Sable said, keeping her tone even.

"You should have had sugar in your urine. But the urine tested negative. Nora had the lab run a pregnancy test. That also came up negative."

Sable couldn't help herself—she laughed. "That is too rich, doing a pregnancy test on Jacob's urine."

"You used Jacob Martinez's urine? And you think that's funny?"

"I'm sorry," she said, racing for an explanation. It came to her, fast and perfect. Oh yeah, she could still outthink everyone around her.

"I need to know the truth. Are you on drugs, Laurel?"

She nodded. "Diet pills."

"What?"

"They were made with all-natural ingredients, so I assumed it'd be okay for the baby."

"Why would you take diet pills?"

"Look at me! My stomach's bigger than a volleyball. I wanted to get my weight under control. I knew Nora wouldn't approve, so I had Jacob give me some urine for my last test."

"I want to see these pills."

"I flushed them a couple days back. I read about this study online, the one about how ephedrine increases heart rate. That scared me— I would never do anything to endanger Hannah." Sable started crying. It was a gift, being able to perform on demand. Though somewhere deep inside, she really did regret putting Kyle through it.

Kyle handed her a sample container. "I need a urine sample. Right now."

A minute later, she came out of the bathroom and handed Kyle the bottle. She was surprised, almost impressed when he went into the bathroom and checked the waste container to make sure she hadn't made some sort of substitution. She hoped her own urine would pass muster this time. She had stopped the weed three weeks before—Anthony had made her.

"I'd better let you get to bed," Kyle said. "You look wiped out."

"Yeah. I am."

Kyle stopped at the door, looked back at her. "Laurel, are you sure you're okay? After this thing with Anthony?"

She shrugged. "I've put it behind me already. You should too."

He smiled, then closed the door. Sable laid her head on the table, too tired to move. She would miss Anthony, but what did she expect?

Nothing good ever lasted.

15

aurel had pulled him into her arms and screamed rape.

She hadn't used the actual word, of course. She left that up to Kyle Dolan. Not much of a jump there, Anthony knew. Laurel hollered and cried, Dolan bashed his face in, then Mrs. Dolan dumped him back into the trash heap he came from.

Anthony could barely see the computer screen. He knew he should just shut it down, forget Laurel Bergin ever existed. But there must be some clue somewhere to explain why she would turn on him.

The monitor flashed. SearchMaster.com brought up over a hundred hits. Anthony straightened his shoulders, blinked hard, and began reading. Most were from the Southwick University Web site. There she was in the alumni register—that golden-haired, blue-eyed liar. He read through four years of scholastic and sports accounts, reading every line to find some explanation for what she had done. After hours of reading, he still wasn't any closer to the mystery that was Laurel Bergin.

"Anthony, you're up early. Or is it late?" His mother stood in the doorway. She was still dressed in her scrubs, coming off the overnight shift in the ER.

"Just some homework," he said, tilting the computer screen away.

"You okay?"

The truth was that he was ripped to shreds. But he couldn't tell his mother that. She'd resisted taking any help from the Dolans in the first place.

"Rich people like them—it always comes with a price," she had said when Kyle had first visited them after the attack on Anthony, proposing a move out of state.

Was this the price? *A fair-haired girl cries, "Get off me," and the Dolans leap to the obvious conclusion about a kid with a Latino name and dark skin?*

"Anthony. I said, are you—"

"Honestly, I'm not feeling well. Probably should stay home. Tell you what—let me get Jacob off to school so you can get to bed early. Then I'll go back to sleep myself."

She wrapped her arms around him, this hardworking woman who worked her tail off to keep her sons on the right track. "Okay, baby," she whispered. "But if you need me, just wake me up."

An hour later, Jacob was on the school bus and Anthony was back on the computer. He backtracked the references to Laurel's high school years. She had led her softball team to a state championship. He brought up the photo of her, curious as to what she had looked like at his age.

Except it wasn't her. Though it was a fuzzy shot and taken from the side, that girl was too broad and too dark to be the girl he knew. Anthony clicked on an even older reference. The year earlier, Laurel had been named Scholar-Athlete of the Year. There was a long article, telling all about the records she had broken and the honors she had earned. And a clear head shot of a solemn Laurel Bergin.

Anthony stared at the picture for almost an hour, his head throbbing, his anger high in his throat. Even when he collapsed onto his bed and closed his eyes, Laurel Bergin stared back at him.

"You know how I feel about sexual predators," Nora said. "I'd like to take a knife to—"

"Not Anthony. He's always been so gentle. I want to believe—I *have* to believe that it just got out of hand and Anthony couldn't . . . " The truth was that Bethany didn't know what to believe.

"Any man can and should stop. There is no excuse for rape, Bethany. Though whether you should believe Laurel on anything—

well, that's a whole other discussion." Nora banged out a vicious sequence of minor chords.

They had sat down at the piano for some four-hand piano, a favorite activity since they were girls. Nora usually played the chords while Bethany did the elaborate fingering.

"Why do you say that? Do you think . . . "

"Honestly, I don't know what to think." Nora squeezed her hand. "Come on, girl, let's forget it for now. Which piece are we doing first? Nothing too hard now."

"Bach's 'Arioso.' That's easy."

As Bethany set the music out, Nora dramatically flexed her fingers, fluffed out imaginary tails. "You know, I always enjoy this. Until I actually begin playing and blow it left and right."

"All you need is a little practice."

"All I need is twenty more hours in the day. Or maybe a couple of clones," Nora said, laughing. "One-two-three-and . . . "

They played through the piece twice. Not the best performance ever, Bethany knew, but the music and the companionship created its own unique beauty. "Let's do the Clemente piece next," she suggested.

"The 'Allegro'? I don't think I'm ready for that one." Nora picked at the keys, playing a little Schubert instead.

Bethany followed along, improvising as they went.

"What's up with Jenny and Kate?" she asked, once they had settled into a comfortable rhythm.

Nora filled Bethany in on the girls' lives—Kate's novel about dead rock climbers who haunted Cathedral Ledge and Jenny's romance with a Romanian prince who turned out to be a pizza delivery boy. They were laughing so hard, it took them a moment to hear the doorbell. Their laughter died as soon as Bethany opened the door.

Anthony stood on the front step.

"Tell me why. Why you would do this to us." Bethany's voice was brittle.

"I can't. Maybe after the baby's born, but not now. I beg you, Bethany, please just let it go for now. I promise you—" Sable had hoped this moment would never come, but she had prepared for it. Yet her fine-tuned story was stuck in her throat, blocked by dread. And yes, regret that Bethany and Kyle had had to find out.

Sable had hated it the first time Bethany hugged her, had to stop herself from pushing the woman away. She had learned to endure Bethany's touch, her fingers brushing back her hair, the sisterly kisses on her cheek. She became accustomed to Kyle's jokes, his constant pouring out of sports lore and business wisdom, his Southie stories, his outright enthusiasm for this God who loved him beyond imagining.

Kyle had also said that God loved Sable beyond imagining. Maybe that was why she *couldn't* imagine it. Where was God now, in this moment when Bethany's fear and Sable's fear twined like a noose, strangling them both?

"Bethany, you weren't lying, were you? When you said you . . ." Sable wanted to bite the words back. And yet, they had a life of their own, pushing out of her mouth in fits and starts. "When you said you liked me and that I was part of the family?"

"I said I *loved* you. As did Kyle."

"Were you lying?"

"No. But you were." Bethany's face was horrible to see, drained of color and life.

"Okay, so maybe I borrowed Laurel Bergin's name. But it was me. And it still is me. Just let me be Laurel for two more months. What could it hurt?"

Bethany stepped toward her, and Sable instinctively raised her hand, expecting a blow. Bethany brushed Sable's hand aside and put her own hand on Sable's shoulder. Not hurting her, though when Bethany had first burst into the apartment, her anger shone through her skin so powerfully that Sable could feel its heat.

"You tell me what it would hurt," Bethany said. "Tell me what you're running from."

"I can't."

"Then just tell me who you are. I beg you."

For a moment, Sable considered it. But no, she couldn't. Bethany and Kyle just couldn't even imagine the darkness that was out there. Their lives were too perfect, too good to ever have been touched by—

He was near now. Sable couldn't see him, but she could feel his breath, moist and hot, on her neck. She moved across the living room, trying to put space between herself and whatever hole he was sliding out of.

Bethany followed her. "We know who Laurel Bergin is. Now, please, tell me who you are. If you're in trouble, there might be something we can do to help."

"Look, just give me some space for a few more weeks. That's not too much to ask, is it?" Sable looked out the window. Storm clouds had turned the afternoon to early night.

She felt Bethany's fingers dig into her shoulder. "We've entrusted you with our daughter. I beg you . . . "

Sable wanted to clasp that hand, but before she could, Bethany let go. She left the apartment, disappearing like a ghost into the first burst of snow sweeping down from the mountains.

"Would it be too much to ask that you forgive me, no questions asked?" Sable whispered to the window.

But Bethany was out of sight.

16

yle was numb with rage. "Tell me your real name."

"Why? You don't like Laurel? I think it fits me quite well."

Laurel—or whoever she was—munched on potato chips, as care-free and glib as if Kyle had just asked her to name her favorite Red Sox player.

"I don't know who you are, but you are not Laurel Bergin."

Bethany had called him at Dol-Pak, absolutely hysterical. Kyle cursed himself for not investigating Laurel Bergin any further back than her college years. He was furious with himself for buying her story that her parents were dead, that she needed the surrogacy to pay for medical school. Sure, her references had checked out, because the real Laurel Bergin was a girl above reproach. Three thousand miles away, no one thought to mention that she was dark haired and brown eyed. Why would they, and why would Kyle ask, when the picture in the Southwick directory showed her as blond and blue-eyed?

A look at the Web sites that Anthony had clued them into, fol-lowed by a few phone calls to Laurel Bergin's real hometown, had confirmed that the woman carrying their baby was a fraud. The real Laurel Bergin had been adopted as an infant from Korea. She was doing a year of missionary service in Africa before heading off to U.Conn. Medical School. By the time Kyle drove back from Boston, Bethany had been stunned into silence. She sat in the dark, unmov-ing and pale, her eyes staring straight ahead. Nora volunteered to go up to the apartment and talk to Laurel. Kyle had to shake the truth out of the girl. Who knew what secrets she might be hiding?

Kyle paced; if he stopped moving, he would explode. The surrogate was now as unyielding as the granite mountain ranges that surrounded them. He could see no way to crack what had to be the real Laurel—or whatever her name was. For months, she had put on sweetness and light, perfectly masking the hard woman underneath.

Nora sat in the chair across from the girl. "What was your real interest in this surrogacy?"

"I told you the truth last summer, and it's still the truth. To make some money for myself. And to carry a baby for Bethany and Kyle."

"Why did you lie to us?" Kyle snapped.

"Why do you think?" Laurel pointed at a pillow on the chair under the window. "Can you get me that? My feet are so swollen."

Kyle tossed her the pillow. "I'm not in the mood for guessing games. You tell us."

"Hmm . . . sorry, but I'll pass on that. It's not in my best interest. Or yours."

"We could find out easily enough," Nora said. "Lawyers, private investigators—"

"That is not in anyone's best interest. Not the Dolans', and certainly not the baby's."

"It's my baby. I'll decide what's in her best interest," Kyle said.

"It's your baby—but she's in my body. What's that old saying? Possession is nine-tenths of the law?" Laurel stood, arching her back to get her balance.

"What are you doing?" Kyle said.

"Taking a walk."

"Where?"

"Maybe I'm going to the bathroom. Maybe I'm going to Conway Village. Or maybe I'm going back to where I came from. It's not your business."

"You can't just leave."

"Why not?" The girl widened her eyes in exaggerated innocence.

"You signed an agreement," Nora said.

"Laurel Bergin signed that agreement. You said I'm not Laurel Bergin. So I'm free to go."

Kyle grabbed her arm. "I'll have you arrested."

"Get your hands off me!"

"Kyle, calm down." Nora guided him away from the girl.

Laurel moved to the recliner, sitting heavily, then pulling the lever to put her head back and her feet up.

As though she doesn't have a care in the world, Kyle thought.

"What would you be arresting me for?"

"Try fraud," Kyle said.

"That won't fly. I am doing what I said I would—having your baby. Your little girl, Kyle. I can feel her now, kicking inside me. She can hear us, you know. You keep shouting, she'll be born being afraid of her daddy."

Kyle breathed evenly, trying to keep from putting his fist through the wall. He unclenched his hands, ashamed that he had struck Anthony, both with his fist and with that ugly accusation. He knew better, knew the kind of young man Anthony was, a gentle boy who had also been taken in by this—Kyle could barely stand to even think the word—this *impostor*.

"Identity theft, then," Nora said, as if she had climbed onto the same wavelength as Kyle. "You're certainly guilty of that."

"You could stick me with that, I suppose. But since I haven't stolen a dime from Laurel Bergin, the most I'd get is a slap on the wrist. On the other hand, the publicity could be very profitable. Book and movie deals, that kind of thing."

"How about statutory rape?" Kyle said, fighting back the anger that seemed to burst from every cell in his body. "You seduced a high-school kid. Then had the nerve to claim he assaulted you."

Laurel laughed. "Kyle, *you* claimed Anthony was assaulting me. I just tapped into that prejudice you're too righteous to think you have. Besides, Anthony turned eighteen in December, so he's of legal age. Then again—"

"Then again what?" Nora snapped.

"You don't know how old *I* really am. Wouldn't that be a kick, if I turned out to be the minor child in this mess we've got here?"

Kyle sank into a chair. His head felt as though it was about to blow apart. *Lord, please don't let me lose it. Give me patience, wisdom, guidance. Things I should have asked for before we got involved with this girl.*

"We'll be contacting the police to see if there's a warrant out for you. It's highly possible you're a fugitive of some sort," Nora said.

"Go ahead. Take my picture. Fingerprint me. Interrogate me. And if there is a warrant—or two or three—they'd put me in jail. Dear me, just thinking about it gives me contractions."

"What do you want?" Kyle said.

Laurel flipped the recliner forward. "The same thing you do. To give you a healthy baby and then to leave you to live happily ever after with that healthy baby."

"Okay. Let's say things just go on as they have been. Will you agree to continue staying here and doing what is best for the baby?" Nora asked. "Will you stay clean? Out of trouble?"

"Given the proper incentives—sure."

"What kind of incentives?"

The girl just laughed.

"You have to rephrase the question, Nora," Kyle said. "How much?"

"I won't be greedy. Let's keep it neat—say, double my fee."

"That's robbery!"

"That's good business. Surely you can appreciate that, Kyle."

Business. That's what it had all come down to, and it was all his fault. If anything happened to his baby, he'd never forgive this girl— whoever she was. And he'd never forgive himself.

———— ∞ ————

Flurries of snow swirled on the wind. From the deck, Kyle could see Laurel stretched out on the sofa, watching one of her stupid game shows. So cool and in control. He slammed his fist against the railing. "How did she get by the screening?"

"Motivation. And apparently, ample intelligence," Nora said.

"But the questionnaires, the physical exam, the psychologist—we looked at her from every angle. She got a clean bill of health!"

"Pathological liars and psychopaths know all the twists and turns of our testing. They routinely beat us at our own game, if they choose to. If I remember, she displayed just enough neurosis to make her seem entirely normal."

"Can we do a Caesarean section, get the baby out, and just be done with this girl?"

"It's too risky at thirty-two weeks."

"You said the baby was viable now."

"Viable, yes. Optimal? Nowhere near. Besides, what makes you think she would agree to a section? Or do you plan to hold her down while I take a scalpel to her?"

"Don't tempt me."

"Your best course is to give her what she wants and just let the pregnancy proceed. Don't you agree, Kyle?"

"I'm concerned about why she lied about her identity."

"Do you think she's hiding from something? Or someone?"

"I'm almost afraid to know," Kyle said. Had that home invasion last October had something to do with Laurel? He had not forgotten the menace in the thug's voice. *Next time, it won't be pretty.*

The wind gusted. Night had fallen and brought a storm with it. "We'd better get inside before we freeze to death," Nora mumbled. "Talk to her and get something settled."

"You go. I need a minute by myself." He gripped the railing, staring into the clouds.

What do you say to the stranger who is carrying your baby?

———— ✖ ————

It was a miracle that Sable had held it all together under Kyle's and Nora's questioning. But what choice did she have? It wasn't as though the Dolans and Nora were in a forgiving mood.

They were finally gone. They hated Sable now, that much was clear. What had she expected, getting involved with those people? She should have kept it a business relationship. Anything more was trouble. Trouble and hardship and grief.

Hadn't her mama taught her that?

———⚬⚬⚬———

She could hear Crooked Teeth trying to get the Big Man to leave. "Hey, man. Take a number and come back later."

"I had an appointment. Ain't that true, Angie?"

"Give me a minute." Mama came out to the kitchen then, cursing under her breath as she lit a cigarette. Big Man followed her out, fists clenched, face red. Sable made herself as small as she could, trying to press into the wall behind the stove.

"Hey, cowboy, I am so sorry," Mama said. "I got my nights screwed up. Can you give me a few minutes, let me get rid of dog-face in there?"

Big Man grabbed Mama's arm. "I can ditch him a whole lot faster than you."

"Please, babe. No trouble. I can make him—what? What are you looking at?"

Sable. He was looking at Sable.

17

ethany was missing.

"The Volvo is in the garage," Nora said.

Kyle went out to the back porch. "Her snowshoes are gone."

"She's out in this storm? Should we call someone? The police, maybe?"

Kyle rubbed his face. "No. Not yet. Look, her snow gear is gone too. She must have thought this out." He pulled on his ski pants. "I think I know where she's gone."

"Maybe you should just wait, Kyle. I don't need both of you missing."

"I'm not letting her face this alone. I'll call you when I find her or if I need help." He pulled the hood over his head and was out the door.

Nora watched him trudge through the backyard toward the woods. The snow came down sideways in the strong wind. She closed the door, went into the house, and sat down to pray.

Even in the blinding snow, the trail to Thor's Falls was easy to follow. Snowmobiles had pressed the path into a wide, hard swath through the trees. The wind howled down the mountainside, bending the trees, cracking dead branches. Within the hour, the going would get very tough.

Kyle pushed harder, working up a sweat. The roar intensified—not just the wind now; he was getting close to the falls. The water was a mighty force, hurtling over the granite boulders and ledges. There were places where the cascades had worn the rocks smooth.

There were even holes in the vast boulders, molded from centuries of swirling current—holes deep enough for a man to step into and disappear.

Bethany loved to scramble high into the cascades where she could watch the water go by on every side. *How easy it would be for this wind to carry her off, to lift her off her perch and drop her into the icy water.*

The storm came off the mountain now in a thunderous roar. Kyle couldn't tell which rumble was wind and which was water. Both were so savage that he couldn't hear himself think.

And then he heard it. The voice of an angel, singing against the wind.

———⊗———

For the first three years, she had struggled to know *why*. Begged God to show her how to get past the pain. Sought to find, if not a place of comfort, at least a place of rest.

She was long past seeking any answers that would make sense. She had gone up there to find that which was greater than she was. But her heart was blinded by a desolation far more powerful than the storm.

God's face was veiled by a pain that gripped every part of her being.

God's heart was as unreadable as the granite in the heart of the mountain.

God's mercy was harder to grasp than the water rushing under her feet.

God's will was fiercer than the wind sweeping out of the sky.

Her hope was in the womb of a dangerous stranger. Her prayers were strangled in her throat. Her faith was frozen under a mass of pain that had been plowed under like snow and left in a crusted, filthy pile.

All she had left was her music, little more than a sliver of song flung against the storm.

Great is Thy faithfulness, O God my Father . . .

She kept singing, scraps of words and notes thrown into the sky, because if she stopped singing, she would cease to exist. For the longest time, the water and wind and storm swallowed her song. Then, out of the growing darkness, another voice—off pitch and rough—joined hers.

There is no shadow of turning with Thee . . .

Two voices joined together—one ragged but strong, one weak but pure.

Thou changest not, Thy compassions they fail not . . . Bethany felt her husband take her hand and stand with her in the storm.

As Thou hast been, Thou forever wilt be . . .

They sang together until her heart thawed. Then she let her love take her home.

———∞———

You hem me in—behind and before;

You have laid your hand upon me.

Such knowledge is too wonderful for me,

Too lofty for me to attain.

(PSALM 139:5–6)

———∞———

18

As Cade Parker stared at a million dollars, he muttered a string of words descriptive enough to melt paint off the walls.

"Good morning to you too," Hailey said, laughing. "I'm glad you're enjoying our new computer. But you don't have to check that account every hour."

"What if she decides to pull the plug?"

"That is why we have to find her," Hailey replied.

"If your little stooge could get us the password, we could just make our own withdrawals."

It had taken Hailey's computer jock a month to retrieve the account numbers from the server. The kid had been hacking on the password for weeks now. Hailey had used up all their money already, but she had found other ways to keep the nerd working.

"I know this was my idea, but it's taking too long," Hailey argued. "The money could be long gone when we finally get the password."

"Got another bright idea?"

"Put the pressure on."

Sable pulled the shades, then jammed the door shut with a chair. While her laptop booted, she hooked up the modem to the phone line. It was a real waste, using a land line when she had high-speed cable. But she couldn't do her work on the desktop computer. She needed to keep her accounts and passwords completely secret.

She shifted in her chair, trying to get comfortable. The baby jumped around so much, it was like having a puppy crawling inside her skin. She knew one way to calm the little one. Bethany reminded her constantly to play the tape for the baby. "I am," Sable would say. And that was kind of the truth.

The baby kicked and punched and tried to turn over the first few times Sable had put the tape player to her stomach. Clearly, the woman made people nervous, even her own baby. So Sable made a change to the tape. A baby needed her mother's voice. And at least for now, Sable was the mama.

Bethany would have freaked out if she had known, but it had to be done, that much was sure. Though that was the only thing Sable was sure of. More and more, her thinking was muddy and skewed. Did pregnancy make everyone stupid? Even now, she saw things out of the corner of her eye, shifting in the shadows.

No! She would not go there. She was just tired, that was all. On edge, with Kyle and the rest of them breathing down her neck all the time. This was the best part of the day—the business hour. Sable's mind seemed sharper, maybe because as she worked her accounts, she knew her future was brighter. *Nothing like a million dollars to clear one's head.*

She planned to move twenty thousand dollars, spread among twelve batches. These small transfers were annoying, but it would be worth it if it meant the trail would be impossible to follow. After escaping the clutches of Bernard, Cade, and Hailey, Sable didn't need the IRS coming at her.

She executed the transfers and was about to close when she noticed a message in her bank e-mail account. GUNGHO@smart-send.com. *Cade.* She had deleted him from her life, so she should delete the stupid e-mail. Then again, it might be important. Maybe Bernard was sniffing around again, and Cade wanted to warn her. She double-clicked to open it.

Hey Kid, How come you're ignoring me? I miss you. You okay? Did you have that baby yet?

Love and kisses, Cade. P.S. Need help baby-sitting? $1,104,934.35 can get into a lot of trouble by itself.

Sable didn't even feel the floor when she hit it.

———⏳———

She would have cried out for help, but she knew she was already beyond saving.

She would have begged to die, but anything that was good in her had already died.

He gained strength from her weakness. She could hear him speaking now, in the hum of the refrigerator, in the whir of the clock. A low voice, congratulating himself for finding her yet again. His words unwound from the ceiling fan, peeling off like notes on a staff, regrouping like dust bunnies with fangs.

Hello, sweetness.

His breath was on her check now. Impossibly cold, burrowing through her skin. If she could only turn her head, she might escape. But no, he would burrow into the back of her head and rip through her brain like paper. If she turned to him, she could swallow his voice, that twisted symphony of raw sound, a parody of words to anyone except the initiated.

Those words made perfect sense to Sable.

Come back. Back to Papa.

The same force that left her with no power to resist—to lie motionless on the tile, cold and abandoned—also left her with no power to accept. Yet, she was not so muddyminded that she didn't know inaction bred submission.

Just *being* meant agreeing.

She felt the child in her, moving where she couldn't flee, kicking where she couldn't resist. Protected by some hand that was not hers, a hand that pushed *his* back.

The child refused *him*. So she must also refuse, even though he was moving into her pores now.

Don't resist, sweetness. That will make it harder for you.

He was in her now. Burrowed into her capillaries, beating with her heart. He could move on a thousand feet, feed with a thousand teeth, swallow and consume her a thousand ways, and still come back for more.

"No," she said with the last ounce of will. "You can't make me."

I already have.

19

"oxemia," Nora Hemlow pronounced.

"What's that?" Laurel was in bed, hovering at the edge of consciousness, a blood-pressure cuff strapped to her arm.

"It's a condition that can occur late in pregnancy," Nora explained. "A challenge to the kidneys, characterized by high blood pressure and protein in the urine."

"Hmm," Laurel said, rolling over.

Nora gently rolled Laurel back. "You need to listen to me so you can understand what is happening to you. And what we have to do to help you."

Laurel screamed, her eyes suddenly stretched so far open that Bethany feared they would burst. Kyle moved forward, but there was no foe to fight, at least none that they could see.

"Laurel, what's wrong? Are you in pain?" Nora asked, keeping her voice steady.

"No, I just . . . where am I?"

"You're in the apartment. I'm Dr. Hemlow. Kyle and Bethany are here with me. We've been discussing your condition, remember?"

She nodded, her eyes heavy now. "Yeah. Okay. I was lost there for a moment. This thing I have—is it something bad?"

"It can be."

Laurel's eyes opened again, for a moment perfectly clear as she stared down Bethany. "You. See what you've done to me?" She rolled over, curled into as tight a ball as her condition would allow.

Nora motioned Kyle and Bethany into the living room.

"Why is she so irrational?" Kyle said.

"Toxins circulating in her blood. Her kidneys are not keeping up with the demands made on them. The medication should clean that up, help her become more oriented to reality. If only we had her real medical history."

"This is very serious, isn't it?" Bethany said.

Nora jammed her fingers through her hair. "It can be life threatening. Out-of-control blood pressure, kidney failure, the possibility of stroke or aneurysm. We do have ways of relieving the symptoms, but it bears watching. Very close watching."

Fear and anger surged in Bethany. Guilt followed quickly, a damp and musty emotion that could only blanket the panic, not quell it. Her first and thousandth thoughts had been of Hannah. Bethany had given little thought to their surrogate, so sick now that she could die in the instant it took a blood vessel to burst.

"What's the best way to treat it?" Kyle was asking.

"She's at thirty-six weeks. We should consider a Caesarean section," Nora said.

"No!" Laurel stood in the hallway, her face deep red.

"Laurel, please. Sit down." Bethany tried to lead her to the sofa.

Laurel yanked away. "Forget that. I'm out of here."

Bethany wanted to block the door, to hold on to Laurel until she agreed to have the section. But she didn't dare touch her—what if Laurel fought back and blew an aneurysm?

"Please, just calm down," she said as gently as she could.

"Calm down? You want to gut me like a stinkin' fish, and you want me to lie down and play dead while you do it?" Laurel staggered to the closet.

Kyle went into the kitchen and got a drink of water. *He's blocking her exit,* Bethany realized. *Has it come to this? Holding our surrogate hostage?*

"You've known that a surgical birth was a possibility all along." Nora positioned herself in front of the slider. The deck was the emergency exit for the apartment.

Laurel struggled into her coat but couldn't button it over her stomach. "You're not cutting me open."

"Laurel, no one's going to do anything to you, except take care of you," Bethany said, trying to keep her voice steady. She couldn't let the girl go outside. The previous night's rain had been followed by a frigid Canadian air mass that coated the world with ice. If Laurel didn't have a stroke or kidney failure, she could break her neck on the stairs. Slip in the driveway. Get in a car crash. Catch pneumonia. Life was too blasted fragile.

Laurel stormed into the kitchen and pushed at Kyle, trying to get to the door. He stood firm, taking her blows without reacting.

Bethany risked another touch, carefully putting her hand on the girl's back. "You're in danger. And we do care what happens to you."

"You don't." Laurel's voice was weak now. The trip from the closet to the kitchen and her feeble blows had exhausted her.

Bethany took the coat off her shoulders, then guided her to the sofa. She pulled the afghan over the girl's lap, then stuck pillows under her feet. Her ankles were so swollen, her skin looked like an overripe tomato. "Isn't this better?" Bethany asked.

Laurel shrugged. Her stomach loomed large under the blanket, but the rest of her seemed to fade into the cushions.

Bethany tried to smile. "How about I get you some supper?"

"Whatever you want," Laurel said, her voice no more than a whisper now. "That's the way it always is, right? People like you always get what you want."

Sable stretched out on the sofa. Her head throbbed; her feet felt as if they were about to split right open. She was a prisoner—of Bethany and Kyle, of the baby in her belly, of the toxins in her blood. And of the mud in her mind. She couldn't think straight. But one thing she knew.

No knives. Knives were a terrible way to die.

God, why all this? Kyle prayed. *Is it because we used a surrogate? If You have to punish us, I understand. But why punish Hannah? Punish me, please. Not my baby.*

"Is our baby going to die?" Bethany asked, her voice a raw whisper.

"No one is going to die," Nora said. "We'll watch Laurel closely. Take away her potato chips, keep her on bed rest, and you'll see that blood pressure come down."

"I'm so sorry, Nora," Kyle said.

She raised her eyebrows at him.

"For dragging you into this."

Nora's eyes were lost in shadows that hadn't been there a year ago. "Nothing to apologize for."

"You've got a family and a practice to attend to, and now you're having to come here and baby-sit Laurel all the time."

Nora shrugged. "I've been waiting for my godchild for a long time now. It'll all be worth it, in the end."

If there is an end, Kyle thought.

20

Kyle knocked until his knuckles stung, but Laurel did not answer the door.

He slipped his key into the lock. It didn't turn. The girl had been on bed rest for six days, and she still had managed to get the locks changed without their knowing it. What kind of person were they dealing with?

"Laurel! Open up!"

No response. Kyle jammed his elbow through the side window, kicked out the shards of glass, and climbed in.

Laurel's boots and sneakers were still in the closet. She hadn't gone out walking, then. The expensive desktop computer that he had insisted on buying was booted up and running. The desktop was loaded with icons for video games. Kyle double-clicked on the Internet icon. Maybe he could get some clue as to how she spent her time online.

The program demanded a password. Kyle swore in frustration.

"Does Jesus know you use dirty words like that?"

Kyle whirled around to see Laurel standing in the door.

"By the way, Kyle, someone broke into my apartment. Some security you got here."

"Where have you been? You're supposed to stay in bed."

"Yeah. Whatever." She sat down, grabbed her pant leg, and hoisted her left leg onto her right knee. She struggled to reach her foot.

"Let me help you." Kyle quickly untied the laces. He yanked off one boot, then knelt to remove the other. He couldn't believe she had been out, after she had been told she had to stay in bed. "Where have you been?"

"My feet stink, huh? I need a bath."

"It's not safe for you to get into the shower or bath alone. Bethany volunteered to help."

"She'd try to drown me. She hates me, if you haven't noticed."

"Laurel, for goodness' sake." Kyle tossed the boots into the closet. "She's disappointed, yes. Hurt and scared. But she doesn't hate you."

"It eats at her that I can carry a baby and she couldn't."

"Thank you for your expert psychoanalysis. If you're finished, I'll go run you a bath. I can sit outside the door while you're in there." Kyle went into the bathroom, stoppered the whirlpool, and started the water.

After a few minutes, he stuck his hand into the water. Too hot. He let the cold trickle in.

"Is it ready?" Laurel called from the other room.

"Almost." He turned on the jets to let the water mix. Nora had warned about hot baths raising the body temperature and endangering the baby. The irony struck him—soon enough, he'd be checking the bathwater for his baby girl instead of for the woman carrying her.

"Can I get in?"

"Sure. Let me get out of your way and you can get un—" As Kyle turned, he bumped right into Laurel. She wore a sheer nightgown that stretched over her pregnant belly.

"Excuse me," he said, trying to step by her.

"Wait." She grabbed his hand and pressed it to her side. "Feel that? It's Hannah's foot."

He snatched his hand back. "Get in the tub, Laurel. I'll wait outside, make sure you're all right." He touched her arm, trying to move her aside. She grabbed both his hands and clutched them to her stomach again.

Kyle wanted to push her away, but he was afraid of toppling her. Her grip was like iron.

"After Hannah's born, you'll want a little brother for her, won't you?" she said.

"Get away from me." Kyle jerked away, and she staggered sideways. He caught her, making sure she was stable before he left the bathroom.

"Don't go too far," she called after him, laughing. "I might need you."

∞∞∞

Sable laughed to herself. Kyle had left the apartment in such a sweaty huff, it'd be hours before he remembered he had had to break in because she had gone missing. She loved the feeling of being back in control, on top of her game. The new medication was helping clean her mental windshield. Okay, things were still fuzzy, but at least she had enough wits about her to rent the house.

Jacob had sent Switch by that morning, just as she asked. She met the guy around the bend in the river, out of sight of the farmhouse and other prying eyes. Switch drove her to the sweet place Sable had found on the Internet three weeks ago, before this whole toxemia thing popped up.

Let the Dolans blabber on about heaven. Sable had gone out and rented her own piece of paradise. Her new home was a secluded cottage about thirty miles from North Conway. Tucked deep into the woods, the place had come furnished, complete with cable and high-speed Internet. She had paid in cash so she wouldn't leave a paper trail.

The cottage was all windows, flooding every corner in the house with sunshine. She was tempted to just stay there, especially now that Nora was harping on doing surgery. But what would she do out there in the woods, a baby ready to burst out of her?

Besides, Kyle still owed her over twenty thousand dollars, once she unloaded the baby. It didn't matter that she had a million dollars in the bank. Every penny counted, Sable knew. Because you just never know when someone will take what you have and still want more. She would stick out the surrogacy. No Caesarean, though. She'd spit the baby out before she allowed that to happen.

She got into bed and pulled the blanket up over her head. Even the whirlpool hadn't relieved the pain in her back. Her body ached most of the time now. She spread her fingers over the expanse of her stomach, feeling a foot on one side, her baby's bottom under her ribs. Then she bent her knees up as far as they would go, bringing her stomach close to her face.

"I'm your rental home, little one," she whispered. "A safe place for you to wait until it's okay to come out."

Sable was no musician, but it was clear to her that the baby enjoyed the tape she had made more than Bethany's original one. And why not? Sable was the mama, at least for now.

"Close your eyes and sleep, dream of wishes sweet," Sable said. Then she held the tape player to her stomach and pressed PLAY.

———

Cade pushed back from the computer with a smug smile. "It took a week, but she's offering to 'loan' us the money. Which we all know won't get repaid."

"How much?"

"Five thousand."

"Not enough," Hailey said.

"It's five thousand more than you got. Or me, for that matter."

"We need more than that to approach Bernard. Tell her ten and promise her we'll get lost."

"But we won't, will we?"

Hailey laughed. "As long as your little Sable is sitting on that cool million, we're gonna be on her like a thirsty leech, sucking her clean."

21

*I*n the beginning, there was the music. Or was that God, in the tones her infant ear had heard? Had angels whispered the songs Bethany could sing before she could even talk? And whose Spirit guided her hands over the keys before her father had formally introduced his baby girl to his beloved piano?

Yes, there was God and there was music.

Then, when it seemed that was all life needed to be, there was Kyle.

Kyle was twenty, Bethany a year younger, when he walked into her life. Nora had dragged her to a dorm party at Dartmouth—something neither of them usually indulged in, but they were giddy from exams, looking to just let loose.

Kyle's hair was so gold at that age, he looked as though he wore a halo. His eyes were clear and cool, like a stream running in the deep woods. He smiled so often, it would have been easy to think him a fool or worse—a jerk on the prowl.

But when he turned that smile to her for the first time, she knew into her toes that his joy was so real, it could move worlds. And so it did hers. They walked the next twenty years at each other's side and would walk together as long as God asked them to before they soared.

So, another beginning. Kyle, bringing more music, bringing her closer to God—though she knew, in every measure of her being, that it was God who brought her closer to Himself, God who allowed her to dance and sing and love as she went.

Four years before, they had opened another door. They started in hope, stalled in tears. When Bethany thought she could bear it no more, there was Hannah. Unseen yet loved thoroughly. Bethany had to believe that she would hold Hannah in her arms, had to believe that Kyle would hold them both in his arms, had to believe that God would hold them all.

She just wished she could muster the faith to ask Him to bring the surrogate—whoever she was—into the family that He had ordained, a family that bore the name and spirit and love of an uncomplicated man and a glorious God named Jesus.

Bethany slipped away from the piano and onto her knees. *Gracious Father, please hear my prayer . . .*

The apartment was a stinkin' war zone, Jacob thought. The only thing keeping his mama from slapping Laurel silly was the baby in her belly. And the only thing keeping Laurel from slapping his mama silly was—well, the baby in her belly.

A few days before, Mr. Dolan had had to break into the apartment because Laurel had gone missing. So he had hired Jacob's mom as a "personal care attendant" for Laurel. Nice title, but they all really knew she was Laurel's bodyguard.

Which meant Jacob got to hang out with Laurel again. When Anthony blew the whistle on Laurel, he also ratted out Jacob.

"Buying pot for a pregnant woman? For anyone at all!" his mother exploded in a rant that had lasted for a week. She forbade him to get anywhere near Laurel.

Well, there he was. If his mama was going to baby-sit Laurel and keep him off the street, she'd have to do both at once. Of course, his mama was always in their faces, but they had their ways around that. Laurel had set up a secret messaging system between the big computer and her laptop. His mama thought he was doing homework, but he was really IMing Laurel.

The two prisoners had a lot to say to each other. When his mama ran to the main house to get clean laundry or work in the kitchen, he'd sneak into Laurel's bedroom. Mostly they'd jaw on how cool they were and how stupid the whole rest of the world was. Sometimes they'd talk about what they'd do when they broke out of there, the kinds of lives they'd have.

Laurel was the only person in the whole stupid world who understood where Jacob was coming from. And where he was going.

Joan was in the kitchen then, testing Laurel's blood for sugar. Once she got the result, then she would prepare a shot. She loved sticking that needle in Laurel.

"Joan, can you make me an egg sandwich while you're there?" Laurel had asked. "Maybe a green salad too. Oh, and some mashed potatoes."

His mama mumbled at Laurel under her breath. As soon as she went into the kitchen, Jacob sneaked into Laurel's bedroom.

Laurel told him what she needed and how to make it happen. "I'll give you a thousand bucks," she was saying. "Cash. Switch might need up to five hundred to pull this off, so the rest will be for you to split."

Jacob could only sputter. "But-but-but—"

"But nothing. This is New Hampshire—everyone's got these things. Switch can do this in his sleep. All you have to do is take the money his way and bring the package back to me."

"I don't know. Switch just might . . . " He couldn't find the guts to tell her he couldn't do this because it *scared* him.

"You can work Switch, no prob. You are the smartest kid I know." The way she was looking at Jacob made him believe her, as if she were pumping *cool* into his engine.

"Hurry up; take this before your mother comes back in." *This* was a roll of bills.

"I don't get why you need something like this," he said.

"I already told you! I've got an angry ex-boyfriend on my tail. The kind that beats you silly for burning the coffee. Know what I mean here?"

"Oh, yeah." He had seen plenty of that, back in Forge Hill.

"Anyway, word is that the dude's closing in on me. I want to— *need* to—be ready, in case he catches me by surprise. Whaddya say, Jacob? Can you be my man on this?"

"Sure," Jacob said. He would do anything to help Laurel.

꧁꧂

They were closing in on Sable, coming from all sides now. She had paid Cade and Hailey off, but she knew they'd be back after her when the ten thousand dollars was gone. Kyle was on her every minute—either baby-sitting her himself or siccing Joan Martinez on her. That woman would hang her upside down out of the window and rattle her senseless, given any excuse. If it weren't for Jacob, Sable would have gone ripping nuts.

But it was Anthony she missed. He hadn't answered any of her phone calls or e-mails. She thought about him, especially at night. His touch, as if she was as fine as the music he made. She was fooling herself, she knew. The truth was that in the end, men all wanted the same thing.

Even the baby pushed at Sable. She locked her feet on her ribs, then battered her head against the floor of her pelvis. The little peanut wanted out, that was sure, and Sable would be happy to accommodate her. But the right way—not with surgery.

Nora had promised that the epidural would make it a painless delivery. Sable was all for that. No way was she going to let them do a section. The thought of being cut open made her mind spiral into a tight, hot wire.

That was the worst—her own head closing in on her. Nora said that the toxemia and the medications might make her feel a bit fuzzy. But this was beyond fuzzy. Sable was losing control, and she didn't like it. She needed to know she could get away if it became necessary, which was why she recruited Jacob to do one last favor.

That little house in the woods was just waiting for her. Her, and maybe—just maybe—the baby. Sable would have to see about that.

22

$\mathcal{B}$ernard DuBois knew men like Cade Parker. Good looks, sweet talk, confident swagger—slime like Parker drew women and easy living as roadkill drew flies. Bernard ground men like Parker under his heel and stepped away without a second thought.

But not today. Bernard smelled something big. Something profitable. "How much are you offering?"

"Two thousand dollars." Parker leaned back in his chair, grinning.

"And what is that going to buy you, Parker?"

"Information."

"What makes you think I'm selling?"

Cade looked straight at Bernard. "You're a businessman, Mr. DuBois. You won't turn down good money."

"Two thousand doesn't even open a discussion."

"Five, then."

"Seven."

"Seven? But you don't know—"

"You'd be surprised what I know," Bernard said. "Show me the money."

"But we don't have a deal yet."

Bernard was up from his desk in an instant. He dragged Parker toward the door, banging him against a steel bookcase on the way.

"Wait!" Parker cried.

"Either you show it it, or you blow out of here."

Parker pushed an envelope at Bernard, who opened it, counted the money, and smiled for the first time. "What do you want to know?"

"I need to find someone," Parker said. "And I think you know where she is."

—⊱⊰—

Sable woke from her afternoon nap, soaked with sweat. Her mind was like frosted glass, letting in light but nothing of shape. Where was she? Some woman snored from the other room. Like a lumberjack with the television as background noise.

Was she back in the institution? Why was her stomach so big? Then she remembered. She was going to have a baby. And that big woman was her baby-sitter. More like a prison guard. What was that lady's name? And why were they keeping her there? Why couldn't she remember?

Sable staggered into the bathroom and ripped off her T-shirt. Even her bra was wet. She unhooked it, cringing at how tender her breasts felt, how tight and full. And what was this white fluid leaking from them?

She stumbled to the toilet, sat down before she fell. Did she have some horrible cancer? She touched the droplet, then sniffed her finger. Suddenly it all came clear.

She was the mama. And this was mother's milk.

—⊱⊰—

The knife should do the trick, Bethany thought. She was in the nursery, hacking open a large carton of diapers. The diapers were the easy part. Décor was proving impossible; there were just too many options. Plush or Berber? Lilac or mauve? Balloons or bunnies?

Kyle had offered to help her, but Bethany wanted to do it herself. First she painted the walls a subtle cream. That was as far as she had gotten in the color scheme—no color. She still couldn't decide on anything else.

"Hannah will be in college, and you'll still be trying to decide," Kyle had said on the phone the night before. He was driving up from Boston, planning to stay until the baby was born. Then they would all go back to Boston. It wouldn't be long now. Laurel was due in a week.

Bethany hacked at the end panel of the box. A splash of honey caught her eye—sunlight on the oak floor. Sunflowers! She had seen the perfect border at the wallpaper store, had passed by it because it was too bold. For her, maybe. But not for Hannah, who, despite everything, was strong and vigorous and only days—maybe hours— away from being in her mother's arms.

Bethany just let the music pour out of her, filling the nursery with Hannah's lullaby. It felt so wonderful to use the gift God had given her to sing of the gift yet to come.

When the birds of spring come alive to sing . . .

<hr />

The sun was bright and warm. Mount Washington was still swathed in snow, but the woods behind the farmhouse were mostly dry. Green shoots poked out of the wet carpet of leaves. Sable could hear the trickling of the stream that broke off from Thor's Falls and passed through the back meadow. Then she heard something else.

When the birds of spring come alive to sing, in the golden wonderland.

A lullaby, she knew, though she couldn't remember how she knew.

I will dance for you as the sky turns blue.

She followed the music into the main house. Up the stairs.

Close your eyes and sleep, dream of wishes sweet.

Down the hall, stopping outside the room where the singing came from.

Because I will love you forever and I'll be here with you, for always.

Sable pushed the door open. A dark-haired woman leaned over a crib, a long knife in her hand.

"Laurel? Oh, good grief, I've cut myself." Bright blood stained the sleeve of the woman's blouse as she pressed her hand to the wound.

Sable backed into the corner. An icy hand grabbed her ankle. She looked down, stunned. *He* had come. Drawn by the blood.

"Are you okay? You're supposed to be in bed," the woman said.

The ice was in her brain now, shattering her thoughts. She tried to gather them back, but it hurt her to try to think.

"Look at this mess." The woman grabbed a paper diaper and

wrapped it around her arm. "What are you doing here? Where's Joan?"

"I don't know." She didn't know where Joan was or even who Joan was. She only knew that the blood had made *him* come. Or had he made the blood come? Where was he now? There—behind the woman with the knife.

"You look faint. You need to sit down." The woman stepped toward Sable, still holding the knife. There was blood on the blade, blood on her arm, and suddenly all Sable could see was red.

The woman came closer. Too close. There would be blood on Sable if she didn't do something to make her stop.

He smiled.

Do it now.

Kyle wouldn't stop pacing. "She's got to be locked up!"

"No! You send Laurel—or whoever she is—to jail, you're sending our baby with her," Bethany said.

"Then we'll have her committed."

"That's a better solution? Your daughter born in an institution?"

"You're bleeding again."

"I know." She stuffed a paper towel to her nose.

"She claims you threatened her," Nora said. "She ran back to the apartment and tried to call the police. Joan yanked the cord on the phone."

"She's nuts. Punching Bethany in the face for no reason," Kyle said.

"She's toxic," Nora said. "Maybe even psychotic . . . there's no way to know without getting her medical history."

"What are we going to do?" Circles of light swirled past Bethany. She had probably gotten a concussion when she hit the floor. No way would she tell Kyle that.

Nora shook her head. "Her blood pressure is climbing again, and there's protein and albumin in her urine. We need to induce labor and, if that doesn't work, force the Caesarean."

"She won't agree to that," Bethany said.

"I've got durable power of attorney, which includes medical

decisions. Can't we use that? It's not like we're doing something to hurt her. She's in as much danger as the baby," Kyle said.

"You can't use that unless she's in a coma or brain damaged," Bethany said.

"Or mentally incapacitated. Which she clearly is."

"Slow down, you two. That durable power of attorney is useless now," Nora said.

"Why?" Bethany said, already knowing the answer in the pit of her stomach.

"She's not really Laurel Bergin," Nora said. "So all the contracts that she signed as such are invalid."

"But only we know that," Kyle said. "Right?"

Nora bowed her head. "Kyle, please don't ask me to go along with some ruse . . . "

"The girl herself asked us to keep up the Laurel ruse, didn't she? So in effect, it's her choice, not ours. The point is—we can't mess around any longer," Kyle said. "I've already called Peter Muir. He'll have a motion for the judge for tomorrow."

Bethany couldn't bear the thought of Hannah being held hostage in that toxic body for a moment longer. "Nora, can't you slip her something to induce the labor?"

"Hold on a minute, both of you. I could lose my license, and you two could go to jail. Not to mention that it would be a very ungodly thing to do."

"It's godly to protect the innocent," Kyle said. "Please, Nora. You know that."

Nora was silent, the stricken look on her face enough reproach.

Bethany hugged her. "We've really dragged you into a mess, haven't we?"

Nora sighed. "Let's give it overnight. Let Joan go home—I'll stay with Laurel, so if her condition suddenly worsens, I'll be right there. Let's pray she'll go into labor tonight. Otherwise, Kyle, I guess you'll have to make sure Peter gets that court order. I'll book an operating room for late afternoon."

"Thank you, Nora," Kyle said. "For everything."

Bethany left them to their phone calls. She went outside to the front porch and slipped into the wicker rocker. In the woods, an owl whoo-ed itself up for a night of hunting. The first star appeared, a weak glimmer in an inky sky. She dropped her face into her hands. Her nose bled again, now mixing with her tears.

Dear God, we can't take any more of this. Please let my little girl be born tomorrow.

<hr />

The knife! The woman hadn't succeeded this time, though she had set her dogs—Kyle and Nora—on Sable. Demanding that Sable undergo a Caesarean section.

Maybe even that was a ruse. Maybe they'd knock her out and let Bethany do the dirty work. Things were becoming clear. Oh yes, she was remembering things again. Like Bethany at Christmas, working a carving knife. That woman was good at cutting.

All that talk about religion and faith and God. Sable had heard the other words too. *Sacrifice. Blood. The blood of a perfect Lamb.*

What had Bethany told her about God? That sweet little baby Jesus was born to be a sacrifice. *He* would be after another sacrifice, Sable knew. Hadn't she seen Bethany over the crib, knife in hand? Sable could not let that happen.

<hr />

Jacob was so scared, he thought his skin would bust open. His mama thought he had the stomach flu, with all the hard-core puking. It started after she had come home from a long day at the Dolans', her shoulders down like a dog caught in the trash.

"After all they've done for us, and I let them down. I can't believe I fell asleep on the job."

Joan went into her room and fell on her knees. Praying, Jacob knew, though he didn't understand why until Anthony told him. Laurel had attacked Mrs. Dolan and busted her nose. They might lock Laurel up somewhere, either jail or the nuthouse. His brother's eyes were red at the corners as he told Jacob all this.

No one was going to be locking Laurel up, Jacob knew, because he was the one who had made it so she couldn't be taken. He and Switch. Now he was scared. Scared for her, scared for the Dolans, scared for his mama, scared for Anthony.

Scared for the whole world, it seemed like. And why not? The whole world could end tomorrow. It could be ending as he sat there, his stomach rumbling out of his ribs.

He ran to the bathroom, trying to rid himself of another bunch of being scared.

23

The moon was down and the night was dark. It was time to go. Sable pushed to the edge of the bed and draped her arm off the mattress.

"You okay?" Nora mumbled from the armchair in the corner.

"Uh-huh." Sable had taken all the pills Nora had forced on her except the Valium. She had watched Sable swallow, then looked under her tongue to make sure they were gone.

Sable had learned how to palm pills by the time she was thirteen. The other pills would help her think more clearly, but no way would she take the Valium. They wanted her out cold so they could cut her open, steal the baby out of her. That was not going to happen. She had to get out of there, and she had to do it now.

Sable slipped her hand between the mattress and the box spring.

"Something the matter? What are you doing over there?"

Sable heaved into a sitting position. "Getting out of here."

"No, you are no—" Nora's words died when she saw the gun in Sable's hand.

"Where's the Valium?" Sable asked.

"In my medical bag."

Sable tossed Nora the pill bottle. "Take five."

"Five! But that's—"

Sable stuck the gun to Nora's temple. "Beats a bullet to the brain, wouldn't you say?" She handed her the water from the bedside and watched Nora swallow each one.

"Open up," she said. Nora opened her mouth.

"The tongue too." Sable looked satisfied. "Good. Now we wait for you to go nighty-night."

"Please don't do this, Laurel. You don't understand how much danger you could be in."

"I'm in more danger if I stay."

"Think of the baby, then. Do what's best for her."

"I am," Sable said. "I really am."

----∞----

Bethany moved numbly through the house. When she and Kyle had gone up to the apartment with breakfast, they found Nora unconscious and Laurel missing. Kyle had raced to the hospital with Nora. Bethany stayed back at the farmhouse in case the girl returned.

The phone rang. Bethany jumped out of her skin, almost dropping the receiver. "Laurel?"

"It's me."

"Oh, Kyle, how is Nora? Is she okay?"

"She'll be fine. She was just doped up."

"Does she know where Laurel went?"

"She doesn't even know what day it is."

"We've got to find her."

"We will. I've already given the police the photos we took at Christmas. They've got an APB out on Nora's car. I've got a pilot and a spotter going up, looking for it. Peter Muir is lining up some private investigators to go to the airports, bus station, and car rentals in case she makes a switch."

"Kyle, what did you tell them about her?"

"The truth. That she's nine months pregnant, that the toxemia has made her mentally unbalanced, and that her life's in danger."

"We need to tell them that she's not Laurel, that we don't know who she is. Maybe she's got a criminal record or something. We've got her fingerprints on everything, we could check and—"

"Bethany, stop. Stop and think. If we make it known that she's not Laurel Bergin, then the adoption papers she signed—naming us as parents of the baby—are not valid."

Bethany pressed the phone against her skull, trying to drive the churning out.

Lord, can't You see where this girl has driven us? I'm so stretched, so pushed and pulled and twisted that my body is just going to explode.

"Bethany? Do you agree? For now, we keep silent on that?"

"Even silence can be a lie."

"Don't you think I know that? But do you want Hannah put in the same limbo we're in?"

Bethany let out the breath that she felt she'd been holding since they discovered Laurel gone. "She's driven us to this, hasn't she, Kyle? Bringing us down to her level."

"Yes. She has. Listen, I've got to get over to the police station."

"What can I be doing? I can't just wait here."

"Go up to the apartment. Maybe you'll find a bus schedule in the trash or a reservation for a hotel. Check that computer of hers. And Beenie, please pray. God has to understand. He's just got to."

"Okay." Every breath, every heartbeat now was a prayer that Hannah would be safe. Later, when it all was over—if it was ever over—she would add her plea for forgiveness.

Bethany went up to the apartment and straight to the computer. A waste of time, as she had known it would be; Laurel had reformatted the hard drive and erased all her files.

She slumped onto the sofa, smelling Laurel on the cushions—the lilac shampoo the girl used, the salty scent of potato chips. She closed her eyes, trying to imagine herself in Laurel's place. All she saw was darkness.

Mrs. Dolan looked like a corpse. Her face was white, her eyes wide open but not seeing. Jacob stared through the window for a full minute before he spotted the tears. *Okay. Good.* So she wasn't dead. He took a deep breath, then knocked.

Mrs. Dolan wiped her face, got up, and opened the door. "Jacob?"

The words he needed to say were stuck deep inside him.

"Laurel's not here," she said.

"I know."

"We don't know where . . . " Mrs. Dolan staggered against the door.

Jacob grabbed her arm to keep her from falling. She felt like tissue, ready to just blow away.

"Do you know where she is, Jacob?"

He shook his head.

"Is there anything you can tell me, anything to help . . . ?"

It choked him now, from inside. He had to get rid of this sick feeling, this whacked idea that this was all his fault. "I got it," he whispered.

"Got what?"

"The gun."

"She has a gun?" Mrs. Dolan started shaking as though someone had suddenly dumped ice water over her.

"I'm sorry. Honest."

She bit at her lips but she couldn't stop the *click*ing of her teeth.

"I'm sorry," he said again.

She leaned down, kissed his forehead, pressed her hands onto his face to stop the shaking. "I can see that you are. And I forgive you."

It was as if she had broken a hole in Jacob, the way the words came up and out, starting way back in Forge Hill where his mama hadn't gotten it, hadn't gotten who he was supposed to be. By the time he told Bethany about the gun, he was the one shaking.

"She was wicked scared. An old boyfriend tried to kill her, which is why she was hiding out, using someone else's name. He was closing in again, she said, and this time he would kill her. She was afraid you'd think she was a sinner—"

"Jacob! Did she say that?"

He nodded. Actually, she had used words that packed a real punch, but he knew that what Laurel had said would blow Mrs. Dolan right out of her shoes. "Anyway, she was afraid you'd make her leave. She said she needed protection. Asked me if I could get her a gun."

"Why would she ask you? You're just a child!"

"That don't matter, not if you've got the money and you know the right people. Which I do. Maybe we left Forge Hill, but guess what, Mrs. Dolan? People are the same here."

She stood there, her eyes closed, her face turned to one side as if he had just slapped her. He hadn't meant to hurt her, but she had to know what the real score was, for once.

"I'm sorry, Mrs. Dolan. Really sorry."

She hugged him. "We all make mistakes, Jacob. I've made too many to count. It's amazing, but God loves me anyway."

He just nodded.

"Do you have any idea where she might have gone?" Mrs. Dolan asked.

"No clue."

"Oh."

"But I bet Switch does."

Switch was a very frightening individual.

The man was hairy everywhere, from his long, unkempt beard to the gray tufts sticking out from his T-shirt to the braid down his back. He towered over Bethany, a mountain of muscle, leather, and chains. Switch's hangout was a motorcycle-repair shop two blocks north of Main Street. The garage was stocked with used engine parts, greasy tools, and broken bikes. The air was thick with motor oil and cigarettes.

"Don't know nothin'," Switch said.

"You been drivin' Laurel places," Jacob said. "Tell this lady where."

Switch grabbed Jacob's arm and lifted him off the ground. "Man keeps his word, you little nose-wipe."

"Put him down!" Bethany said.

Switch opened his hand. Jacob tumbled down, then backed up until he was next to Bethany.

"How much will it take to persuade you to help us?" Bethany said.

Switch squinted at her. "Man's word don't come cheap."

"What did she pay?"

Switch ground his cigarette under his boot. "Enough."

"A thousand," Jacob whispered.

Switch showed the back of his hand.

"I'll pay you two thousand dollars to tell me where you've been driving her."

"She promised me another thousand in a month—if I don't blab her business."

"Three thousand, then. Will you take a credit card?"

"What, do I look like Wal-Mart? Cash, lady. Or no deal."

"Fine. You'll have to give me five minutes to run to the bank."

"I'll come with you," Jacob said.

Switch snorted.

Ten minutes later, cash in hand, Switch had plenty to say. "The girl looked like Mary Sunshine, but that one knows how to play the angles. She had me on retainer. She'd call, I'd pick her up in the Thor's Falls parking lot, take her wherever. She was too big in the belly to ride my bike, so I used the old truck there."

The "old truck" was a bucket of rust. Bethany felt her knees go weak, imagining Laurel—with Hannah—in that piece of junk.

"Where did you take her?"

"You'd better write this down," Switch said. "It ain't no picnic to find."

"I'm sorry, Mr. Dolan. The baby didn't survive the crash."

It took everything in Kyle to keep from crumbling. "Are you sure it's Laurel Bergin?"

"We're not sure of anything. The responders on the scene couldn't make an identification. The injuries were too . . . extensive." Captain Rau rubbed his face, sweat breaking out on his forehead.

Kyle had driven down to the state police barracks in Concord, thinking personal contact would induce the police to act quicker. Captain Rau was in the process of notifying Maine, Vermont, and Connecticut when the call had come in about an accident in Nashua.

"Accidents like this—there's fire—"

"Oh, please, God. No."

"Look, Mr. Dolan. Chances are it's not her. But with a stolen vehicle, no identification on any of the kids, no survivors, it might be best if you take a look. So we'll know how to proceed from here."

Kyle nodded. His hands flared with pain. He had dug his fingernails into his palms.

"I'll take you down to Nashua myself," Rau said. "Meanwhile, we'll keep the other units on alert."

Kyle nodded and followed the big man out to the cruiser. His cell phone buzzed as he got into the front seat. *Bethany.* What could he say to her? *Our child is heading to a morgue in Nashua, and I'm meeting her there?* He let the phone ring.

"Seat belt?" the captain said.

"Oh. Sure." Like any of that mattered now.

The phone buzzed again.

"You gonna answer that?"

"It's my wife. I don't know what to tell her."

Captain Rau held out his hand. Kyle passed him the phone. "Please, don't—"

"It's okay." Rau stared at the phone for a second, then figured out how to open it. "This is Captain Rau. State Police." There was a pause, then he continued. "Of course, Mrs. Dolan. Your husband stepped into the men's room, left the phone in case anyone called. No. No definite news, not yet."

Kyle clenched his fists.

"Do you need your husband right away, or can I have him call you back? We're heading down to Nashua. There's been a possible sighting, and we want him on hand in case we need an identification."

Accidents like this—there's fire—

"We'll call you in about a couple hours' time, then. Thank you, ma'am." Rau handed the phone back to Kyle. "We don't know that this is your surrogate. Try to hold on to that."

I'm trying, Kyle thought. *But Lord, my hands are slipping fast.*

Bethany hadn't told Captain Rau about the address that Switch had given her. She was embarrassed to think she had just paid three thousand bucks for irrelevant information.

She dropped Jacob off at his house.

Anthony had been frantically looking for the boy. "Any word?"

"They think they might have her in Nashua. Kyle's going down to take a look."

"I am so sorry, Mrs. Dolan. If I had known what she was like sooner—"

"Anthony, she fooled every one of us. It's not your fault. Kyle and I will never be able to apologize to you enough."

He tipped his head to the side and smiled sadly. "You already have. Just let it go."

She hugged him and Jacob one more time, then turned the car east, toward Maine. She had at least an hour to kill before Kyle got to Nashua and identified the girl who—*please, God*—might be Laurel and called her. She might as well check out the address that Switch had given her.

It might be interesting to see what kind of secret life their surrogate had led.

24

*B*urned flesh.

Even with the menthol salve under his nose, Kyle could smell the charred bodies. There were three of them in the morgue. Four poor souls, if you counted the unborn baby. Kyle spotted the pregnant victim right away, even with the body draped.

"Too late to even try to save the baby," the medical examiner explained. "By the time the EMTs got there . . . "

Kyle already knew the story. A stolen van, with three young people, rear-ended a truck carrying a log splitter and four bottles of propane gas. The van, stuck under the truck, caught fire. A horrific explosion followed.

"Mr. Dolan?" The medical examiner nodded at the middle table, the one with the pregnant girl. "You understand—she's been burned pretty severely."

"Yes, I understand." But he understood nothing. How could God bring them so far, then let this happen? He took his place next to the medical examiner, breathing hard through his mouth to block the stench.

The medical examiner lifted the edge of the sheet. Kyle tried to force his gaze on the body under the drape.

He could see strands of hair, blond under the blood. A naked shoulder, impossibly twisted. Black edges on the skin where the burns started. Slender neck, laced with cuts from the windshield exploding.

Her ear—

"That's enough!"

"Are you all right, Mr. Dolan?"

"It's not Laurel. Thank God, oh, thank God, it's not her."

The medical examiner glanced over at Captain Rau. The big man came to Kyle's side. "Are you sure? You haven't seen much—"

"I'm sure. Yes, I am sure." Kyle felt as though air was rushing back into his body, bringing him to life. "This poor girl has pierced ears. Laurel Bergin doesn't."

"We'll need you to look at her face. Just to be absolutely certain."

"Of course," Kyle said. He wanted to laugh, to cry, to dance, to collapse. Not appropriate in this place, of course, where three young people lay dead.

The medical examiner lifted the sheet again. Kyle glanced at the girl, then turned quickly away. Her jaw and nose were burned into a black mass, leaving only the forehead and eye socket clearly identifiable.

"That is definitely not Laurel Bergin," Kyle said.

"Thank you," Captain Rau said.

Show common courtesy for the dead, Kyle told himself, suppressing the urge to run out of the room. "Thank you, Doctor. And you, too, Captain Rau."

"Sorry to put you through this," Rau said.

Kyle waved away his apology. "It had to be done."

The medical examiner pulled the sheet back over the burned Jane Doe. It slipped off the side, exposing the victim's pregnant abdomen.

Shame washed over Kyle. Even though this wasn't his baby, it was someone's child inside the pregnant girl. Someone's child that would never take its first breath.

Sable throbbed with exhaustion. Up all night, she didn't dare to sleep until she had been through every corner in the place just one more time. It had to be the island of safety for her. And for the baby that she had brought with her.

It had been the best thing to do. Sable knew that now. She

couldn't have left the little peanut with those women—the hard-faced doctor and the soft-haired singer. Not with those knives.

She collapsed onto the sofa. "It won't be much longer, little one." Sable wrapped her hands under her belly, feeling the pulse beat in her abdomen. Two hearts, beating as one.

Her mind was muddy again, but one thing was clear, so clear it was like deep footprints pressed into the mud, leading the way. She would do whatever she had to, to protect the baby.

Because that's what a loving mama did.

"Come out of there, where I can see you," Big Man said.

"Let her be. She's just a little girl."

Big Man inched closer. "She's big enough for me."

Mama pulled at his jacket. "Hey. Come on, let's you and me party."

The Big Man smacked her clear across the kitchen. Crooked Teeth walked in, looking confused. One glance at Big Man and he backed out the door—hands up in surrender.

Big Man moved in on Sable. "You and me gonna have a little party. You like parties, don't you, sweetness?"

She was stuck to the spot. Willing her stomach to freeze so she didn't get sick. Begging her feet to thaw so she could run.

He wrapped his hand around her neck and pulled her to him. Her skin shrank from his touch. Wanting to turn inside itself. "Mama," she whispered.

Mama was up then, leaning against the kitchen table. Just staring.

"Mama."

"Come to Papa, little sweetness." He pressed against her, all salt and smoke. She couldn't breathe. Didn't want to breathe, didn't see any way out . . . except . . . on the stove . . .

A knife. A big knife that Mama had used to cut through a whole chicken.

She reached out. Too far away. Big Man pushed her against the wall. "Get off her," Mama yelled.

She saw Mama's hand, taking the knife.

As Switch had promised, the place was difficult to find. Bethany drove the back roads out of North Conway, tracked around the lakes and ponds in Fryeburg, until she came to the village of Cornwall. She had to trail through farmland until she found the small dirt road, marked only with a broken mailbox and a tattered yellow ribbon.

After driving almost a mile into the woods, dodging potholes and washouts, she spotted the house through the trees. She went the rest of the way on foot, finally discovering Nora's Camry parked under a tree.

Did that mean that Laurel was there, and not in Nashua? Or had the girl met someone there, then gone off in a different car? She needed to take a closer look.

Beyond the stand of trees was a small A-frame house. Bethany cut into the brush to keep out of sight, not even noticing as the briars ripped at her slacks. When she reached the house, she crept quietly along the side where the roof extended to the ground. When she reached the back, she slipped under the railing and rolled onto the deck.

The back wall was all glass, a triple set of sliding glass doors with a large window above them. Bethany could see clearly into the kitchen and dining area, divided from the front of the house by a huge stone fireplace.

She pressed her ear against the slider and heard people talking over each other and shouting, then applause. *It must be a talk show— Laurel's favorite entertainment.*

Bethany speed-dialed Kyle. No answer. Should she wait to confront the girl? No, she didn't dare. What if she was unconscious, or worse? She stayed low, moving around to the front of the house, then slid onto the front deck and took cover behind a lounge chair. She could see the television against the east wall.

Laurel was sprawled on the sofa, eyes closed. Bethany waited a full minute, but the girl didn't move. *Call the police,* she told herself. *Let them deal with it.* But what if Laurel was in some sort of crisis? It had been over fifteen hours since she had her last meds. What if she had had a stroke or was in kidney failure?

Bethany counted out another slow minute. Laurel still didn't stir.

She ran around to the back deck again, checked each of the sliders. All locked. She crawled under the deck, found a rock the size of a baseball. She took a couple steps back, praying as she went. If Laurel was sick, this was absolutely necessary. If she was merely sleeping, it was madness.

Once Bethany threw the rock, Laurel would know she was there. And she had a gun.

She heard a crash, then tinkling of glass.

That cannot be. This was her home. Surely she was safe here.

You think you can hide, sweetness?

Sable jolted off the sofa. She thought she had left *him* back in North Conway. But she could smell the cigarettes and his sour sweat.

No way, baby. No way out.

Bethany sucked in air, trying not to cry out. She had gotten caught on the broken glass and reopened the cut on her forearm. Was it only yesterday that Laurel had attacked her in the nursery? It seemed like years ago.

She pressed her arm against her side and pulled the door open with her uninjured hand. She stepped into the kitchen, walking slowly over the broken glass. As she moved toward the living room, she could hear the television. She crept around the fireplace and looked in. The sofa was empty.

"Peek-a-boo!"

Bethany whirled around. Laurel stood framed in the back slider, gun in her hand.

25

Kyle seemed to have absorbed the smell of burned flesh into his pores. Captain Rau's face was impassive as he drove. Just another day at work for him.

Kyle popped two pieces of gum into his mouth, then checked his phone. Three more calls from Bethany, all from her cell phone. Why wasn't she at the farmhouse? They had agreed she should wait there, in case Laurel returned or called.

He punched in her number. It rang on the other end, then kicked into the mailbox.

"Calling your wife again?"

"Don't know why she's not answering." He punched in the number at the farmhouse.

"She's probably in the bathroom."

"She'd take both phones with her. What if the girl came back home and is holding Bethany hostage or something?"

"Whoa, there. It's one thing to run away. It's another thing to kidnap someone. What makes you think this Bergin girl would go that far over the line?"

Kyle bit at his lip. He knew it was wrong, withholding the information that Laurel was a fraud. But the thought of having to contest Hannah's parentage when they already had signed adoption papers—it was too much for him to deal with right then. Even his attorney, Peter Muir, didn't know the details of the surrogacy. For now, Kyle saw no other choice but to keep it that way.

"She's just been so irrational, that's all. We didn't want to say anything, but yesterday she attacked my wife."

"Hormones gone bad, huh? Well, give your wife a few minutes. If you can't connect, I'll contact the locals and have them stop in. Okay?"

"Okay," Kyle said, surprised that he could dive any deeper into the dread that Laurel had spread over them all.

Why didn't that woman stop moving so Sable could figure out who she was?

"Are you all right? We've been so worried about you," the woman said.

"Shut up!" Sable had to think. Except she couldn't think—there was a haze over her mind, like a spiderweb that caught everything, letting nothing escape.

That was what *he* waited for, any show of weakness.

Yeah, baby.

The woman rubbed her face, spreading blood across her forehead. "What do you want? Is there something we can give you, pay you to just—"

"Peace and quiet, that's what I want! Is that too much to ask?" Sable sighted the gun right on the woman's forehead. She wouldn't last long, not with all that blood. It was smeared on her face and across her belly.

Maybe she'd have the courtesy to go out in the woods and die there.

He was coming now, drawn by the blood.

"Don't you know who I am?" the woman asked.

Sable knew, all right. The woman was Crooked Teeth and Bernard and Bethany Dolan and Cade and yes, *him*. She sighted down the barrel now. She knew how to use a gun—Cade had made sure of that.

The woman stepped back against the stone hearth. "Don't do this," she whispered. "I'm Bethany, remember? I'm here to help."

"Don't do what?"

"Don't shoot me. Please."

"What would it matter?" Sable swallowed hard. She hadn't meant that sob to come out.

"If you have to kill me, then do it. But please, afterward—get yourself to a doctor or a hospital, so you and the baby can get the help you need."

Why was this woman still babbling on? She should have bled to death by then.

Sometimes we have to help them along, sweetness.

Sable tightened her finger on the trigger.

First Laurel, now Bethany. Where had they gone?

Kyle pulled into Conway Village, squealing his Mercedes to a stop at the Martinez house. Jacob opened the door before Kyle even knocked.

"Did you bring Laurel back?" the boy asked.

"That wasn't her in Nashua. Where's Bethany?"

"Uh-oh," Jacob said.

Bethany struggled to bring Laurel back to some semblance of reality. "If I knew your story, maybe I could help you."

"If you knew my story, you'd put a bullet in my head. Except that I have the gun, don't I? Wait a minute! That's a great idea! I'll put a bullet in my own head." Laurel raised the gun to her temple. "That's what he wants, anyway."

Bethany started forward. "Don't. Wait—who is he? You don't mean Kyle? We want what's best for you. Or is it Anthony? He doesn't hate you. He wants you to be well."

The gun came down, leveled now at Laurel's own heart. "I don't know how much longer I can take—no, please, don't touch me! Oh, please . . . "

Bethany had to keep her engaged, keep her somehow oriented toward reality. "I understand. Life can be so dark, so cruel that sometimes it seems impossible to take your next breath."

Laurel laughed bitterly. "What do you know about life?"

Good. At least she was looking at Bethany again, rather than at some unseen demon.

"Four children died inside my body. You can't even imagine what that was like. I kept asking God, what did I ever do to deserve that happening to my babies? There were days that seemed so cruel that Kyle and I couldn't bear to face the next one. Only our faith kept us going."

"What is with this know-it-all, do-it-all God of yours? Where is He when you really need Him?"

Lord, Bethany prayed, *help me to help this girl.* "Laurel, if you just open up a bit, ask Him, He'll be right here—"

"Hey, God. Where Ya hiding? Time to come out now." The girl rolled her eyes dramatically. "Whoops. Listen to that silence. Guess He went home without telling us."

Bethany hated the laughter, but at least Laurel was communicating. "He is here, Laurel. And He loves you, loves you deeply, even if you don't know it."

Laurel grabbed her head, pressing the gun hard against her temple. "Stop the talking. You're making my head hurt."

She looked around again, her head jerking so rapidly that Bethany stepped forward to try to stop her before something awful happened.

"It's your blood pressure that makes you feel like that. You're in danger if—"

"I said stop!" Laurel pointed the gun back at Bethany's face.

That gun is going to go off and kill her or me or—please, God, not Hannah!

"I beg you. For the baby's sake. Don't do this—"

"Shut up! Can't you just shut up! You don't own me!" Laurel looked at the gun, slid something on the top of the barrel.

Click.

The safety was now off, Bethany realized. She closed her eyes and waited for the rush of pain or darkness or silence that death would bring. *Lord—*

The gunshot cracked like thunder.

※

He should have been dead after Sable put the bullet right through his face. But she knew better, knew how hard it was to kill him. How impossible it was to stop his laughing.

You blew it again, sweetness.

"Shut up or I'll shoot you again! Next time, I might get you."

"I don't understand. Are you talking to me?"

The woman shook like a guitar string someone had twanged. Surely she must see *him* now. He was everywhere, hanging from the ceiling fan, climbing up the fireplace, even slithering in and out of the hole she had shot in the wall.

"Him, He's mocking me. He wants it, you know."

"Wants what?"

"The blood. Oh, he pretends to play nice, but he comes for the blood. He's so thirsty, after all."

"Who? Who comes?"

Sable wanted to scream. Was the woman stupid as well as blind! How could she miss him, his long tongue licking at the blood on her arm?

Who's it gonna be, baby! Her! Or you?

"Not me. Please. Not me, this time."

The woman reached out a hand. "I beg you, Laurel. Let me help you."

Her, then.

That made sense. The woman herself admitted she killed her own babies, even while they were still in her body. If even good mothers died for their children, surely bad mothers must. This woman, this BethanyBernardCadeHaileyNoraEveryoneLEGION deserved to be punished for all their sins, all her sins, all the sins in the whole world.

Sable pointed the gun at the woman's face.

Not that way. That's too easy.

"Why not?" Sable asked. She was so confused. If *he* would only stop moving, she might make sense of it all. But he was on Bethany, on her, rubbing the whole world red, it seemed.

She doesn't care if you kill her.

"Yes, she does!"

"What?" Bethany said.

"You care if I kill you, right?"

The woman's eyes went wide. "The only important thing is that you and the baby are safe. What happens to me doesn't matter."

The only important thing . . .

Now you're thinking.

"Me and the baby. Safe." Sable liked the feel of the words in her mouth. *Safe.* The sound of it, the thought of it. The little baby was so innocent. She had never done anything to her but kick Sable's ribs now and then.

But Sable had tried to make her safe—the little baby—and herself, hadn't she? And looked how it turned out. The whole world seemed to be closing in on them.

"I tried that," she said.

He ran through her pores now, trailing darkness. She was trying to think, but he pressed on her, blocking all sense, all senses.

"Tried what?" Bethany said.

"Shut up. I'm not talking to you."

Sable took a giant breath and held it. Okay, she thought she had made herself and the baby safe. She rented the house, got a gun, gone there in the middle of the night. She thought she could control it. She had done everything right, hadn't she?

She found you. Like I found you.

"She did find me, didn't she? You should have left me alone! Why did you come after me?" she screamed at BethanyMamaAnthony KyleLEGION.

"Because I was concerned about you."

Liar.

"Yes. Liar. She is, you are. A liar, dancing in the golden wonderland, under skies of *blood blood blood.*"

"I swear . . . " The woman was gasping now. "Laurel, please, stay with me."

No, baby. Stay with me.

Sable could just pull the trigger, make that woman go away. She knew how it would be—how it was last time—when he had come for her mama, but he had stayed for her.

"Kill . . . "

"Kill who? Oh please, Laurel. Please!"

I'm just gonna keep coming, sweetness.

Sable got away from one, and there was another one just waiting to move in. Big Man. Cade, again and again. All those doctors. Bernard. Nora. They just kept coming. Even if she made Bethany go away, Kyle would come for her. What made them like that, so persistent?

Why hadn't she realized it sooner? She rented the house thinking she'd be safe. But *he* found her here, would find her anywhere. All along she'd been fighting, running, fearing, but there was only one smart thing to do. Sable could see that, now. For her and the baby.

What're you waiting for?

She pushed the gun into her belly. The baby pushed back. Yes, the baby would understand. This was the only way to safety.

The woman—Bethany—fell to her knees. "Do you want me to beg? I will. Please, please. Don't do this. Tell me what I have to do to save my baby. I'll do anything."

"So will I. Even this."

"No. NO!"

26

Kyle pounded the Mercedes into junk, flying over rocks, caroming through brush. What did it matter now? He had no one to blame but himself. The surrogacy had been his idea. He had wanted to heal Bethany's pain. His stubbornness, his insistence on doing things his own way—had he somehow blocked God's hand from their lives?

Nora was with him, an ambulance following. She was convinced the girl had gone far beyond the bend, worried that Laurel might use the gun and that Hannah was in grave danger. "The buildup of toxins will make Laurel irrational. Combined with what I suspect is an underlying psychological pathology—"

Kyle finished the sentence for her. "There's no telling what she might do."

He jammed down the gas pedal. The car lurched forward, spitting out gravel. How far into the woods was this cottage? Over a mile, that slime Switch had told them.

The longest mile of Kyle's life.

She was bathed in blood, death spilling from her as she clung to life.

Breathe.

Beat.

Breathe again.

Beat. Beat. Beat. Beat. Beat.

Kyle kicked in the front slider.

He could smell the blood before he even got the door all the way open. Then he could see it, crimson splattered against pine walls.

He heard strangled gasps before he saw the two of them—Bethany and Laurel.

Swimming in blood.

Nora got quickly to work, getting an EMT to take on the compressions while she struggled to find an airway. It seemed like a lifetime before Nora looked up at Kyle.

"At least the baby is stable," she said.

Kyle fell to his knees. "Thank God," he whispered, covering his face with his hands.

Bethany stood in the shower, letting the water wash the blood away. Decisions were being made, but she couldn't deal with that, not now. She needed to believe that she could get clean. That water would be enough to rid her of the blood on her hands and her face and her chest and her stomach and her legs and in her hair and inside her mouth.

Cleansed by the blood. Cleansing the blood.

She looked down at the drain and saw red. As it swirled into the darkness, she followed.

Hello, sweetness.

No, she cried. Her voice slapped back at her.

Don't fight. We were meant to be.

I suppose, she sighed, but no, the *other* sighed. The tiny one—not of *him*, not of anything but the golden wonderland and skies of blue.

She reached deep inside and found the hand that held her fast.

"My heart can't take this," Kyle said. He was barely able to stand. The adrenaline surge during the rush to the hospital had drained every muscle in his body.

Bethany smiled weakly as she lay on the stretcher.

"You should have let them stitch up your arm before you took the shower. You could have gotten a concussion when you fainted. Broken your neck, even."

"Once I knew Hannah was okay, I couldn't stand the blood on me a moment longer." By the time Nora and the EMTs had taken over the CPR, Bethany had blood everywhere, even in her nose and mouth.

"When are they going to start the section? I want to be sure I'm there."

Kyle kissed his wife's forehead. "They're insisting on doing an MRI first. When that's done, we'll meet with the neurosurgeon. Until then, why don't you try to get some sleep?"

"I can't, Kyle. I keep hearing the gun go off. Seeing the look on her face. Not fear—more like resignation. I never wanted anything like this to happen. No matter what she's done to us, I never wanted to hurt her."

Kyle carefully put his arms around Bethany, avoiding the injured arm. "Beenie, you did the only thing you could do. You saved our baby's life. And Laurel's too." What was left of it.

The girl was in a coma, a bullet in her brain.

Kyle had pressed for an immediate Caesarean, but Nora insisted that they defer to the neurosurgeon.

"The baby's stable. We can't force anything, not before Dr. Chasse gets to examine her," she had said.

Nora wouldn't even look Kyle in the eye. She had been against it from the beginning, and now he knew that her worst fears had been realized.

Far beyond anything any of them could have imagined.

"The section could kill Ms. Bergin if we proceed without knowing all of her injuries," Dr. Chasse said.

"Ms. Bergin? We don't even—"

Kyle squeezed Bethany's hand, and she closed her mouth. No

one, at least outside of their closest friends, knew that the surrogate was *not* Laurel Bergin.

"Surely the baby has to be the priority here," Kyle said.

Bethany marveled at the calm in his voice. Going to battle, she knew. Using every weapon at his disposal, honed through years of wrangling, first on the tough streets of Southie, then with vendors and employees and customers.

They were in Dr. Chasse's office—the neurosurgeon, Nora, Kyle, and she. How could Chasse and Nora be so calm? With Laurel on life support, Hannah's own life hung by a thread.

Please, God, Bethany prayed in a steady stream.

"Dr. Hemlow tells me she's stable for now," Dr. Chasse said. "With the mother on a ventilator—"

"I am the mother," Bethany said. "Not her."

"Bethany, please." Nora touched her arm.

"We're all under tremendous stress here," Dr. Chasse said. "Which is why I don't want to rush into any surgery, be it obstetric or neurological. Since she's not in labor, I can't consent to any drastic procedures until I have a clearer picture of the brain damage. And because she's not able to determine her own care, it falls on me to decide—"

"Actually, it falls on me," Kyle said.

Dr. Chasse looked over her glasses at him. "I don't understand, Mr. Dolan."

"I have durable power of attorney. Including a health-care proxy."

"Kyle, do you really think it's appropriate that you exercise the proxy, given the circumstances?" Nora asked.

"I think it's absolutely imperative." Kyle unfolded a document and slid it across the desk. "When Laurel contracted the surrogacy, she agreed to give me a health-care proxy, in case she should become incapacitated. Obviously, we never envisioned using it."

Dr. Chasse scanned the document, frowning as she read.

"You'll see in section 2.4 that the power of attorney includes all aspects of medical care," Kyle said.

Bethany could see the doubt in Dr. Chasse's eyes.

"She's young. Did she understand what she was signing?"

"She's twenty-three years old, a college graduate. And yes, we discussed each section of the contract in full. We urged her to go over them with her own attorney, even giving her one thousand dollars to pay for the consultation."

"What about her parents? Have you, or has anyone, called them?"

"You'll see that she didn't list anyone as 'next of kin.' Some sort of falling out, I'm afraid. She specified that we not try to contact any of her relatives. Even so, I've instructed my lawyer to do his best to find them as soon as possible."

"This is just too irregular for me. Mr. Dolan, I understand how distraught you and your wife must be—"

"No. You cannot understand," Bethany cut in. "What this girl has put us through was simply hell on earth. We welcomed her into our home, and she—"

Kyle drew her to him. "Stop. Let me. Please."

Bethany dug her fingers into his shoulder to let him know she understood. For better or worse, they had to continue the deception the surrogate had foisted on them—that she really was Laurel Bergin, the woman who signed all the contracts. Only she, Kyle, and the Martinezes knew the truth.

And Nora.

Bethany looked across the desk to her friend. *Please don't betray us*, she thought, trying to put it all in her eyes.

Nora looked down at her hands.

"Not only do I have the power of attorney for Laurel Bergin, but I also have a court order to deliver the baby as soon as possible," Kyle said. "My attorney, Peter Muir, went to court this morning, before we knew what a tragic turn this situation would take. Nora, you gave him an affidavit, right?"

Nora nodded. Her mouth was tight. She wouldn't look at him or at Bethany.

"The judge ruled that the toxemia has rendered Laurel incompetent to decide for herself. That the baby's interests are paramount.

The court order gives Dr. Hemlow permission to either induce labor or perform the Caesarean. Those conditions still exist. I'm sure Dr. Hemlow agrees."

Kyle turned to Nora, his face open and expectant.

"She is stable but precarious," Nora said. "Her blood pressure is down because of the blood loss, but her kidney function remains compromised."

"All I'm asking is to delay the procedure for a few hours, overnight if we can," Dr. Chasse said. "Let me run some more tests, determine the extent of her injuries. So far, there's no significant swelling in the brain. Rushing her into surgery while she's neurologically unstable could prevent any hope for recovery."

"We're talking about an innocent life here, a life that has been endangered over and over by this girl's drug use, her promiscuity, and now this—kidnapping and attempted murder! Surely the balance must be on the baby's side," Kyle said.

Dr. Chasse turned to Nora. "Are you ready to proceed, Dr. Hemlow? Even if I recommend against it?"

Nora looked at Kyle. "In the end, it's your decision. Is this really what you want to do, Kyle? To order the Caesarean against Dr. Chasse's counsel?"

"Yes. For my child's sake, this is what we must do."

Nora turned to Bethany. "Is this what you want? To proceed now, risking any chance of recovery for this young woman?"

Bethany closed her eyes. She should pray, she knew. But the only direction in which she could turn her heart was to her child.

"Yes," she said. "Deliver my baby. And please, hurry."

"We're just doing what's best for Hannah." Kyle was slack against Bethany. She tightened her arms around him, trying to give back some of the strength she had sapped from him. "Nora went along with us. She knows it's necessary."

"She loves us," Bethany whispered.

"And we love Hannah. I don't see any other way to protect her."

"Maybe we should pray about this."

"What do you think I've been doing? And things have just gone from bad to worse to desperate." Kyle took her face in his hands. "Beenie, I'm afraid. I thought I could control the process, give Hannah life, give you happiness. I told God about it, sure—but then I just went ahead and did it."

She pulled him to her. "We all do that, Kyle."

He buried his face in her hair. "What if God has . . . I don't know . . . lifted His hand from us? Leaving us to suffer our own consequences?"

His heart pounded against hers. *Such a good heart,* Bethany knew. *And God must know that too.* "Surely He wouldn't leave us—leave Hannah—without His mercy."

"No. He wouldn't. But where does that leave Laurel? Where is God's mercy for her?"

"I don't know, Kyle. I just don't know."

In less than half an hour, Hannah would be born. Meanwhile, Bethany was alone with Laurel. It was insane, she knew, to be keeping watch, but she had a terrible fear that somehow the girl would pull out all her life support, slip out of bed, and just disappear.

Kyle was with the hospital's attorney, signing all sorts of forms. Nora prepped while an operating room was readied. A neonatal specialist was on hand, as was a helicopter, in case Hannah needed to be life-flighted to Concord for intensive care.

"Hannah looks fine," Nora had assured Bethany. "Her heartbeat is a little slow, but that's to be expected with Laurel on the ventilator."

"Nora, can you forgive—" Bethany began.

Nora put her finger to Bethany's mouth. "No. Don't. We'll get Hannah born and worry about the rest later. I've got to go scrub."

Nora took a last look at the monitors, then left Bethany alone with Laurel.

The girl looked lost in the sea of tubing and monitors. The ventilator tube was taped to her mouth, forcing her chest to expand on regular intervals. Both arms were strung with intravenous lines. The poles at the head of the bed were heavy with bags of fluids, including a unit of blood.

A nurse came in. "Are you family?" she asked Bethany.

"No."

"Oh. I'm afraid the ICU is off-limits, except for—"

"There isn't any family close by. We're . . . her guardians."

"Oh, sorry. I didn't know. A shame, isn't it? Young, pregnant, everything to live for. And she gets shot in the head. So much needless violence these days."

The woman adjusted the flow on one of the IVs, then checked the cardiac monitor. Ragged peaks shot across the screen. The nurse leaned over the bed and looked into the girl's face. "We'll take good care of your baby, honey. You just worry about getting better. Your baby will be waiting for you."

Bethany kept silent, swallowing back anger. She was grateful when the nurse finally left. *Do the right thing*, she told herself. *Pray.* She took Laurel's hand. It was ice-cold. Bethany closed her eyes and bowed her head.

Dear God, I put this girl—whoever she is—in Your hands. I don't know what else to do with her. But as we do that, Lord, please put Hannah Hope Dolan into our hands. I promise we will be good parents. I swear . . .

Laurel's hand felt lifeless in hers. How had it come to this, this nightmare of deception and fear and violence? There must have been something they could have done to prevent it. But what? They had given Laurel everything. Not just computers and televisions and money, but their time, their interest. *Oh, God, even our affection. We tried!*

This couldn't be her fault, hers and Kyle's. How could they have known what this girl really needed if they couldn't know who she really was?

Click.

Bethany startled, almost knocking over an IV pole. *It's just the ventilator*, she told herself. But she knew she would hear the other sound, the click as Laurel slid the safety off the gun, hear it forever—the *click*, then the gunshot.

Bethany opened her eyes. Laurel stared back at her. She gasped, tried to pull away, but the girl held her like a vise, her fingers twisted around Bethany's. Tight as wire.

Bethany grappled for the bed rail and found the call button. The nurse came running in, her eyes keying immediately in on the monitors. They moved on as before.

"Something wrong?"

"Her eyes—" Bethany turned back to the bed. Laurel's eyes were closed.

"Did she rouse?"

"I thought she did. But . . . I guess it was my imagination. Except—" Laurel's hand was still locked on her own.

The nurse bent over, rubbed the back of Laurel's hand. "It's involuntary. Called a 'tonic seizure.' The muscles tensing."

Laurel's fingers loosened. Bethany pulled her hand away.

"Anything else?" the nurse said, giving Bethany a bright smile.

"No. Thank you."

"They're on their way to get her now. Won't be long before we'll be welcoming a new life into the world. It's so sad our little mommy here has to miss it."

"Yes, it is," Bethany said. The nurse smiled, then left.

There was a flicker on the screen of the cardiac monitor. Was something wrong? The nurse had explained that the machines had alarms and would go off if the girl's breathing or heart failed.

Another flicker.

Bethany moved closer. The ragged lines of Laurel's heartbeat seemed to diverge, then come together. Making a definite pattern. Letters, it seemed.

M. Then A. Then M. Bethany watched as the screen filled with blips forming one word, over and over. MA MA MA MA MA

Bethany leaned over the bed, putting her face so close to Laurel's that she could feel the air leak from her mouth as the ventilator drew it out. She could see the blood, crusted under the bandages that covered the girl's wound.

Bethany glanced back at the monitor. The screen was filled

with MAMAMAMA. She leaned closer, putting her mouth to the surrogate's ear. "No," she said. "She is my baby, and I am the mama." Then she got up and went to the door.

"Good-bye, Laurel. Or whoever you are."

He held her down as he put the knife to her stomach. If she wouldn't let go of the little one, he would cut her out of Sable.

What then? Would the little one be free? Was this a plan to divide and conquer? Two for the price of one? Too hard to think. Too dark. Too hot too cold too late too lonely too many too sharp too bloody bloody bloody.

She held fast to that tiny hand, but *he* pulled too hard.

Let go, sweetness. You all come to me in the end anyway.

Oh, Mama, what do I do?

Hold her tight, baby.

No. She knew one thing in this chaos of screaminghowlingbitingcrushing darkness. It was not hers to hold tight.

She let go.

The little one floated into a speck of golden wonderland. She wished she could one time see her face, but no, the darkness rushed into the speck that the tiny one had filled.

Mine at last, sweetness.

OH MAMAMAMAMAMAMAMAMAMAMAM—

Where can I go from your Spirit?

Where can I flee from your presence?

If I go up to the heavens, you are there;

If I make my bed in the depths, you are there.

(Psᴀʟᴍ 139:7–8)

27

*H*annah wasn't in her cradle.

She cried on and on—loud, ragged howls that shook the walls. Not cries of hunger or displeasure at being wet or ignored. Bethany knew those as well as she knew her own voice. And she knew this as well—her baby was terrified.

She ripped through the nursery, pushing aside boxes of diapers, opening drawers, even searching the toy box. She had to feel her way through the room—it was almost completely dark. She had turned on the light, hadn't she?

Bethany flicked the switch again. Nothing. The bulb in the fixture was intact. Was the electricity off? No, she could see the hall light, coming under the crack in the door.

Hannah wailed louder.

"Mama's coming!" She would be there in a heartbeat—if she knew where *there* was. Where was her baby? She was only an infant who couldn't even turn over, let alone crawl away.

Bethany ran out to the hall. It was dark there too. The only light came from under the door to her office. Kyle must have gotten up with Hannah and was trying to settle her in there. But hadn't Kyle still been in bed when she got up? It had been too dark to see him, but she had felt his warmth.

She flung open the door. A heavy gloom flowed around her, wrapping her with hands so icy, she trembled. She couldn't get free, couldn't find the light, couldn't save her baby.

All she could do was scream.

⸎

Kyle shook Bethany awake. "You're dreaming again."

"My throat—" She touched her neck.

"Can't hurt nearly as much as my ears. You were hollering to wake the dead."

She bolted upright. "Don't say that. Ever."

"It's just an expression."

"It's one we can't joke about. You know that."

"You're right. I'm sorry. Can I do something?"

"Just let me sit a minute. Where's Hannah?"

"She's fine. Slept through your—dreaming. Was it the same?"

"Pretty much. Darkness so thick, you wade in it. But this time Hannah was crying, and I couldn't find her." Bethany fought, but the tears came anyway.

"Okay, okay, Beenie. Everything's okay. It's over now. Just a dream." Kyle took her into his arms. Her skin was cool to his touch, almost cold. "Want me to turn the air conditioner off?"

They had gone to Boston with Hannah six hours after she was born and had been there since. Summer was brutal in the city, but the noise and traffic were preferable to the memories North Conway held.

"No, it's too noisy outside," she said. "When is that stupid construction going to be done?"

"Hey, Dorothy, you're not in Kansas anymore. When every politician's brother-in-law has a job, that's when."

She laughed and nestled into him.

"We could go up to North Conway for the weekend," Kyle suggested.

"No. Not yet."

"When?"

"Soon."

"How about the Fourth of July?"

"Maybe."

He kissed the back of her neck. "Speaking of fireworks . . ."

She kissed him back. "How 'bout we celebrate early?" Suddenly her body stiffened. "Where's the baby?"

"Sleeping." He dug his fingers into her hair, rubbing her scalp.

"I don't hear her breathing."

Kyle pressed the baby monitor to Bethany's ear. "Hear that? She snores louder than I do."

"You took her out of the cradle?"

"I didn't want your screaming to wake her. Besides, she doesn't fit in that thing anymore. I took her into the nursery, rocked her, and in a minute she was asleep. In the crib, where she belongs."

"Kyle, we agreed—"

"That she could sleep in here with us for the first week. It's been almost two months."

"I need to check on her." Bethany bounced out of bed.

Kyle went into the bathroom. He splashed his face with cold water, then toweled off. Just because he didn't want to sleep in the same room with Hannah, it didn't mean he was a bad father.

When he got back into bed, Bethany was there, lying with her back to him. He could hear Hannah, those little squeaks that were so cute—except in the middle of the night. "You went in and got her?"

"She was fussing."

"No, she was not fussing. For heaven's sake, Bethany. You never wake a sleeping baby. And she was sleeping peacefully."

"But I wasn't."

"And now I'm not. Thanks a lot."

Hannah quieted. Kyle knew she was taking the milk now.

"I'm sorry," Bethany whispered.

"Yeah. Whatever," Kyle said, digging his head into the pillow.

"Kyle, I get scared. I'm sorry. I'm trying, but . . . "

Kyle rolled over, draped his arm over her shoulder. "I do too. But we've got to get over it, for the baby's sake."

"We're quite the pair, Dolan."

"No, Beenie. We're not. We're quite the family."

—∞∞∞—

Bethany leaned back against the pillow, enjoying Hannah's little head nestled into her arm, the warm body curled around her ribs. The blessed moments of her baby sucking at her breast. No one thought she'd be able to do this. Nora had even warned against it. "Taking that many hormones—you're increasing your chance of cancer."

"I don't think I have to worry about uterine or ovarian cancer, do I? Considering I don't have the plumbing anymore."

"There's always breast cancer. And other delightful things to consider, like bone loss. Inducing lactation in a nonpregnant woman requires a hormonal blast that could screw everything else up."

"It'll be for a little while, Nora. Not a lifetime." Bethany had started the regime of shots and pills in March, when they still thought Laurel Bergin was who—and what—she said she was.

She nursed Hannah the day she was born. She didn't have any milk then—Hannah's sucking was needed to stimulate milk production. La Leche League had fitted Bethany with a lactation aid that allowed Hannah to take formula from a little pouch by sucking at her breast and a feeding tube simultaneously. It wasn't any more complicated than the shield some nursing mothers used. The first drop of milk appeared when Hannah was eight days old. Kyle laughed as Bethany danced around the kitchen, her shirt open.

"Just don't go on a milk run across the Common," he teased.

Now Bethany was producing at least three ounces of her own milk per feeding. The rest came from the tube of formula, which allowed her the sublime joy of having her child at her breast.

Heaven indeed, Bethany thought. *Thank You, Lord, for small miracles.*

28

ell, well, well. What do we have here?"

"Excuse me?"

The woman looked as if she were about to jump out of her skin. Which would have been all right with Cade. Her skin was something else. Sure, there were a few miles on it. But she was sleek, dark, exotic. Like a cat. And the hair—he could imagine wrapping up in that cloud and staying there for days.

"Your baby. She just winked at me."

"I don't think so. Winking is an advanced skill," the woman said, laughing. "She's just starting to smile, though half the time, that's just gas."

"I swear. She looked me straight in the eyes, then did this." He gave the woman a slow wink. "She's really pretty, your little one. What's her name?"

She stiffened. "If you'll excuse me, I have an appointment to get to."

Cade nodded, then stepped aside to let her pass. The woman hurried down the sidewalk, heading into that huge expanse of grass known as Boston Common, moving like music—her slender legs, her full, swaying hips. Oh yeah, Cade could sing that song.

"That must be the baby," Hailey said. She had been sitting across the walk, hidden behind a Yankees cap and a racing form.

"For sure? That is the Volvo chick? The one you saw in Troy?"

"Madame Sad Eyes. Yep."

"I could make her smile. Oh, baby, I could."

Hailey twisted the skin on his forearm, leaving a deep red welt. "She ain't the one we're lookin' for. Remember?"

Cade slumped onto the bench Hailey had just vacated. He shook out a cigarette, lit it, dragged hard, and held the smoke, letting it mellow him. He'd love a joint about now, maybe even a hit of smack. But he had to get back to Albany the next day and pee in the cup for his probation officer.

Stupid Hailey. He had a mind to whack her one, right there with all of snooty Beacon Hill watching. She was the one who brought home the blow, then complained because they sniffed it in minutes. If he hadn't gotten stopped speeding with that dime bag in his pocket, they would have made it to Pilgrim Road two months before. Maybe they would have found Sable before she had a chance to split.

Cade pleaded out on the drug charge, served a quick thirty days to get it done with. He didn't have the money left for a lawyer anyway, not after paying off Bernard. He cooled his heels in the county jail while Hailey made weekly trips to Boston, trying to track Sable at the address Bernard had given them. No luck there. Where had she gone? The girl was more slippery than motor oil.

The bigger question was, why hadn't she touched her money in over two months? They had monitored the account, watching as she made steady, small withdrawals. Suddenly, in mid-April, the transactions stopped. With the interest it was gathering, the account was back up to over a million. Just sitting there. Waiting for the person with the password.

Why didn't Cade have the smarts Sable did? He'd have cracked the puzzle or found some other way to grab the money. Then again, even the computer jock at Rensselaer never figured out the password. Cade needed to find Sable. Or at least, he needed that laptop of hers. That would be the key. That little computer was her best buddy.

If only Sable loved him the way she loved that piece of electronic garbage. Then he wouldn't be here, hanging out in Boston, trying to figure out who Lady Sad Eyes was. And what she was doing with Sable's baby.

Kyle found Bethany in the bathtub, in tears.

"Tell me," he said, kneeling down next to her. "Tell me what's wrong, and I swear, I'll make it better."

"I hope it's hormones. If it's not, then I'm losing my mind." Her face was puffy and red, her eyes almost swollen shut. Goose bumps dotted her arms and chest.

Kyle stuck his fingers in the water. It was cold. "Are you ready to get out of there? I could pour you a glass of wine, make you something to eat."

"Let's see. Do I want corn chips? Or your leftover fried rice? Hm, salt or grease? Hard choice." She forced a smile. "No, not yet."

He turned on the hot water. After a minute, he swirled it with his hand. Bethany sat staring straight ahead. Kyle grabbed the bath cushion from the shelf and stuck it behind her head. "Here. Relax."

"Did you check on Hannah?"

"Out in the hall, sleeping soundly. Why is she still in the stroller?"

"Someone gave me very sage advice: don't wake a sleeping baby."

"Beenie, I—"

"No. Don't apologize."

"What makes you think I was going to apologize? Maybe I was winding up for an argument." He splashed a finger of water her way.

She grinned and kicked some his way. "You stink, Southie."

"I showered this morning. Of course, I slaved all day over a hot conference table."

"I'm thinking you need a bath."

"Okay, I confess. I do stink. I'm almost fainting from the odor. Maybe I need a bath," he said, laughing.

"Definitely you need a bath."

"If you insist." Kyle yanked off his tie, pulled off his shirt and pants, then tossed his underwear aside. He slipped into the tub with his wife, grateful as always that she had talked him into the oversized tub instead of the two-headed shower he had wanted for the master bath.

The hot water made Kyle feel fresh, even though it was eighty degrees outside. "How long have you been in here?" he murmured after they had sat for a long time.

"More than an hour," she said, leaning back against his chest. "The last half of which has been heaven."

"What about the first half? What was that about?"

"Nothing. Just something stupid."

"I do stupid really well."

"Okay. There was some man on the Common, making small talk. I didn't like the way he looked at Hannah."

Kyle leaned over her shoulder so he could see her face. "What do you mean? Exactly how did he look at Hannah?"

"He just seemed more interested than you would expect a stranger to be. It's no big deal. I just overreacted."

"Was he some kind of street person or something?"

"Not at all. He was dressed casually but well. He was actually very attractive, almost like a movie star. Really bright-blue eyes, great hair and smile—the whole package."

"And this hunk made you cry? I guess I should be grateful."

"He was just making baby talk at a cute baby."

"So what's the issue? Other than me thinking I'm going to have to beat the boys off my beautiful daughter a whole lot sooner than I expected."

She took his hands and crisscrossed his arms around her. "The issue is—I think I'm losing it, sometimes."

"If anyone has the right to, it's you, Bethany. But you're not, I assure you. You're just—adjusting to life being normal for once."

"Normal? If you only knew, Kyle. The bizarre things that swirl in my head."

"Tell me."

"I had this terrible notion about this man. That he wasn't just some guy in the park. That he was there waiting for Hannah."

"Okay, now you're scaring me. Should I be calling the cops, hiring some security?"

"Of course not. What're you going to say? 'A man said hello to my wife while she was pushing our baby in the carriage'? It's just—it felt like a premonition almost. The way he smiled at Hannah, then me. Gave me a shiver so deep, I'm still trying to warm up."

"What kind of premonition?"

She sat, so silent that the drip of water from the faucet sounded like thunder.

"Bethany."

"I just felt—that he was going to take Hannah away from us."

Kyle tightened his arms around her. He should be telling her that it wasn't true. That the movie-star man in the park or Laurel or anyone else would never take Hannah from them. It just wasn't going to happen. He should tell her that, right now.

But he didn't dare speak. Even if she didn't see his face, she'd hear it in his voice.

He had the same fear. That their happiness would never be complete because someone was going to take Hannah away from them.

"Tell me about the dreams, Bethany."

Patrick leaned back in his chair, feet up on his desk. *Always at ease*, Bethany thought. She was more comfortable with him than with anyone except Kyle and Nora. And Hannah, now.

"The dreams are like a symphony. Lots of variety, but the same melodies and countermelodies."

"What's the theme?" He smiled but listened with intensity.

"Two themes. A baby crying—Hannah, of course. And darkness. The location can be anywhere, from the townhouse to the Boston Public Library to David Hemlow's workshop. In fact, I'm never in the same place twice, it seems."

"Tell me about the most recent one, then."

"I dreamed about Fenway Park two nights ago. The whole stadium was dark. I could make out the lights on the poles, but I couldn't get them turned on. I hated the shadows, especially the ones under the seats. I tried to shine a light under there, but my flashlight wouldn't work.

"Then the crying started. At first it was a lonely little voice. Remember the crying I told you about last year? The wailing I heard that night in North Conway? It was just like that. I ran down the rows, even crossed the bleachers, trying to find Hannah. Then it grew in volume, echoing off the scoreboard and the left field wall, the monster thing out there."

"The Green Monster?" Patrick said with a smile.

"Yes, that high wall—the cries just bounced back at me. But it was too dark to see what was happening on the field. I shouted for someone to turn on the lights and turn off the sound, but no one helped me. I woke up screaming, Kyle said. As usual."

"Let's start with the crying. How do you know it's Hannah if you can't see her?"

"Patrick. I'm her mother. I just know."

"Think carefully now. Listen to the dream—does it sound like her voice?"

Bethany closed her eyes. She hated remembering. She could live with darkness, but the crying was unbearable. Hours after she woke up, that wailing would still ring in her ears. She feared sleep now. She didn't even want to nap with Hannah during the day. If she could sleep with her eyes open, gazing at sunlight instead of night, she would.

"You know, maybe it isn't Hannah. I just assumed that, because it was a child and all. But the cry seems deeper than Hannah's voice. Kyle teases that she's going to explode all our crystal someday with that high-pitched howl."

"Is it deep enough to be an adult's cry?"

"No. I'd say it's definitely a child's cry. Enough lung capacity to deepen the tone, but no maturity of the larynx."

"Whatever you say."

She laughed. "Can you tell I teach voice? Or at least, I used to."

Patrick looked down at his hands. His fingers were long, strong—expressive. The hands of a musician, she told Kyle once. "No way," Kyle had said. "The hands of a pitcher. Or a quarterback."

They had known Patrick socially from church for years. Bethany had never expected to be in his office as a patient.

"So, is it possible that it's not Hannah you're hearing?"

"Who else would it be?"

"That's something we need to think about. And pray about. So— how is your prayer life going?"

"I spend all my time praying that Hannah will be safe and that I'm not crazy. I'm ashamed to say, there's little room for anyone else. Even my husband."

"I'd tell you if you were crazy. In hundred-dollar words, yes. But you're not. So let's put that behind us. What you are is coming off an incredibly stressful time. Just parenting an infant boosts anyone high up on the stress table. You've had a year—four years, really—of intense wear and tear. We can walk through those times together, air them out, if you'd like."

She wanted to bury the past year in the deepest grave and shovel in the whole earth to cover it. She couldn't change any of it. And she did have Hannah. And Kyle. Always Kyle.

"I don't like," she said. "But you're right, it probably would help even things out a bit. But what about the dreams? What do they mean?"

"That's your journey, your discovery. I'll help you get there, if you're willing to make the trip. We'll go together."

"Of course," she said. What choice did she have?

The laugh was familiar to Bethany, but she couldn't place the voice or the content—meaningless talk, splattered with profanity. She walked more slowly, straining to hear more.

The bandstand had become a popular nesting place for the homeless, with a roof and clear view across Boston Common. Competition for space was tight. Homeless people gathered on the platform during daylight hours to keep their spots. The police chased the bandstanders out on concert days, but otherwise, they let them be.

Bethany went by there frequently, walking to the downtown shops, getting out for exercise, or seeing Patrick. Even with Hannah in the stroller, she felt no anxiety. The bandstanders had their own code of honor and let people pass by without bother. Occasionally someone would ask for a handout, and she'd give the person a certificate for a nearby market.

Today there were four people in the bandstand, arguing about their favorite fast food. "Them Big Macs, they'll kill you, man. All those trolls in there, runnin' 'round your blood. Choking you up."

"You mean cholesterol, B.J.?"

There it was again—that woman's voice. Husky but melodic. Bethany could almost hear that voice working through the octaves, rich and strong. Why was it so familiar?

"I be meanin' fat, man. Gobs, rolls, chunks, lunkers of fat."

"Oh, come on, Blue Jeans. I saw someone buy you two the other day."

"Hey, a freebie is a freebie."

"So you think it's a conspiracy, then? People passing off Big Macs to you?"

"If they's wantin' to knock us off, they'd be passin' us bottles now, wouldn't you say?"

They were all laughing now, play-punching Blue Jeans, a withered man in overalls and railroad cap. The one woman in the group—the voice that had sounded so familiar—had her back to Bethany. She wheeled the stroller closer, tracking around the bandstand so she could see the woman straight on.

"Want fries with those fries?"

"How 'bout we super-duper-size it?"

The girl's hair was cut almost to her scalp. She was pierced from eyebrow to navel. Dressed in tight shorts that barely covered her backside, she wore a tank top that left nothing to the imagination.

And yet, Bethany remembered a girl who smelled of bubble gum and baby powder, a girl who could sing like the sea. The wonderful voice that had anchored the alto section of the Forge Hill Chorale. A lifetime ago, it seemed. "Charissa?"

The girl turned, looked over the railing at Bethany. "Omigosh!" Her face flashed with the shock of recognition.

"Come on down," Bethany said, smiling. "I want to introduce you to someone."

A half hour later, she and Charissa sat in Biff's Sandwich Shop. Charissa wolfed down a steak and cheese sub while Bethany picked at a garden salad made with iceberg lettuce and drowned in bottled dressing. Hannah had nursed and was now drowsing. Bethany put the baby to her shoulder and patted her back. Hannah burped noisily.

"Can you tell she takes after her father?" Bethany said, laughing.

"Is that who she looks like? 'Cuz she doesn't look like you, Mrs. Dolan."

"We're not sure yet."

Hannah's eyes were muddy and darkening by the day. Kyle thought they'd turn to brown, but Bethany wasn't sure. Hannah had been born with very dark hair, but what was growing in underneath seemed many shades lighter. Her skin was fair, even more so than Kyle's. Bethany had already begun searching old family photos to see whom she resembled, since she didn't look like her and only vaguely resembled Kyle.

Charissa had been staring at the baby the whole time they were together. "Can I hold her?"

"I think she wants to drop off to sleep now. Let's give her a little time to rest." Bethany put Hannah back in her baby seat, grateful that Hannah had nodded off. She wasn't sure when Charissa had last showered. She had a rash across her right shoulder and chest, and dirt under her nails.

"Sure. I understand."

Bethany flagged down the waitress. "A cup of tea, please. Honey, no milk. Anything else for you, Charissa? Maybe some dessert?"

The girl looked down at her hands. "No. That's okay."

"Come on. I remember how much you love chocolate."

"Sure. Okay."

Charissa dug into a huge piece of fudge cake. She was much thinner, Bethany realized, than when she had last seen her. It had been more than a year, a year that seemed like a lifetime to Bethany. And apparently, to Charissa too. What had happened to throw her so far offtrack that she was now hanging out on the bandstand with home-less people?

"How's your little girl? Tawndra, right?"

The tears started. Bethany held her breath, hoping the girl would say her baby was in school or day care, that Charissa didn't live with the bandstanders but was just visiting. But the girl was crying too hard to say anything now.

Bethany reached across the table and took Charissa's hand. Charissa looked everywhere but at her.

"Tyler and me, we tried to make a home for her. I tried to stay in school, and he was working a lot so we could get a better place. The best we could afford was a dump in Forge Hill. One room, hot plate and cooler. Had to share a bathroom, those stupid junkies leaving their needles . . . " She broke off in a sob.

Bethany gently squeezed the girl's hand.

"Tyler was really tired all the time. But there was this one time, he had worked a double shift. I was late for school, so I just shoved her into his arms. Had to catch the bus, you know."

She was crying so hard, she couldn't continue. Bethany patted her hand and waited. Finally Charissa gulped it all back.

"He dropped her, Mrs. Dolan. He didn't do worse, I swear. She just pushed up in his arms and tumbled onto the floor. She was kind of stunned at first, but soon enough she seemed okay. No crying or anything. So I didn't take her to the doctor. I mean, babies are so squirmy. I dropped her a couple times myself. It's awful, but things like that happen, don't they?"

Bethany nodded. Things like that—and much worse.

"She passed out the next day. Tyler called 911, then he freaked, just left her in our room there with the door unlocked so the ambu-lance could get her. They took her to the hospital, said she had a fracture in her skull. But underneath, she had this thing in her brain, where blood was leaking. We didn't know, Mrs. Dolan, or we would have done something. It was nothing we could see.

"They were gonna make Tyler go to jail, but they let him go to an anger management course and be on probation. They put Tawndra in foster care. They said I should have known that she was so sick. I only get to see her on Saturdays. It's been over half a year. She barely remembers me. I lost the welfare, on account of I no longer had my baby. Lost the one-room dump. None of it matters anyway, not without Tawndra."

"I'm so sorry, Charissa. I had no idea. Is the school helping you with counseling and legal services?"

Charissa finally looked up at Bethany. "Oh, come on, Mrs. Dolan. Do I look like I'm in school?"

"Why did you let school go? After all your hard work?"

"Why did you let school go, Mrs. Dolan? After all your hard work?" Charissa pushed away from the table and stood up. She grabbed the rolls from the basket and stuffed them into her jacket. "Thanks for lunch."

"Charissa. I'm so sorry. There must be something I can do."

Charissa collected the sugar packets and the unopened packets of salad dressing that had come with Bethany's lunch. "That's okay, Mrs. Dolan. We all can't be special like Anthony. I really understand."

She turned and walked out of the restaurant. Before Bethany could get Hannah into the stroller so she could follow, Charissa had crossed the street and was heading toward the bandstand.

We can't all be special like Anthony. Bethany had been so focused on the surrogacy, so concerned with getting the Martinezes to safety, that she hadn't given more than a moment's thought to the kids she'd left behind.

She had to pray it wasn't too late for Charissa.

29

The doorbell rang.

Jenny looked through the peephole. "It's some woman, Aunt Bethany."

Bethany opened the door. "May I help you?"

A woman of medium height and chunky build stood on the stoop. Her lank brown hair and creased face didn't seem to fit with the well-tailored navy suit she wore. "I was looking for the young lady who just came in here. I passed her on the sidewalk, then realized she had dropped this. I turned to call for her, but she was already inside. Anyway, here it is." The woman held up a peach-colored silk scarf.

Bethany turned to Jenny. "Were you just out?"

"Not me."

"No, not her," the woman said. "This girl was taller. You know, with shoulder-length hair, lots of sun streaks. She looked like she might be pregnant."

"How did you say you knew her?"

"Why, I don't know her at all. I just wanted to return her scarf. Are you all right? You look like you're going to faint."

Bethany stiffened. "I am perfectly fine. And there is no one that fits that description here."

"Are you sure?"

Jenny stepped between the woman and Bethany. "Yes, we're sure."

The woman looked from Jenny to Bethany, confused. "Look, can I leave this here? I don't know what else to do with it."

Jenny took the scarf. "Fine. Thank you." She closed the door in the woman's face, then turned to Bethany. "That was weird, huh?

She must be one of those cult people. Trying a new technique to get into people's houses."

"Give me that," Bethany said.

"Why don't I just toss it?"

"No. Give it to me."

"Okay. Sure. Hey, I hear Hannah. Want me to get her up?"

"Please." Bethany smiled weakly as Jenny trotted up the stairs. Without realizing it, she put the scarf to her face. It smelled like lilacs.

"Aunt Bethany is not a raving maniac!"

"I didn't say 'raving maniac'," Kate Hemlow said. "I said she was a drooling lunatic."

Jenny laughed. Typical Kate, making everything high drama. That was the novelist in her. "I feel so bad for her. She is losing it, honest. Like this morning, this woman comes to the door, looking for someone. Mistaken identity, that kind of thing. But afterwards, Aunt Bethany is shaking so hard, I think she's gonna pop right out of her skin."

"You sure you want this job? She already shot one live-in in the head."

"Stop dramatizing. They were fighting for the gun. And yes, I want this job. At least I'm out of New Hampshire for the summer. Unlike some hicks I know."

"Who you calling a hick?"

"You, Lulu. You still have cow manure stuck to your sandal."

North Conway had its own culture and sophistication, Jenny knew. But a summer in Boston had its attractions. Jenny was far away from her stickler mother and her observant father. It was awesome to live in an elegant place like the Dolans' townhouse. And being a nanny beat slaving at Burger Boss. She'd be working few hours and making lots of money.

So what if Aunt Bethany got a bit excessive at times? She was entitled, wasn't she? Having a real lunatic living in her house, carrying her baby, threatening to kill everyone, including Jenny's own mother—that would rattle anyone's brains.

Kate was in Boston for a couple of days, visiting colleges and her sister. On that beautiful summer day, they walked through the Public Gardens, heading for Copley Plaza. They had intended just to window-shop, but Uncle Kyle had slipped Jenny a couple hundred bucks that morning. "Just for fun," he said.

Hannah was in the stroller, sound asleep. What an angel, sleeping most of the day, crying only when she wanted to be changed or fed. Not that Jenny had much to do anyway—just baby-sit while Bethany went to church every afternoon to work with that chorale of hers. Otherwise, she was a real hands-on mother.

Kate was making eyes at some built dude, sunbathing on a bench in cut-off shorts and nothing else. The guy had terrific abs and pecs, and a killer face. "He's hot, huh?"

"He looks barely out of junior high."

"Yeah, well, I like my guys with some life left in them. Not the doddering fools you go after."

"I like my men mature," Jenny said. "So sue me."

A man's voice cut into their conversation. "Sue you? For what? Having a cute kid?"

Jenny jumped, startled. A good-looking guy bent over the stroller, smiling at Hannah. The baby was awake and smiling back.

Now, this is what I'm talking about, Jenny wanted to say to her sister. *Look at this guy.* The eyes were to die for, bluer than the Caribbean. Jenny could imagine diving in there and floating around. His hair was dashed with sun, tousled just enough to look carefree and not styled. And the smile. Even if the guy had been ugly as a wart, the smile would have been enough to blow Jenny off her feet.

"Is she yours?" he asked Jenny.

"No. I'm the nanny."

"Is it hard, being a nanny? Do the parents drive you crazy?"

"The parents *are* crazy!" Kate said, laughing. "At least, one of them is."

"Don't listen to her," Jenny said. "It's really an easy job. Gives me lots of free time."

"Really?" The guy raised his eyebrows as if he was maybe interested in her free time. Jenny checked quickly—no wedding ring.

"She has lots of it, you know," Kate said, giggling.

Jenny stepped on her sister's foot. "I'm from New Hampshire. So it's a treat for me to be in the city," she said, looking for some way to extend the conversation.

"Then I'm sure we'll see each other again," the guy said. "I work over on Boylston, but I come here a lot to brainstorm."

"Really. What do you do?" Kate said.

He shrugged, smiled. "Have fun, mostly. I'm a movie producer."

"Wow," Kate said.

He bent over the stroller. "Bye, sweetie. See you soon. And you two, as well."

Wow, Jenny thought as she watched him cruise away.

<hr>

Bethany excelled at many things, but Kyle had never suspected she had such a talent for organizing. She had gone to him only a week before, agonizing over finding Charissa on the street. Guilty about having abandoned the chorale.

"You didn't abandon them," he said. "You found a replacement."

"Geoffrey Aaltonen is a great musician, but a lousy teacher. I knew that, but I was so caught up in my own problems—"

"I won't have you beat yourself up about this. Everything is forward from this point on."

She hugged him and told him what she wanted to do. He hugged her back, then watched as she secured the church hall for every afternoon, recruited musicians and teachers she knew would connect with the kids, made phone calls, got the word out, and made that afternoon happen—the first rehearsal of the new Forge Hill Chorale.

No longer attached to the charter school, they could sing hymns, gospel, and anything else that caught their fancy, as long as it was decent and uplifting. Bethany had twisted the arm of the acclaimed rock musician, Stan Todd, to conduct. Stan was also a classically educated pianist and saxophone player, but the kids didn't know that.

They were more impressed about singing for the front man of *Weeping Willow* than by Stan's years at Juilliard. In Boston for the next two years to produce a CD, Stan was thrilled to be working with the kids.

The hall filled with their warm-ups, silly sounds to open airways and stretch mouth, throat, and chest muscles. Kyle recognized many of the kids from the old Forge Hill Chorale, but there were lots of new faces too. Thirty kids in all, who would sing as a chorus and study voice privately with a host of volunteers that Bethany had mustered in seven short days.

The only gap was Charissa—Bethany had returned to the bandstand and called her grandmother, but she'd gone missing. Kyle hired Harry Stevens, a private investigator, to try to find her. They prayed it wouldn't be too late.

Bethany finally spotted Kyle, went running to meet him, and greeted him with a kiss. The kids in the chorale hooted. He bent her backwards and kissed her with gusto, giving the spectators their money's worth. "Well. I have to get out more often," she said as she came up for breath.

"Makes coming home all the sweeter. Hey, the kids are psyched."

"You should have heard them when Stan stepped up to the podium. Dead silence. Then they burst out with applause. He told them to save it for themselves—if they earn it."

Kyle laughed. "You trained him well."

"Wish I could train you half as well."

"What? I got mustard on my tie or something?"

"Try chocolate on your shirt. Ice cream, I presume?"

"Low fat. I swear."

"Supposed to be *no* fat, remember? You'll be too fat to teach Hannah to ride her bike."

"I'll never be too fat to teach you to—"

"Kyle Dolan! We are in the presence of children."

"Oh, yeah. Children who could teach us a few things." He put his arm around her waist, watching with her as Stan introduced the first piece of music.

"Did you check on Hannah?" Bethany said.

"I was wondering when you'd ask that."

"I waited a good five minutes. Aren't you proud?"

"Always proud." He kissed her hair. "Yes, I stopped home before coming over. Jenny and Kate had her strapped in the stroller. Something about taking her to drag race down Beacon Hill."

Bethany punched him.

"Hey, I did my part. Threw some weights in the basket so Hannah would be the fastest."

Bethany shifted away from him.

"I'm kidding!"

"I know. I mean, my head knows. But the rest of me wants to strangle you."

"All that fresh air, she'll be starving by the time we get home. Looking for her mama."

Bethany leaned into him. "And I'll be looking for her."

Kyle stood with her for the whole hour, watching Stan work with the kids. Listening to music in the making, thanking God for the music of his life.

Hannah and her mama.

30

*H*ow could she do this to him? Didn't she know it would rip his heart out?

"You're a man now, Anthony," his mother had said. "Time for you to take some responsibility."

Anthony was willing to do anything the Dolans asked. They were paying him well to house-sit the farmhouse. He had moved into the guest suite on the first floor. No way would he live in that apartment. He did his fair share—weeding, mowing, even painting the barn. But to be asked to do that?

"I'm loaded down with this strep throat," Joan had complained. "I can't go driving over to Maine, all germy. It wouldn't be fair to all those people up there at Hale."

"Then wait until next week, when you're all better," Anthony had said.

"Kyle expects me to go every week. We aren't gonna let the man down."

So Anthony was on his way to Maine, driving Kyle's old pickup truck. He stuck in a tape so he could practice his Italian. He'd do anything—even homework—if it would take his mind off what was ahead.

Laurel had been a vegetable for almost three months. She deserved that living hell, mostly for what she had put the Dolans through. But also for how she had lured Jacob into drug-running between her and that guy Switch, and buying that gun. She also deserved it for what she had done to Anthony, pumping up all that love in his heart, then shattering it like it was nothing.

It *was* nothing, to her. Anthony had made it nothing for himself, throwing himself into his music and language studies, preparing for the conservatory. Trying to forget the way she laughed at his jokes and felt against his skin. Trying to forget—because he couldn't forgive her. Or himself.

⌘

Laurel was jivin' him from beyond the grave. She had to be, Jacob thought after he opened the e-mail. Okay, maybe she wasn't really pushin' up daisies. But she might as well be, lying like a stone up in that nursing home. Except a stone didn't wear diapers or have a machine breathe for it.

Jacob was at Sean's house when he got the e-mail. Switch had skipped town, but the judge came down hard on Jacob. Sentencing him to join Boy Scouts! Sean Richards had taken him on as a project, trying to get Jacob through all his badges so he wouldn't look like some sissy at Scout day camp when it came time to start a fire. Jacob could teach these wusses something about starting fires. But that was a whole other life.

Day camp beat the Division of Youth Services, Jacob supposed, though he heard it was easier to score dope in one of the DYS homes than it was on the street. Anthony had moved out. They said it was to help the Dolans and to give him some space, but really, it was a plot to let his mama get her little boy all to herself. She had the notion that she hadn't paid enough attention to Jacob, which was why he got in trouble. The only places she let him go by himself were to day camp and to Sean's house.

Oh, yeah, Sean's house. With three computers, all on high-speed Internet, Jacob kept his action going there, keepin' it cool and teaching that nerd Sean to do the same. Except for that afternoon—Jacob almost upchucked when he saw an e-mail from Laurel's address.

"Whassup, bro?" Sean sat at his worktable, trying to construct a catapult. Jacob was teaching Sean all boss stuff, like how to speak street and how to catapult water balloons and rotten tomatoes at tourists from the top of Cathedral Ledge.

"Just someone punkin' me. An e-mail from someone in a coma."

"No kidding! What does he say?"

"She. I didn't open it yet. Gotta be bogus. Right?"

"No. Might be a delayed transmission."

"Yo. Speak English, bro."

"You tell your server to send it at a later date," Sean said. "Like months, maybe years later. As long as your account is open."

"Okay, but how could she keep an account going if she ain't?"

"She probably either paid in advance or used automatic with-drawal on a credit card. So what's she saying?"

"Nothing." Jacob sent the e-mail directly to the printer without reading it. He'd grab it off and find a private place. This was his business and his alone.

"Laurel?"

Her eyes were open but empty, rolled partly back. Her hand was warm to the touch, but as unmoving as dead meat.

Anthony couldn't stand looking at Laurel and couldn't stop look-ing at her. Laurel—but not Laurel. They had never even learned her real name. She was still beautiful, even with no makeup and a breathing tube taped over a hole in her throat. Her hair was brushed and her lips touched with gloss.

A bag of white, thick fluid hung on a pole, trickling into a tube that disappeared under the sheet. The feeding tube, going into a hole in her stomach. His mother had prepared him for what he would see—but not for what he would feel. The *click click click* of the ventilator made Anthony want to scream.

"Hi, there!" A nurse entered the room. "You must be Joan's son. Anthony, right? I'm Laurel's nurse, Marjorie Owens. Call me Marj."

"Hi. Yeah, my mother's got strep. So I came up to check up on . . . um . . . her."

"There's no change since last week, I'm afraid."

Anthony was about to get up out of his chair, when Marj stepped in front of him to check all Laurel's tubing.

"No one really expects a change, I suppose," he said, hoping she'd be quick, or at least get out of his way so he could get out of there.

"You haven't given up hope, have you?"

"No one has any hope, not for her."

The nurse turned around, surprise on her face. "Both Dr. McDonald—she's Hale's medical director—and Dr. Chasse, the neurologist, do. I do too. Has your mother explained her true condition to you?"

"She's in a coma."

"She's not in a coma."

"So what is she? Playing dead?"

"Oh, what's happening to her is real. It just can't be classified as comatose. Her electroencephalograph readings are almost normal. Diagnostically, the condition looks much more like deep sleep than coma."

"Nobody said anything about that to us."

Marj frowned. "The Dolans have been informed. If they don't want to act on the information . . . " She turned away from Anthony again, her movements sharp.

Anthony sat for a long minute, listening to the ventilator click away. "I'd like to know more," he finally said.

Marj glanced back. "You sure?"

Anthony nodded.

She sat down, took Laurel's hand, rubbed it. "This will be good for you to hear, too, Laurel. The bullet grazed across her skull, fractured it a bit, but really didn't do much damage. It was stuck more in the bone than the brain tissue. The EEG shows almost normal brain function. She was expected to wake up in a few hours after the neurosurgery."

"But she didn't," Anthony said.

"We've tried everything—even tried weaning her off the ventilator. It's as though she's gone somewhere else and just doesn't want to come back. Or maybe she can't. Who knows for sure?"

Anthony rubbed his arms, trying to shake out the creeps. "Does my mother know this?"

"Of course she does. I've encouraged her to spend some time here, talk to the girl." Marj leaned very close to him. "But she told me, in no uncertain terms, that she has nothing to say to Laurel."

"She has her reasons. Trust me." Anthony remembered his mother's ravings. *You should have known better, Anthony. But Jacob, he's just a kid. Bad enough she got him to buy her marijuana. But to allow him—persuade him—to help her buy a gun! That is the devil's working, pure and simple.*

"We try to spend time with her," Marj said. "But she's just one of many. Maybe you could talk about things you used to do together. You did know her, right?"

"Yeah. Kinda."

"Tell her what you're doing now. What she could be doing if she'd just wake up."

"I don't know. I have to—"

"Please. It breaks my heart to see her alone like this." Marj blinked hard as she rolled Laurel onto her side.

"I suppose. Since I'm here anyway."

"Thank you so much." She covered Laurel, then gave Anthony a bright smile and left.

What was he supposed to say? *Remember the time you made Kyle Dolan think I was raping you? Or how you threatened to shoot Mrs. Dolan, then tried to shoot Hannah?* It was stupid. Laurel could be a bloody murderer, for all anyone knew. One thing Anthony was sure of—she had crawled out of some gutter somewhere.

Then again, so had he. And he hadn't done it on his own. The Dolans were there, boosting him and his family up.

He knew what life was like for some of the kids in Forge Hill. Some born already hooked on drugs. Some beaten. Some raped. Abused, abandoned, burned, stabbed, shot. Was that why Laurel stayed in the coma? Was it better for her there than where she came from?

What could he say to this girl he really didn't know? A girl no one knew. Anthony had no words. So he sang.

If you're reading this, then I'm dead.

How whacked, Jacob thought. *How totally cool.*

Bethany cut me open and took out the baby. That's the likely scenario. The woman is insane.

Talk about the pot calling the kettle greasy.

Or he's caught up to me—he's been after me for a long time. In which case, it would have been a slow thing. I hope it didn't hurt too much. Though I gotta tell you, man, I can take a lot. Watch out for him, man. He's bad, badder than even you can imagine.

Whoa, creepsville. Maybe he'd better show the e-mail to Anthony. Or just toss it.

Anyway, I gotta thank you for being the only friend I ever had. Because of that, I'm gonna give you something unbelievable. Something that will set you up for life.

Then again, maybe he should just keep reading.

I can't out and say it, in case this falls into the wrong hands. I have arranged everything so you can have it legally, fair and square. I named you as beneficiary, Anthony as your guardian. There had to be someone over eighteen. Not your mother. She hates me, you know. I can't blame her for that. I want you to listen to her. There's things you wanna be doing, things you saw me doing, that you're better off without. Listen to her, even if she's making you nuts.

I gotta tell you in code about this awesome thing I've left for you. You might have to think a little, but you'll get it soon enough. Here's the trail you have to follow.

Step One. Play up to the castle level in the game that we first played. Think hard to the Labor Day picnic. The game we played that day.

Okay, when you get to this level, play to the top of the tower. Up there, you'll see something hanging. This is what you'll be looking for. Inside is the information that will let you get the awesome . . . well, you'll know in a little while. Just be trusting me on this.

Step Two. Once you know what you're looking for, here's where to look for it.

Remember the game I got you for Christmas? I know, I gave you five. This one is in keeping with the spirit of the holidays, if you get my drift. Yeah, now you know.

Play to the very top level. You love this game, so you must be almost there by now anyway. When you get up there and you find the ultimate villain of the game, you'll be shocked at who it turns out to be. This game's the bomb, for sure. Anyway, look how the dude makes his entrance. That's how he gets away with all the bloody stuff without being caught.

That's where I hid the thing you'll see in the other game. I know it sounds complicated, but I gotta make it so only you can get it.

Step One. Figure out WHAT you're looking for.

Step Two. Figure out WHERE I hid it.

Step Three. Be happy for the rest of your life.

You need to look for it with everything that's in you, man. I tried to build something special for myself, but I should have known it wasn't gonna work out for me. Never has. But if I can't have it, I want you to. 'Cuz you the money, man. In every way.

Live large, J. I mean, someone has to, so why not you?

I guess I didn't.

31

*B*ethany wanted to wring Kyle's neck. "Hey, Southie. Get in here."

Kyle walked into the nursery, a towel wrapped around his waist, his face smeared with foam. "What?"

She pointed at Hannah, gurgling merrily in her infant seat.

"So she's beautiful. I knew that. Now can I finish shaving?"

"The safety bar is up," Bethany said.

"So?"

"I told you to put it down." Kyle had played with Hannah while she showered, then put her in the seat so he could shower.

"I did. You must have lifted it."

"No. I've been busy doing laundry," Bethany said. "You did it. Except you didn't do it."

"I strapped her in the seat, put the bar down, and went into the bathroom," Kyle said, his voice testy. "Once there, I grabbed my safety razor and the shaving cream from high up on the shelf where a kid couldn't possibly touch it—"

"I'm just reminding you to be careful. That's all."

"And I'm telling you that you must have flipped it . . . oh, forget it. She's strapped in. No harm done."

"Maybe next time you'll forget the strap too."

"I did not forget the bar!" Kyle shouted.

Hannah startled, then cried.

"Look what you did," Bethany snapped.

"No. Look what *you* did. Now, if you'll excuse me, I'm going to finish shaving."

"Fine." She unbuckled the strap and lifted Hannah from the seat.

"Fine." Kyle left the room.

Moments later he was back, hugging Bethany. "No, it's not fine. We shouldn't be yelling at each other, especially in front of the baby. I'm sorry."

"Me too. I'm sorry I'm turning into such a nag."

He kissed her, then kissed Hannah. "Nag me as much as you want."

"You sure you didn't do this?"

"What does it matter? One of us did and forgot. That's all."

"Maybe that's not all." Bethany trembled, hated herself for what she was about to say, but she couldn't stop. "Kyle, is she still in the coma?"

"Anthony saw her yesterday. Our family is safe. Believe it."

"Yes, I do. I love you, Kyle."

"I love you. And you, little fuzz ball." He kissed Hannah again, then went off to dress.

"Come on, little love. Let's change those smelly pants." Bethany lay Hannah on the changing table. Hannah kicked and gurgled. The night before, Kyle had gotten a belly laugh out of her, the first one ever.

That was the thing about kids, Bethany thought. All the amazing firsts. Judging by Hannah's prolific drool that week, her first tooth might be ready to break through, even though she was only three months old. It would only be minutes before she lost that first tooth, got her first braces, had her first kiss, diapered her own first baby. The cycle of life ran too fast sometimes. Now that Hannah was there, Bethany wanted to slow it down so she could savor each moment.

After cleaning her, Bethany sprinkled Hannah's backside with powder—that day was supposed to be another humid one. Bethany pulled the diaper up, then lifted Hannah into a hug. Before Hannah had been born, Bethany hated the scent of baby powder, because it reminded her of what she couldn't have. Now it was better than expensive perfume.

Such a mess, though. Bethany strapped Hannah in her seat, dropped the bar, and went looking for a cleaning cloth. She returned, wet cloth in hand. Hannah's bar was up.

"Kyle? Kyle!"

She could hear the water going downstairs in the kitchen. Kyle would be making coffee. She knocked on Jenny's door. Jenny answered, bleary-eyed. "Did you come into the nursery just now?"

"Nope. What's wrong?"

"Nothing. Go back to sleep."

Bethany went back to the nursery. Hannah fluttered her hands as if they were the most fascinating thing in the world. Maybe she was just making too much of it all. She must have left it up and forgotten.

She went to the changing table to clean up. Her hand stopped midwipe. Letters were scrawled in the spilled powder.

M A M A M A M A

Cade met Jenny Hemlow every afternoon in the Boston Public Gardens. The girl was plain, plump, and smart—and she was in love. Cade had made sure of that.

"So what are you working on today?" Jenny asked. The baby was in the stroller between them, playing with her feet.

"The same old thing. That little film about the psychic nun."

"I thought you said she was a psycho nun."

The girl listened too well. "Everyone thinks that, because of the visions. Hey, I talked to Meg's agent today. She's interested, big-time. Reese is after us, too, though I think she's too perky. Even so, I'll slip her the script once we get the financing. Of course, then we'll need twice as much financing. Hire one of the top stars and you get to pay for her hairdresser, her chef, her manicurist, stylist, masseuse, astrologer . . . "

Jenny laughed. Cade laughed with her, making sure to catch her eyes.

"Glamorous job," Jenny said.

"Nah, it's the same as yours."

"Being a nanny?"

"Except my babies whine louder, make bigger messes, and instead of spitting up milk, they spew booze." Cade took Jenny's hand. He could feel her tense, then relax as he stroked her palm.

"It's so exciting. I would love to break into the business."

"You'd be a natural, Jen."

"Not in front of the camera."

"Forget acting. A pretty face is just skin-deep, a dime a dozen out there in la-la land. The real passion is in getting a story to the screen. Producing."

"How would I do it?"

"Well, you can either indenture yourself to some slave-driving producer—like me—which means getting my car washed, picking up my dry cleaning, and maybe, just maybe, meeting some important people. Or . . . "

"Or what? Sell my soul to the devil?"

"The second option is to find a great story. Pretty faces come and go, but a compelling, intriguing story is to die for." She was circling his bait—he could tell by her inward gaze.

"I might know a story that could make an amazing movie," she finally said.

"Really? I'd love to hear it."

"It has to do with . . . " She pointed at the stroller.

"Not a talking baby, I hope."

"Hardly. It was a tragedy. Close to unbelievable."

"A family-in-jeopardy thing? We could sell that in an instant."

"Totally. But my parents have been friends with the baby's parents since the Dark Ages. They're even my godparents. It could be like this huge betrayal."

"You can disguise locations and characters, change enough facts so no one can really pin it down."

"Oh my gosh, it is such a great story. But . . . I just don't know . . . "

"Tell me. If there is a movie there, I can help you develop the story, then introduce you to some of the money people. Imagine, you could be producing your movie by next year!"

"At my age?"

"How old are you?"

"Um . . . twenty. One."

Cade took her face in his hands. "Hollywood worships youth. You're right where you need to be." He looked deep again, letting her drink in his sincerity. "Right now."

"I know." Her tone was dreamy, her eyes closing.

He touched his lips to her forehead. She'd be disappointed, but that would ensure she'd come back for more.

She sighed. "I suppose as long as you don't tell anyone . . . "

"Between us. I swear."

"Okay." She moved close to him, her eyes bright. She'd been dying to tell, Cade knew. Whatever it was, he knew Sable would be the main character. "Here's what happened. The people I'm working for couldn't get pregnant. So they hired a surrogate . . . "

<hr />

Midnight in Forge Hill was about as dangerous as you could get. Jacob had dodged cops on the beat, slipped by dopers in the alley, danced around prostitutes on the corner. He'd even ducked a few bullets in his time.

But that night, up there in North Conway, Jacob wanted to run home and jump under his bed until the sun came back up. He was going around the side of the Dolans' farmhouse when a hundred bats dived at him like thirsty demons. He batted them away and caught his breath. Then there was a *whoo-hoo* from the big oak tree, like Jacob might not be too big for owl to try to take down. The wind in the trees should have been familiar by then, but in the dark, that *whoosh* that turned the leaves on their sides felt like a mighty hand passing by, ready to strike.

Jacob slid the key in the door, jiggled and then turned it. The apartment was dark and silent. *Get out,* his gut screamed. *Get to work,* his mind hollered back. Joan had taken away his PlayBox, so he needed to get at Laurel's PlayBox, unravel the clues she had sent him. This was a good time to do it, with Anthony in Boston overnight for his piano lessons.

Laurel's smell still hung in the air, junk food and sweet shampoo.

Lilac, she told him once when she caught him sniffing her hair. *Hey, J, he could hear her say. Think ya can take me in Reign of Chaos?*

Yes! The PlayBox was still hooked up! Maybe he should just take it home. No, it would take his mom about thirty seconds to sniff it out. He could take it to Sean's, but he'd never get enough time there to advance in the levels. Best to play it here. It was easy enough to get out at night, with his mama working at the hospital. His baby-sitter was a dumb farm kid, asleep by ten. Jacob could run a rave and the lump would snore through it.

Time to get to work. This could mean his whole life, the life Laurel wanted to give him for free, if he could figure out the clues. He knew it would be an awesome life, because Laurel had sent him another e-mail four days after the first. No words. None were needed, because the number in the second e-mail said it all.

$897,909

<hr>

It was no dream. "My God, my God!" Bethany cried. Where was Hannah?

They had just gotten home from the chorale's first concert, fol-lowed by dinner out with Stan Todd and his girlfriend. Bethany's first thought on getting home was to check on the baby. She wasn't in her crib. "Kyle. Kyle!"

Kyle rushed in and went pale when he saw the empty nursery. "I'll look. You get Jenny."

Bethany rushed through the townhouse and finally found Jenny asleep in the family room. "Wake up!" She dug her fingers into the girl's shoulder and shook her. Jenny's eyes barely flickered.

Kyle ran in, his face raw with despair. "Did Jen say—?"

"She won't wake up."

Kyle opened his cell phone. "I need an ambulance at 6 Pilgrim Road. Our nanny is unresponsive. Yes, she's breathing, but we can't get her to wake up. And we need the police. No, not that. It's just— our baby is missing."

He looked over at her. "Bethany, stop it!"

Bethany looked at her hands, shaking Jenny so hard the girl's teeth knocked. She let go and raced down the hall and into the kitchen.

She opened doors and drawers, even looking in the refrigerator. "God, save us!" she cried as she opened the freezer and microwave. *The carport*, she thought and raced out the back deck. She stopped cold at the sight of the gas grill, its lid large enough to hide a laundry basket. She lifted it. *Thank God*. Nothing.

She ran down the porch stairs, heading for the carport, when she tripped over something in the walkway. The stroller. Hannah was strapped in her baby seat, sleeping soundly.

Jenny refused to get into the ambulance. "I'm not moving until my parents get here."

The next flight from Harrisburg wasn't until six that morning, so they were making the drive up from Pennsylvania.

"We can't make her go with us," the EMT told Mr. Dolan.

Jenny was in bed, playing the victim. Kate had driven down from North Conway. "Shut the door," Jenny whispered.

Kate sat on the bed with her sister. "Aunt Bethany is totally freaking out. Mom and Dad are storming mad at you *and* them. What happened?"

Jenny shook her head. Big mistake—it went from pounding to near-exploding. She probably should have gone to the hospital so they could do a tox screen, find out what she had been doped with. But then they'd find other stuff too. Private stuff no one knew about.

"You have got to swear this is between us. If any of this gets out, Mom and Dad won't let me go to Brown in September. They'll think they can't trust me. Swear?"

"Swear. Sister's honor."

They linked fingers, then Jenny continued. "You know that guy I've been seeing?"

"Hollywood Harry?"

"His name is Cade."

"Oh, like that's his real name. Uh-huh."

"You're jealous 'cuz I got a hunk and you got—"

"My books to keep me warm. You bet. So, were you with him tonight?"

"Yeah."

"I mean, *with* him."

"No. I wasn't *with* him. Not like that. What a night, though. You should have seen the public gardens. Flowers everywhere. The swans swimming on the pond, people drifting around, hand in hand."

"Stars, moonlight, and violin. Gag me, will you?"

"I'm just telling you—I couldn't resist. The Dolans were out for that concert. You know, that chorale thing that she organized. Hannah and I walked over to the gardens together. Cade had a picnic waiting for us."

"While I spent the night at the library, you're making sweet under the stars. So what's the big secret?"

"Cade, for one. I never told anyone I was seeing him. Aunt Bethany would insist on a background check. And if she knew I had Hannah out after dark, she'd rip my head off."

"What else?"

"What do you mean, 'What else'?"

"That's not enough to keep you from going to the hospital," Kate said.

"Well, he had some munchies and a nice bottle of champagne."

"Champagne? Oh, that's nice. You're not even drinking age. What a creep."

"Not his fault. I told him I'm twenty-one."

"My gosh, Jenny! Okay. So you're afraid the alcohol would show in a blood test."

Jenny felt the flush coming. "That. And the grass."

"What!"

Jenny slapped her hand over Kate's mouth. "It's no big deal. Everyone does it."

"We don't," Kate said.

"Oh, grow up."

"You grow up. We know better than that." Kate got up to leave.

"Wait. Don't. Please. You promised. Sister's honor."

Kate sighed and sat back down. "So you got drunk and doped and passed out. Now, that's something to be proud of."

"No way. I wasn't even high, just feeling a little good, that's all. It's just afterwards that something happened. I think someone gave me that date-rape drug."

"Oh my gosh, Jenny, were you—"

"No. Absolutely not."

"So why would Cade dope you like that?"

"Who said it was Cade? On the way home, we got coffee. The guy behind the counter looked like a stoner. Maybe this was his idea of a joke. Anyway, I remember opening the back door, and that's all. I must have passed out before I brought Hannah inside."

"So why didn't Cade call an ambulance?" Kate demanded.

"We said good night at the back gate. He didn't know."

"You believe that, I got a used Yugo to sell you."

"I do believe it. Which is why I'm just going to play dumb."

"You are being dumb. It's hard to believe you're going to college in a couple of months."

"And you're naïve, little sister."

"I'd rather be naïve than stupid. At least tell Uncle Kyle."

"No. What they don't know won't hurt them."

"You'd better hope so," Kate said.

32

*P*ut on the heels," Cade said. "Those stiletto things turn me on."
It hadn't been easy, shoplifting something that fit Hailey, but it had been worth it. Expensive wool was like silk. Hailey modeled the navy suit and pearl earrings for Cade.

"So, what now?" he asked, nibbling Hailey's earlobe. "We demand custody of Sable so we can get all her 'effects'?"

"Don't be stupid. What if they actually give *her* to us? You want to be stuck with a vegetable all your life?"

"So how do we get at her stuff?"

Hailey grinned. "I've got an idea."

"Tell me."

"First, I'll show you."

Cade just smiled.

"Ghosts?"

"Is it possible, Patrick?" Bethany hated the hysteria trickling at the edge of her voice.

"Well, I've never seen a quark, and I know they exist. Do you believe in ghosts?"

"Stop playing shrink. Tell me what you know."

Patrick put his feet up on his desk, leaning back in his chair. "King Saul hired a spiritualist to raise the ghost of Samuel. We don't know if it was actually Samuel's spirit she raised or, somehow, God allowing a spirit to speak through the apparition. Regardless, Samuel was furious to be disturbed, and the spiritualist was terrified at what

Saul had tricked her into. He also reiterated God's judgment on Samuel.

"So yes, ghosts may exist, as any other supernatural phenomena may, as tools of Satan or, in rare instances, like the voice given to Balaam's donkey under the direction of God. But the cinematic notion of ghosts being souls caught between life and death, with unresolved issues, is simply unscriptural. We don't get to tap-dance around judgment and grace. It is what it is. And thank God for that."

Bethany got up and paced. "Then how do I view these events? Too many weird things have happened just to be coincidences. The woman who came to our door described our surrogate to a T. These images that pop up all over."

"Was there something other than the baby powder?"

"Yesterday I was making bread. I sprinkled the counter with flour, then went to get the dough. When I came back, those squiggles were in the flour—the M A M A thing again."

"Did you get either Jenny or Kyle to confirm that the image was there?"

"It's always gone by the time I get them. A couple days ago, there were tracings in the steam in the bathroom mirror. By the time Kyle got there, it was all just droplets of water. Oh, and by the way—Jenny is gone."

"What do you mean, gone?"

"We're all being closemouthed about it—trying not to let this incident come between our friendship with the Hemlows. Kyle wants to call this thing a 'teenage indiscretion.' He thinks Jenny passed out before she could bring Hannah in from the stroller."

"How do you see it, Bethany?"

"What time of day is it?" Bethany's laugh strangled in her throat. She went to the window. "I want to believe Kyle's theory. But he's as worried as I am that something evil may be at play here. He's just better at hiding it."

"You just said he wants to let it go."

"That's what he wants me to think. I overheard him last night.

He's got a private investigator looking into this. Kyle believes that this could have been a kidnap attempt."

"It's something to be considered. Don't obsess, but be aware."

"I know. We've been so blessed with the financial freedom to do whatever we want, and yet, all this blessing makes Hannah a target."

"Would you feel less anxious if Kyle hired security? Perhaps on a short-term basis?"

"Harry Stevens is starting today. But his presence can't cover all the possibilities."

"Oh. And those would be . . . ?" Patrick leaned forward in his chair.

"Back around to the supernatural."

"Okay. Make your case for it."

"Weird things keep happening. That weird crying, first in North Conway, then in my dreams. The images. The woman who thought she saw Laurel come into the townhouse. This thing with Jenny passing out and Hannah being missing." Bethany looked down at her lap. "Everything's just spinning out of control, and I'm going with it."

"Bethany, you're safe here. You know that."

"I do. Thank you, Patrick. I appreciate that you're not looking at me cross-eyed."

"I'd never do that. Why don't you give me your bottom line here in regard to these strange occurrences?"

"I told you . . . the supernatural." Bethany looked over his shoulder to the window, not daring to meet his eyes. She felt his hand cover hers.

"Be specific."

She kept her gaze averted. "I guess I'd have to call this . . . I don't know . . . a haunting?"

"A haunting." Patrick's voice was matter-of-fact. "That requires a ghost. So . . . whose ghost are we talking about?"

"You know whose."

"A ghost requires a dead person. Your surrogate is alive."

Bethany covered her face with her hands. Her cheeks were burning hot, her palms cold.

"Bethany? You okay?"

She looked up at Patrick. "Technically, she is alive. But the truth is—she's as good as dead. So I have to believe, if I'm being haunted, then it's by her. Because the alternative is worse."

"What alternative?"

"Patrick. What if it's my babies? What if they're haunting me? And haunting Hannah, because she's alive and they're not?"

33

his is heaven, Kyle thought. Hannah on his lap, Bethany at the piano. A tangy breeze coming off the Atlantic, cooling Boston. The doorbell rang. Bethany paused.

"No, don't stop," Kyle said. "Show Mama how much we like her music." Kyle clapped the baby's hands together.

The doorbell rang again. Bethany glanced out at the front hall.

"Harry will get it. Hey, look what Hannah-banana can do. Come on, fuzz ball. Show Mama patty-cake."

Hannah brought her hands together. Kyle beamed. "Isn't she smart?"

"She sure is," Bethany said.

"Takes after her daddy."

"No doubt."

"Plus she's very beautiful."

"Absolutely," Bethany said.

"Takes after her mama."

"No way. Not an Italian bone in that little body. She should be wearing a Celtics shirt, with that fair skin."

"Hey, her Mediterranean looks are there. Just hidden under all the baby fat."

Harry Stevens walked in. "Sorry to interrupt. There's someone here that needs to see you, Mr. Dolan. A business matter."

"I don't do business at home. You know that."

"You need to see this guy. Trust me, Mr. D." Harry kept his voice low.

"Okay, I'll be right out." Kyle passed the baby to Bethany at the piano. Hannah immediately banged on the keys.

"Who is it, Kyle?"

"Just some papers to sign. I'll just be a couple minutes. That should be enough time to teach Hannah her scales. And how to tap-dance. Go ahead and potty train her while you're at it."

"We'll see what we can do."

Kyle kissed his two girls, then followed Harry out.

An ex-Boston cop, Harry Stevens was big, tough, and loyal. Kyle had known him from the old neighborhood, respected his street smarts.

"So who is this guy I just have to see?"

"His name is Cade Parker. And he claims he's—I'm sorry, Mr. Dolan."

"Just say it, will you?"

"He says he's the baby's father."

"What baby?"

"Your baby, Mr. Dolan. This guy is saying he's little Hannah's real father."

———

Dolan looked like he wanted to rip his head off. *Let him try,* Cade thought. *It'd be nice to blow off a little steam.* Then again, Dolan's muscle had his hand inside his jacket—no doubt petting his .38. Another reason Cade left street fighting to the amateurs.

"Who are you?" Dolan asked.

"Mr. Kyle Dolan, I take it?"

"Answer Mr. Dolan's question," the muscle growled, too stupid to realize he just had answered Cade's question.

"Cade Parker. From the Albany area."

"Okay, Parker. You have sixty seconds to tell me why I shouldn't have Mr. Stevens drag you back to whatever gutter you climbed out of."

"I'm Sable Lynde's husband."

"Is that supposed to mean something to me?"

"You know Sable as Laurel Bergin, I understand." Cade handed him a picture from two years before—Sable with her arms around his neck, looking a little drunk and a lot happy.

"Mr. Dolan? You okay?" Stevens looked about ready to administer CPR.

"Let's go into my office," Dolan said, walking down the hall. Cade followed, taking great care not to whoop, holler, or dance. It just wouldn't be polite.

"I thought she loved me," Parker was saying. "She could make any-one believe anything, as you know."

"What I know is none of your business," Kyle said. Yes, the girl was a cruel liar. Which meant that anyone involved with Sable Lynde might also be the same.

"I had always been up-front about wanting a kid—lots of kids. She agreed, but when it seemed to be the right time, she made excuses. Like we needed to have a house. So I took on a second shift, work-ing sixteen hours a day. She starting going out at night. Said she was taking computer courses and was busy with lab work.

"She was busy all right, but not with school. There were guys. Plenty of guys. She just laughed when I confronted her. 'Why?' I asked her. 'Because they're not all over me to knock me up,' she said, laughing right in my face. 'They're just all over me.'

"I threw her out. Missed her something bad, but I couldn't put up with that catting around. Maybe another man could, but not me. I thought love was supposed to be something special." A tear trickled down Parker's cheek.

Kyle wanted to slap it off the man's face. "Did you check on Mrs. Dolan?" Kyle asked Stevens.

"She took the baby up for her bath."

"Okay. Thanks. Mr. Parker? Can you continue?"

Parker sniffed and wiped at his face. "So she was gone, for months and months. Then last summer she came back to New York."

"When last summer?"

"July, I think it was. Toward the end."

When Kyle and Bethany were up in North Conway, renovating the apartment. They had left Laurel—Sable—alone for almost two weeks.

"Anyway, she begged me to forgive her. Said she wanted a baby with me so badly, she just couldn't wait. I mean—you know what she was like. Gets under your skin, a girl like that. So we dug right in. I thought if I could get her pregnant right then, she'd stay."

"And did she?"

"For three days. I tried to find her. Looked all over Albany, even went down to Brooklyn to check out some places we used to hang. No one had seen her. When I found out she was pregnant, I almost went nuts."

"How did you know she was pregnant, if she never made any contact?"

"One of my friends is a real estate agent. She was out snapping photos of some commercial property in Troy. Took this."

Parker passed a photo to Kyle. It was of Bethany, hugging Laurel in a parking lot. "If you weren't looking for it, you might not realize that puffy belly was a pregnancy. But if you knew her before, had seen that tight stomach of hers—then what else could that swelling be?"

"How did you find us?"

"I had a PI circulate the photo. No luck on Sable, but someone recognized your wife. She's famous, huh? A piano player? None of it made sense until I finally tracked you down."

"What didn't make sense?"

"Why Sable would come home, get pregnant, then disappear on me. But now I realize. She sold you our baby, didn't she?"

Don't react, Kyle told himself. *Don't kill this man.* "How much do you want?" he finally said.

"Excuse me?"

"Nice story. Complete fabrication, but it could cause some annoyance to my wife and me. How much do you want, Parker?"

"I'm not following you."

The man's face looked like innocence itself. But so had Laurel's, hadn't it?

"How much money do you want to go away?"

"I don't want any money, Mr. Dolan."

"Then what do you want?"

"All I've ever wanted. My baby."

34

Kyle wouldn't let go of Hannah.

"I have to nurse her," Bethany pleaded. "She hasn't eaten since four."

"If you'd let her take a bottle, I could feed her too." Kyle rocked the baby. She had been asleep for two hours but was rousing.

"You're scaring me, Kyle. Why won't you let me have her?"

"I know Laurel's real name, Bethany. It's Sable. Sable Lynde Parker."

"How do you know that?"

It took Kyle two minutes to tell her, a mere brutal second for her to respond. "I'll die before I let anyone take my baby."

"Now you know," he said.

"Maybe we should call Nora."

"What good will that do?"

"She did the implantation, all the pregnancy tests—"

"She always made it clear that none of this is an exact science," Kyle said.

Bethany had always relied on Kyle's strength, assuming it was boundless. Now she realized that he had been as shredded as she in the last year.

"You hold on to our baby," Bethany said, kissing the top of his head. "I'll go make up a bottle."

She was back a minute later and held her husband while he fed their daughter. Then they made their plans.

"You back again?" Marj asked.

Anthony hunched his shoulders. "Yeah."

"Where's your mother? She's not sick again, is she?"

"No. She had jury duty. The grand jury thing in Concord. Has to stay overnight. So I came up. Don't know why I had to bother. Laurel looks the same as last time."

"We have to work hard just to keep her the same."

"What do you mean?"

The nurse pulled the sheet off Laurel. "Look." Plastic braces were strapped to Laurel's legs, fastened with Velcro straps. "These keep her limbs straight. Because she's not moving, the muscles atrophy and the tendons shrivel. We brace her hands, too, usually overnight. A physical therapist comes in every day, stretches her limbs, works her muscles, even massages her fingers. We're trying to keep her ready, you know."

"Ready for what?"

Marj slid her arms under Laurel's hips and shoulders and rolled her onto her side. "For when she wakes up."

"When will that be?" Anthony said.

Marj pulled the sheet up to Laurel's chin. "When she decides it's safe to come out, I suppose."

— ❦ —

How much cooler could life get?

With his mom out of town and his brother not paying attention, Jacob got to hang out in an awesome apartment no one wanted to go in, with the best video games in the world. Yeah, man. This was living.

Jacob had reached the castle level of Reign of Chaos. Laurel had said there was a clue here, and now he knew what it was. A bell. Well, not just one bell. Thousands of bells. Big, little, tinkling, booming—bells upon bells upon bells. So this was the first clue—Laurel had hidden the instructions for getting the money in a bell somewhere.

He had searched the apartment high and low. He had even taken the doorbell apart, but that wasn't it. He was so desperate he had offered to dust the main house for Anthony earlier that day, just for the opportunity to search there. He found his first bell in the living room—a crystal bell on the mantle.

Anthony freaked when he caught Jacob holding it upside down. "That's not a toy. You break it, and I'll break you."

Searching was a waste of time, Jacob decided. Laurel had said the bell was hidden. To know where, he had to play the game she had gotten him for Christmas. Winter Slaughter. It was a boss game, with lots of white snow and red blood and creative weapons, like icicles and sled runners. His mom had thrown it in the trash.

When he told Laurel, she bought him another one. "Play it here," she said. "I'll take a few swings through it, too, and we can blast each other."

Jacob booted up the game, wishing Laurel were there to blast him then. He had a lot of practice time ahead of him if he was going to make it to the top level, find the ultimate bad dude and where he made his entrance. That's where Laurel hid the bell, and the bell was where she hid the instructions. Lots of clues, lots of work, but Jacob was stoked.

Eight hundred ninety-seven thousand dollars and some change could buy a lot of video games.

35

ailey was fifteen years older than Cade, forty pounds heavier, with a hundred times more mileage on her. But Hailey was smart. She figured that the Dolans would try to book out of Boston. Which is why Cade and his lawyer—a shyster from Somerville named Paul Leonard—waited for the Dolans in their carport.

The sun hadn't even broken the horizon, but it was already broiling, another hot August day. Beach weather. But if Hailey was right, the Dolans would be making tracks a lot farther than Cape Cod or Maine.

A black SUV was parked in back. *The vehicle of choice for beautiful people on the move.* Cade and Leonard sat on the trunk of the Mercedes. Cade smoked one cigarette after another, taking care not to get in sight of a window.

The back door opened. Stevens stepped out first, carrying two huge suitcases. Kyle Dolan was next, lugging a baby seat and a shoulder bag. Bethany appeared last, dressed in a loose jumper that did nothing to hide what Cade saw as her delicious tight body. She cradled the baby in her arms.

Cade slid off the Mercedes. "Going somewhere?"

The wife startled, moving instinctively back toward the house.

Cade stepped between her and the door. "Good morning, Mrs. Dolan. We haven't met. I'm Cade Parker. And this is my attorney, Paul Leonard."

"The man from the park," she said.

"Guilty as charged. The question is—what are you guilty of?"

"Vacation," Kyle snarled. "And you're not invited." He opened the back door of the SUV and put the baby seat in.

Stevens dropped the suitcases and fisted his big hands. "You want I should throw them out, Mr. Dolan?"

"Nothing would make me happier."

"Not a wise move," Leonard piped in. Hailey had scored an Italian suit for Leonard, made him get a manicure and haircut. He looked every bit the five-hundred-dollar-an-hour lawyer he'd never be.

"You heard Mr. Dolan. Move it." Stevens grabbed Leonard's arm.

"Mr. Dolan, it's rash to be leaving like this," Leonard said.

"You can't stop us," Kyle said.

"No, but a judge can—and will."

Kyle jerked up. "Harry. Wait." Stevens let go of Leonard.

"What do you want?" the wife said, her voice as silky as her hair.

"A DNA test will clear this up," Cade said, though he thought maybe it wouldn't be bad at all to drag it out as long as they could. Bethany Dolan would be fun to play cat and mouse with.

"No," Kyle said. "Now get out of our way before we have you arrested."

"For what? Asserting parental rights?"

"For trespassing."

"Mr. Dolan—" Leonard began.

Cade cut him off. "Mrs. Dolan. Are you absolutely sure that she is your baby?"

"Absolutely," she said. But her eyes betrayed her, blinking too fast.

"And I'm absolutely sure she's mine," Cade said. "So you understand, I can't let you leave with her."

"I repeat: you cannot stop us," Kyle said, looking ready to go ten rounds.

Cade laughed, thinking it might be fun to take on the society stud in front of his luscious wife.

"This is just a joke to you?" she said.

"Of course not. I apologize. It's just ironic—even from her coma, Sable tightens the noose, doesn't she?"

Leonard stepped between Cade and Kyle, alerted by the code word *noose*. Hailey had prepared an Oscar-worthy script for him. "Mrs. Dolan, Mr. Dolan. We have no desire to trouble you or put you through any more pain. But if we can't proceed informally, I have an appointment to appear before a judge this morning, to sue for temporary custody of the baby."

"No. Please, no," Bethany said.

"We know the judge will have to take strong consideration of a desperate father's desire to be united with his child. Combined with your obvious flight, the judge will most likely order the baby into foster care until we settle this."

"Foster care?" Bethany tightened her grip on the baby.

"We want to offer a more reasonable solution," Leonard continued. "We propose—"

"Just get it out on the table—how much do you want?" Kyle said.

Cade shook his head, trying to appear infinitely patient. "All we want is to settle this. We'd like to go to wherever you've got Sable, take everyone's blood, determine parentage. If I'm wrong, I'll apologize and go away."

"We don't need you to do that," Kyle said. "My wife and I can take blood tests right in Boston."

"And keep me from seeing my wife?" *Time now for the wounded look,* Cade thought.

"No. We'll be glad to give you her address. But why unsettle her with an unnecessary medical procedure?" Kyle said.

"Unnecessary only if the baby is yours," Cade said. "Here's how I see it: Sable miscarried your baby, then got pregnant right away with me to collect the money you promised. The baby was small when she was born, wasn't she?"

"Who told you that?" Bethany asked.

"So I'm right. She may have been small because she's small. Or because she was born a couple weeks earlier than she was supposed to be."

"We had blood tests, urine tests, all confirming that the pregnancy held," Bethany said.

Cade laughed. "Sable knows her way around things like blood tests." The Dolans glanced at each other. *Bingo,* Cade thought. Sable had been up to her old tricks.

"Even so, we don't need to bring the girl into this. Or you. We can confirm that we are the parents without any of you involved," Dolan said.

"Unless there's a third option for parentage," Leonard said.

"What? The cabbage-patch theory? Or the stork? Either one is as valid as the bull you're shoveling," Kyle said.

Cade smiled and nodded at Leonard. Time to stick the knife in and give it a delicious twist. "There's a third option, which absolutely requires we get a blood sample from Ms. Lynde," Leonard said.

"For goodness' sake, what are you talking about?" Bethany asked.

"You know what my wife could be like, Mrs. Dolan," Cade cut in. "Sable is—was—attractive and cunning. Very persuasive. It's possible that Mr. Dolan is the father all right, and that Sable is the mother."

Bethany slapped him.

He'd have finger marks for days. But Cade just laughed. Just something else to charge to their bill, he knew. And they would pay. He and Hailey would see to that.

———— ✤ ————

"You had to know this would come back to bite you," Peter Muir said.

Nora was silent, her face a mixture of compassion and regret.

"We were desperate," Kyle said. "Going through an agency would have meant relinquishing control—"

"And getting someone absolutely qualified. Not some low-life impostor."

"Fine. I deserve that," Kyle said. "Whatever foolish or unethical or even illegal behavior you want to accuse me of, Peter, I've already slapped myself with. You can't make me any more sorry that I already am."

"No! I am not sorry," Bethany said. "We have Hannah, don't we? Regardless of what this man claims—in every hair on her head, every beat of her heart—she is our little girl."

"Then let's do the stupid blood test and get this over with," Kyle said.

Peter shook his head. He was a small man, precise almost to the point of being dapper. He had an exquisite legal mind and an unwavering loyalty to Kyle and Dol-Pak, which was why Kyle *hadn't* consulted him about the surrogacy. The money and terms Kyle proposed were beyond accepted practice, even outside the bounds of Massachusetts and New Hampshire law. Kyle had written the contracts himself, not wanting Peter to feel compromised. Now they looked to Peter to rescue them from the morass that Kyle had invited.

They sat in the office of Peter's associate in Sanford, Maine, ten miles from the nursing home where Laurel—or Sable—lay in her coma. Nora had driven east from North Conway, Peter had traveled up from Boston with Kyle and Bethany.

Parker and Leonard paced outside in the waiting room, refusing to let the Dolans out of their sight. "If you disappear, I'll have you charged with kidnapping," Parker had threatened.

When this was all over, Kyle thought, he would gladly charge Parker with extortion, harassment, or whatever charge Peter thought would stick. Or maybe he'd just pound the brains out of him.

"We have two choices," Peter said. "Tie this guy up in so many legal knots, it'll cost him a fortune to get out of it. Then force him to name his price."

"What's the second?" Kyle asked.

"Call his bluff. Run the blood tests and establish paternity—and maternity—and go on from there. If Hannah isn't your blood child—"

"Oh, good grief, Peter. Don't even say that. She is ours," Bethany said.

Peter looked pointedly at Nora, inviting a response.

"I'd agree with Bethany," Nora said, "*if* the girl hadn't been so clever in fooling us with her drug screens. We can't put it past Laurel to have used someone else's urine to simulate a pregnancy. Maybe even somehow switched tubes of blood. Kyle, you made it so financially attractive for her to succeed that she would pull anything to continue as your surrogate."

"I just wanted to guarantee her cooperation. Not solicit some sort of fraud." It was painfully clear that what Kyle thought was a wise course had been foolish to the point of recklessness.

"How could Hannah be conceived two weeks later than the implantation?" Bethany asked. "Every ultrasound was in normal range."

"Which is why it's called a range. Don't forget, Laur—Sable— missed the first ultrasound because she had diarrhea, or claimed to. We started the diagnostics late, so we could have been ten days off, or more. There is a tiny chance that this guy is telling the truth." Nora's eyes filled with tears.

Bethany handed Hannah to Kyle, then hugged Nora. "We're doing it again, involving you in our messes. I am so sorry."

Nora forced a smile. "Life is messy. By the grace of God, we deal with it."

"The girl signed the adoption papers, Peter," Kyle said. "Any wiggle room there?"

Peter shook his head. "First of all, they aren't legal. She signed them as Laurel Bergin. Secondly, if the baby was hers and Parker's—"

The pain is like a knife, Kyle thought. *Cutting right through me.*

"Then she couldn't put the baby up for adoption without Parker's permission."

"So we're going to have to go through with the DNA testing?"

"Sure looks that way," Peter said.

"Then let's just do it. Right now," Kyle said. "Okay with you, Bethany?"

"No. It's not okay. It's wicked and horrible and incomprehensible. But we don't have any choice, do we?"

"One more thing," Peter said. "They don't trust Dr. Hemlow to draw the blood and arrange the tests. Leonard and I need to contact a lab together and have someone meet us there."

"I'll come anyway," Nora said.

Kyle kissed her cheek. "No. It's okay. Go home. We'll call you later, okay?"

Nora nodded and grabbed her bag. "I'll be praying."

"Thank you," Kyle said, even though he felt the notion coming up like bile. Why bother when it was clear that God had taken His hand away? Kyle deserved it. But surely, Hannah did not.

Please, Lord, don't let anyone take away our baby.

36

Kyle knew he should feel pity for Sable Lynde. Her eyes were blank, her skin waxy, her hands curled into her wrists. Her only movement was that of her chest, each time the ventilator breathed for her.

But anger left no room for pity. That a stranger named Cade Parker could make a claim on their daughter was unforgivable. And that was the bottom line, wasn't it? Forgiveness was required of Kyle as a person of faith. But as a husband and a father, he couldn't muster forgiveness any more than he could sympathy.

The lab technician finished drawing Parker's blood. She slipped the tube into her basket, then turned to Kyle. "We need the baby now."

He went out to the hall where Bethany waited with Hannah. "It's time."

She shrank back like a trapped animal. "Tell them I took the baby to the car to nurse her. Tell them you're going out to the car to get me. We'll go north, to Canada, Kyle. Keep going, if we have to. Please."

Kyle leaned his cheek against hers. He was fire, she was ice. "They would stop us before we reached the border." He slid his hand under Hannah, trying to take her from Bethany.

"Why can't they do it out here? She shouldn't have to go into Laurel's room."

"The lady from the lab is all set up in there. So let's get this done and get out of here."

Parker was laughing when they went back in. He exuded charm, and the lab technician responded, leaning her arm against his.

"We're ready," Kyle said.

The lab technician blushed. "Sure. Let's lay her down right here."

She motioned to the second bed, kept empty because Kyle paid for a private room. Bethany put Hannah down and rested her hand on the baby's stomach. Kyle went to the other side. Parker smirked from across the room. *He hasn't looked at Hannah once*, Kyle realized. *If he doesn't care about her and won't take money, what does he want?*

"Is it difficult to take blood from babies?" Bethany asked.

The technician squeezed Hannah's upper arm, poking at the inside of her elbow. "It can be. Fortunately, this little one has a decent vein."

"Will it hurt?"

"Just a little pinch. More likely to startle her than to hurt her. If you can help keep her still, we should do just fine."

"You take her legs," Kyle said. Bethany wrapped her hands around Hannah's thighs. Kyle smiled down at Hannah as he rested his hands on her arms. "Hey there, waffle face." Hannah smiled back with her whole body. In that moment, Kyle hated Cade Parker so much that he could have ripped him apart without a second thought.

The technician slipped on latex gloves, then fitted a syringe with a needle. She wrapped a tourniquet around Hannah's arm. Hannah kept her eyes locked on Kyle. He knew the needle was in when Bethany gasped.

"Yes! I got it," the technician muttered. The syringe slowly filled with blood.

Hannah let out a delayed howl. Kyle wanted to throw his head back and howl with her. He didn't know whom he was most angry at—Sable Lynde for her fraud or Cade Parker for coming after them.

Neither, Kyle realized. He was furious with God, with the Lord of their lives, who, in His vast love and mercy, had seen fit to rip out his wife's womb, then allowed them to be drawn into this circle of deception and despair. *Tell me, Lord. How could any of this be Your perfect and precious will?*

⸎

Bethany swept the baby out of the room with Kyle following. She could see the anger boiling under his skin. He would die for her, die for Hannah. That primitive urge comforted her. She put Hannah into his arms. He kissed the baby, then held her close.

The rest of them left Sable's room. "When will we know?" Peter was asking.

"It takes a couple of weeks," the technician said. "Someone from Huntington will contact you with the results."

"Thanks for coming out on short notice," Peter said. "Have the bill sent to my office."

The technician nodded and headed down the hall. As she passed Kyle, she touched Hannah's cheek. "Sorry, little doll."

"Our next step—" Leonard began.

Peter cut him off. "Not here. We'll go to the lobby, discuss further business there."

"I left my purse in the room," Bethany said. "Kyle, take Hannah out; get some fresh air."

He nodded. Neither of them wanted the baby there a second longer than necessary.

When Bethany went back in, Sable looked exactly as she had when they first arrived. The only change was the bandage on her arm where the blood had been taken. Bethany looked closer. There were two wet spots on the front of her nightgown.

"That can't be." Bethany had seen the same spots on herself on some mornings, when her milk let down.

"What can't be?" A nurse with dark hair and a bright smile had come in. "Oh, dear me. Her breasts are leaking again."

"Didn't you suppress her lactation?" Bethany said, appalled.

The nurse shrugged. "We've tried and tried. The milk production should stop on its own because there's no baby—no sucking to promote it. But yes, she was treated with bromocriptine after the surgery to inhibit the release of the prolactin. We even tried that barbarian practice of binding her breasts. This just shouldn't be happening."

"Then why is it?"

"Some sort of neurological thing, Dr. Chasse thinks. Or maybe an urge so primitive, based so deep in her pituitary that it can't be stopped."

The nurse lifted Sable's nightgown and wiped her with a wash-cloth. "Oh, good grief, look at this. I don't know where it all comes from." Milk pooled between Sable's breasts, trickling down on her abdomen.

What Bethany had struggled to achieve, Sable had done mind-lessly.

37

*H*e's at the door again," Harry Stevens said.

"What does that scum want?"

Stevens handed a document to Kyle.

He scanned it, biting back curses. "Okay. Give me a minute to get upstairs. Then bring him into the living room. Don't leave him alone for an instant in there, Harry. He's likely to pocket the silver or something."

"Want me to take him out back, Mr. D? Teach him a lesson?"

"Don't tempt me. But no, we don't live our lives like that." *Not yet*, Kyle thought.

He went upstairs and called Bethany on her cell phone. She and Hannah were out running errands. "Parker is suing for visitation."

"No. Absolutely not! That man is not touching my baby!"

"My thoughts exactly. I want you to take her up—well, you know where—while Peter and I get to court and wring this guy out."

"Nova Scotia is beautiful in July," she said, despair in her forced laugh.

"No. At least, not yet. Just go where we know people, where I know you'll be safe. He won't be able to track us there. Call me when you get there." He gave her Stevens's cell phone number and the number for Peter's office.

"I love you, Kyle."

"I love you too. Tell my Hannah I love her too."

"I will, Kyle. I love you."

"You already said that, muffin."

"Can't say it enough." Her voice changed, a smile coming through the tears.

They clicked off. Kyle stood with the phone against his cheek, wondering how it had come to that—urging Bethany to trust him. There was a time when he would have told her to trust God. A time when he trusted God.

Bethany's hands trembled as she capped the pen. She was grateful that Hannah was sleeping, so she wouldn't pick up her anxiety and Kyle's anger. She stuck the pen back in her purse and went to close the notebook. Below the two phone numbers that she had taken down from Kyle was a scrawl that was becoming too familiar:

MAMAMAMA

Cade Parker was so close, he could taste it.

"We're right there," he told Hailey. "Our lips pressed to a cool million."

"You mean, Sable's million."

"Hey, what's hers is mine. Always has been."

Hailey laughed as she slipped her hands into the pockets of Cade's jeans. "And what's yours is mine. Always will be. Just make sure your little lab technician friend knows that."

"Hey, I walked her to her car, asked for her phone number. That's all the time I needed to do what had to be done."

"Yeah, well, I see you tossed the blood but not the phone number."

"Never know when I'm going to be in Maine again, right?"

Hailey smacked him. Cade grabbed her and nuzzled her neck. "Did you finish going through the stuff I got from the hospital?"

"A pair of maternity jeans and an oversized T-shirt? I opened all the hems, but there's nothing there. I told you there wouldn't be. We need to get all her stuff, especially that little laptop of hers."

"I know," Cade said. "I'm working on making myself such a nuisance that they'll give me anything I want to make me go away."

Hailey laughed. "Just make sure they don't give you that baby."

38

North Conway throbbed with life. Corn stood tall in the fields, wildflowers carpeted the meadows, and birdsong and squirrel chatter filled the air. Tourists roamed the shops and scenic views while the adventurous hiked, climbed, canoed, and camped.

It had taken only two days to make the farmhouse her home again. Bethany filled the vases with flowers, opened the windows, and let the fresh air in. Even Hannah sensed the peace. She slept better, laughed louder, ate more.

Anthony had been house-sitting, staying in the guest suite since Hannah was born. They had offered him use of the apartment, but he refused. "I just can't. The whole place creeps me out too much."

Bethany and Kyle understood.

She was cleaning up the kitchen after baking hazelnut cookies. She'd ship some to Kyle and have Anthony take the rest to Jacob. Anthony said his brother had been very withdrawn all summer. It was terrifying how many lives Sable Lynde had gotten her claws into.

Bethany wasn't going to think about that. She scrubbed the counter, enjoying the feel of physical work, the satisfaction of being in her own kitchen. They had settled in quickly to North Conway. Bethany had stopped at a baby store on her way north and bought diapers, clothing, even some toys. They should have gone north sooner— maybe the whole Cade Parker thing never would have happened.

The baby monitor cheeped. Hannah was awake from her nap. Bethany rinsed her hands, dried them, and went to get her daughter.

The phone rang. Bethany picked up Hannah and hustled down the hall to the master bedroom. It was Kyle.

"How's my baby?"

"Wonderful. Want to talk to her?"

"Later."

"What's wrong, Kyle?"

"Can you put her down for a moment? We need to talk."

"Is it the blood test?"

"Put her in her baby seat for a minute so we can talk, okay?"

Bethany wandered back to the nursery. "Just for a moment, pop-corn," she said, putting Hannah down.

The baby waved her arms and whined, unhappy at being put down again so soon. Bethany grabbed the bag of toys she had just bought and pulled out a set of alphabet blocks. She gave Hannah one for each hand. "Here, chew on these."

Hannah obeyed, happy to be occupied with the colorful plastic blocks.

"What is it, Kyle?" Bethany asked.

"Go into the hall."

"Why?"

"I don't want Hannah hearing our discussions. She may not understand what's going on, but she feels the tension."

Bethany walked numbly back into the hall. "Okay. Tell me."

"The lab lost Hannah's blood."

"That's ridiculous."

"Apparently not. They've got yours, mine, Parker's, and Sable's . . . but not Hannah's."

"Now what?"

"I offered to have Nora draw her blood, but Parker refused. He wants to see with his own eyes that it comes from Hannah. When I refused to tell him where you were, he threatened to go to the police, tell them we kidnapped Hannah."

"That's it. I'm going to take Hannah to London."

Kyle forced a laugh. "We've sunk that low, have we, that we're becoming fugitives?"

"Okay, so it sounds insane. But what else can we do?"

"Parker's after me to give him Sable's belongings. Maybe if we give him what he's asking for, he'll back off for a few days, give us time for our own legal maneuverings. I want you to pack up everything that's in the apartment and ship it out today. Get Anthony to help you. Okay?"

She pressed the phone against her temple. No, it was not okay. Not one bit. But what else could she say?

In the nursery, Hannah whined because she had dropped her blocks. The baby strained against the straps of the seat, looking down at the floor as if she could retrieve them herself.

"Well, I'm glad you like them," Bethany said distractedly. The thought of going into Sable's apartment chilled her all the way through, despite the August heat. She bent over to pick up Hannah's blocks, then stopped.

Bethany clenched her hands to stop the sudden shaking. *Don't be such a fool,* she told herself. *It's nothing. Just a stupid coincidence.* Out of the twenty-six blocks, she had managed to grab the M and the A, that was all.

She tossed the blocks back into the box. Too hard—the box tumbled sideways, spilling out its contents. She bent down to pick up the blocks, then stopped and turned away.

Just ABCs, she told herself as she picked Hannah up and hurried downstairs. *Each block has one letter of the alphabet, as advertised.* So she could not have seen the image that burned into her brain like an instant photo: blocks tumbling out onto the floor . . . all reading M A M A M A.

Jacob almost choked when Anthony showed up at the apartment.

He had stopped going to camp two weeks before, too close to finding the answer to Laurel's puzzle to waste his time playing Boy Scout. His pal Sean had whipped up a letter saying Jacob would be having his foot operated on. The camp thought he was in the hospital. His mom thought he was at camp. Jacob was exactly where he wanted to be. Where he needed to be.

Winter Slaughter might have been a breeze for Laurel, but Jacob was finding it a rough go. He still had not discovered who the ultimate bad guy was. That meant he still didn't know where to look for the bell.

And now Anthony was on the porch, rattling the keys. Jacob grabbed the PlayBox and scurried out to the deck. He'd have to hope Anthony did his business, then got out fast. Otherwise, it was gonna be a long, long day.

Bethany's hands shook so badly, she could barely hold Hannah. How could Hannah's blood just disappear like that? Did Cade Parker take it or bribe the technician to lose it? Or were they back to a half-dead ghost? Maybe she should call an exorcist or something. *No. I am a Christian,* Bethany told herself. *I believe in a sovereign God, I trust in a merciful Savior for my life. And my daughter's life. Please, Lord, strengthen my faith.*

What had Patrick said the last time she saw him? "The only way we could be afflicted by any supernatural occurrence would be if God allowed it. If that were so—and Bethany, it's oh, so unlikely—then you and Kyle would need to pray about it and seek out God's purpose."

O Lord, please. Please show me Your purpose in all this.

Cade was ripping mad. "It's not here. All these boxes of trash, and it's not here!"

"It's your fault," Hailey snapped. "We should have kept the pressure on Dolan."

"I don't want the baby. I want Sable's laptop!"

"Well, let's see. You've got her deodorant, her underwear, her books on programming, her toothbrush. About four thousand bucks' worth of clothes. Look at these labels. Liz Claiborne makes maternity clothes? I gotta get the Dolans to hire me to make them a baby."

Cade grabbed the sweater from Hailey. He was about to rip it to shreds when he caught a whiff of it. Lilacs. He put it to his face, letting Sable wash over him. That funny smile. Her eyes, so clear that you'd think she was empty-headed—until she started talking. She spouted ideas that were complicated and intense, incomprehensible most of the time. But her face would be so alive, her voice so animated that Cade would catch her excitement anyway.

He had hated seeing her wired and tubed in the nursing home. Then he realized it wasn't *her*, it was just some body that she had left behind. Cade didn't know where Sable was—heaven, hell, limbo—who knew? Maybe she was in cyberspace. That would be paradise for her.

"Do you think Dolan got his hands on the account?" Hailey said.

"No one's got their hands on the account. I checked this morning. The money is still sitting there. Growing with that 2 percent interest, but otherwise, no movement. You think Dolan cares about a measly million? He's got his own money, he doesn't need ours."

"Ours? It's Sable's," Hailey said, laughing. "It's not like you made that pile."

"But I'm Sable's heir. I have the marriage certificate to prove it, thanks to your computer jock friend. Tell me again why we can't just go to the bank and get it. Especially now that I can prove she's incapacitated and I'm her next of kin."

Hailey grabbed the sweater out of his hands. "Stupid. So stupid. I can't believe a smart girl like her ever put up with you."

Cade lunged at her, and Hailey raised her fists. "Go ahead, slugger. Take your best shot."

Cade backed off. "No. I won't give you the pleasure. What did I say that was so stupid?"

"Think about it. What if the auditors are still watching the bank? Or what if the feds or someone finally got tipped off to the voice-mail thing and are watching that specific account? We could end up in jail. And even if no one's figured anything out, do you want to have to pay taxes on all that money?"

"Oh, yeah. Taxes."

"Uh-huh. Plus, there's something else to consider," Hailey said.

"What's that?"

"We've been joking about them sticking us with that baby."

"Never happen."

"No. But you go on about being Sable's next of kin and they could stick *her* on us. You want to cart a vegetable around with you for the rest of her life?"

"No." He couldn't do that to Sable. Hailey would have her hand around that breathing tube so fast . . .

"I need you to think, Cade. What would Sable have done with that laptop?"

Cade stretched his shoulders, trying to put himself in Sable's place. She was so smart and so paranoid. "Whenever she wasn't using it, she always hid it. Afraid of someone breaking in, stealing it."

"Exactly. So we go look ourselves."

"Like Dolan is going to let us into that fancy Boston townhouse."

"They have a second house, up in New Hampshire."

"How do you know that?"

Hailey grinned. "Because I made the UPS guy give me a full receipt for all this junk. It had the 'shipped from' address on it. So now we know."

"Now we know," Cade said. "And now we go."

<hr />

Bethany was in the front garden, weeding. They had shipped Sable's effects to Cade Parker—surely he would leave them alone. A couple of days before, when she had gone back up to Hannah's room, the blocks were all as they should be, from A to Z. It was the stress that had gotten to her, made her see things that weren't there. She just needed to get out more, do physical work, enjoy the New Hampshire summer. It was good therapy, getting her hands into the warm soil.

Hannah slept nearby, her stroller covered in mosquito netting. New warnings about West Nile virus had alarmed Bethany. On top of that, Lyme disease was in the area, so she had to be sure not to put the stroller too close to the bushes where ticks might hide. Life was a blessing, and life was a peril.

Hannah sighed in her sleep. Bethany looked over at her and smiled. Her baby was four months old, every day a discovery.

She could hear Anthony from the back of the property, singing an aria as he painted the barn. He had worked hard on his languages and now brought opera forth as if it flowed in his veins. From hip-hop to Handel to Mozart—what an amazing journey.

She hummed along, joining the symphony of bees buzzing in the flowers. Then Anthony stopped singing, midphrase. Moments later, he came around the front of the house where Bethany was working.

"I heard it. Her."

She felt the chill now, even in the August sun. "What?"

"I don't know. I just heard . . . " He looked confused. "Come with me and listen. I think it's Laurel."

"I'm not taking Hannah near there. Tell me where. I'll go alone."

"The back of the barn where I left off painting. You'll have to climb the ladder to hear it, I think. Be careful."

"Okay. But don't you leave Hannah for an instant." Bethany checked for the fourteenth time to ensure that the baby was strapped in and the brake on the stroller was set.

The ladder was positioned at the back of the barn, between the bathroom and bedroom windows. Anthony's paintbrush lay on the ground, bright-red paint splashed in the grass.

Bethany slowly climbed until she reached the place where Anthony had left off painting. She stopped and listened. The breeze ruffled the trees. Far away, a motorcycle whined. Across the river came the muffled hoot-hoot of the sight-seeing train that went around the valley.

And then—a child's voice, high-pitched and tremulous.

Sing to me, Mama, so I'll know you're still there.

Bethany knocked on the bedroom window. "Who's in there?"

Singing now—a familiar tune but not in Bethany's voice.

When the birds of spring come alive to sing, in the golden wonderland . . . I will dance for you under skies of blue . . .

"What do you want? Answer me!"

Because I will love you forever and I'll be here, with you, for always.

Bethany slammed the paint bucket through the bathroom window. There was a tremendous crash as paint splashed everywhere. The singing stopped.

39

Jacob wanted to rip someone's head off.

Why did everyone have to start hanging around, now that he was so close? Just that morning he had blasted apart a herd of fire-breathing reindeer and made it to the secret cave in Winter Slaughter. Jacob was sure he'd find him hanging there, the character that Laurel had called the "ultimate bad dude."

He had just taken a break for a minute when someone threw a paint can through the window. He almost exploded out of his skin, thinking he was back in Forge Hill and someone was doing a drive-by on him. He kept it cool, though. He could see Anthony in the front yard and Bethany running toward his brother. She must have been the one who threw the can. But why?

She was "unstable," Joan had whispered to Anthony. Big hoot. You didn't need a fancy college degree to see that Mrs. Dolan was wired too tight. And then she had gone and trashed the bathroom, splashing the whirlpool with red paint. It looked like blood.

That got him back thinking on Laurel, and how she took a bullet. *Took a header*, they'd say back on the street. He imagined her lying in that bed with a breathing tube in her throat. That made him feel so whacked that he even sent God a little prayer. *Have someone watch her back, okay, God?*

Jacob shut down, hid everything, and waited for Anthony and Bethany to go into the house. Then he climbed down the ladder and ran into the woods to wait. He hoped they would just cool it. He needed to keep on top of everything. Laurel would want him to.

—∞∞∞—

"I can't believe I drove up from Boston to look for some ghost." Kyle stood in the door to the kitchen. "I've searched every inch. There's no one in the apartment."

Anthony and Bethany huddled together on the stairs. Neither one would go into the apartment. Hannah was in the farmhouse with Katie Hemlow.

"May I remind you that you volunteered to come up from Boston? Maybe you didn't look hard enough. It's not like a ghost hides in the cupboard," Bethany said.

"How would I know? I don't have a clue," Kyle said, irritated. "You sure it's not just . . . "

"What? My imagination? Or my psychosis?"

"Hold it! Time out. I heard it too," Anthony said. "You guys have had enough going on, so I didn't want to say anything before. But while you have been living in Boston, weird things have been happening up here. Drawers are left open. Things move, books and lamps. Lights in the apartment. Once I heard what sounded like a video game up there. I know I should have checked it out, but that place gives me the creeps. I'm sorry. I let you guys down."

"You didn't let anyone down," Kyle said. "Anything else I should know about?"

Anthony hunched his shoulders, working out tension. "When I went into the apartment on Monday to pack up that stuff, I sat down to take a quiet moment before I got started. I let my hand just rest on the sofa. There was a warm spot on the cushion. Like someone had been sitting there."

"What do you think, Kyle?" Bethany asked. "We can't both be crazy."

Kyle didn't know what to think. He was supposed to be meeting with Parker's lawyer that moment in Boston. After Bethany's frantic phone call, he left Dol-Pak and drove three hours north to chase . . . what? A ghost? Or some sort of shared hallucination?

Kyle hugged Bethany. "We'll figure this out. I promise. Sorry I was short with you."

"My fault. I should have thanked you for coming. So thank you," Bethany said. "What about that meeting?"

"It's probably better if Peter meets that scum and his lawyer without me." Kyle hated the thing inside him that made him want to strike out and physically damage Cade Parker. And yet, wasn't it a God-given impulse that fathers protect their families?

"Let's change the subject," Anthony said.

"Good thinking," Kyle said. "What's for supper?"

Bethany smiled. "I picked the first eggplant of the season. And it's a beauty." She kissed Kyle and headed down the stairs. "Supper in about an hour. Eggplant parmesan. Maybe some fettuccine. Fresh spinach salad."

Anthony started after her. "You got me sold. My cooking stinks. I get so sick of mac and cheese."

"Anthony. Wait." Kyle motioned for him to stay silent until Bethany had crossed the lawn to the house.

"I'm sorry, Kyle. I don't mean to add to whatever is spooking her."

"No, it's not that. It's just . . . I've never really told you how sorry I was for what happened last February."

"Sure you did."

"Not properly. I was out of line, too quick to accuse you. I'll never be able to express how sorry I am for how I acted."

"Hey, man. Sable knew how to make people think what she wanted them to think."

"I never should have hit you, Anthony. I hope you'll forgive me."

Anthony shrugged. "Sure. It's over and done with."

"Thanks. I've been taking a long look at myself. Seeing how much I was blinded by what I wanted."

"Hey, I was out there too. Doing what felt good. Not what I knew was right."

"I'm glad you gave us a second chance."

"Ditto that." They shook hands, then started down the stairs together.

"So what do you think this stuff is, this weird stuff?" Kyle asked.

"Bethany worries that it might be her—your—babies. The ones who died."

"That's impossible. God would never allow that. Ever."

"Amen to that. I can see why she thinks that, though. The little girl we heard—she sounded young. Very young. The thing is, though . . . " Anthony looked away.

"Just say it."

"I've got an ear for voices, Kyle. This kid sounded really young, yeah. But she still sounded like Laurel. I mean, Sable."

Kyle just shook his head. "That girl has a way of getting into your head. Kind of a genius at that. I just don't know how she could do it from a coma, that's all."

"I'm definitely having a baby for the Dolans."

"Shut up," Cade said.

Hailey danced around the living room. "Look at this place. A barn on the outside, a fancy crib inside. Did you see the size of that TV? A whirlpool bath and walk-in shower. Anything a girl could want. That Kyle Dolan ain't bad, either, if you like the teddy-bear type."

Cade grabbed her by the throat. "Will you quit yakking? We got a job to do."

He had set up an evening meeting to make sure Kyle would be in Boston, so they'd have a clear shot at the apartment. By the time Kyle found out that Cade wasn't showing, they'd have the laptop and be out of there. If they could find the stupid thing. Where was it? He had checked Sable's usual hideouts—inside the box spring of the bed, in back of the refrigerator, under the bathroom sink. Nothing.

Hailey was working her hands down his chest.

"Get back to work," he growled.

"You're getting to be one big yawn."

And you're getting to be predictable, Cade thought. Maybe he'd rethink the partnership—after he got his hands on that million bucks. He ripped off the back of the entertainment center. Nothing but wires and dust.

"In here." Hailey waved him into the computer room. "Under the bottom drawer. Feels like the laptop, but I can't get my arm in all the way."

Cade tried to wedge his hand in. Too tight—only a kid could get in there. "We gotta lift up the whole desk." He lifted while Hailey drew out what was hidden underneath.

"It's a video game player."

"Why would she hide that?" Cade asked.

"Those Dolans are real holy rollers, right? Maybe they wouldn't allow her to play those stupid games. Wait. There's something else back here." She flashed her penlight into the back. "A tape player. With a tape in it."

"Maybe Sable left us a message on how to find the laptop. Or better yet, maybe she just left all her passwords."

Hailey laughed. "Dream on, sweetie. It's probably just her favorite mix tape."

Cade grabbed the tape player and hit PLAY. He couldn't believe what he heard.

⊶∞⊷

Kyle couldn't remember the last time Bethany had slept through the night. Yet she hadn't stirred when Hannah fussed, even though she had insisted on moving the crib into their bedroom.

"There you go, gumdrop," he whispered as he finished changing the diaper. "How can such a big mess come from such a little sweetie?"

He rocked her for a few minutes, kissed her, and put her back into the crib. Her hand went to her mouth almost immediately. *She's the only innocent one among us*, Kyle thought. He'd have to spend a long time on his knees when this whole thing was over.

Not that night, though. No time. He needed to get out and hunt down that ghost.

The night was alive with the racket of frogs and crickets, an occasional cry of an owl, and even the distant howl of a coyote. The moon cast long shadows across the grass. Kyle meandered around the back of the barn, the cold dew soaking his sandal-clad feet.

Growing up, he and his brothers played in the street, dodging trucks as they tossed footballs and hit baseballs. What little yard his family owned had been hot-topped for parking. It had taken him years to ease into North Conway living. He still had uneasy thoughts about snakes and spiders crawling across his toes.

A far-off squeal filtered from the barn. *The bats must be back*, Kyle told himself as he started up the stairs. He'd have to call someone to screen the attic again. Maybe Anthony had disturbed them with his painting. As for the other occurrences, they were probably products of Bethany's and Anthony's fine-tuned artistic sensibilities.

———

Cade felt as though someone had ripped through his insides with a razor.

"Stop that thing!" he said.

Hailey backed away from him. "It's Sable, isn't it?"

"I'm gonna shove that thing down your throat if you don't turn if off."

Sing to me, Mama, so I'll know you're still there.

The voice on the tape began to sing. *When the birds of spring come alive to sing . . .*

"It's her, isn't it? Playing Mummy, sounds like," Hailey sneered.

Cade lunged for her. She darted into the bathroom and locked the door.

"Open up, you cow! I swear, I'm gonna tear you apart!" He could hear it through the door now, Sable in a little voice, singing. *I will bring a light to your darkest night . . .*

He didn't hear Kyle Dolan until it was too late.

"What do you think you're doing?"

Parker turned and swung at Kyle. That was all Kyle needed.

———∞∞∞———

"When will it end?" Bethany cried.

"Only God knows," Kyle said. "I sure don't."

Bethany prayed as the police took Kyle away for questioning. Cade Parker needed an ambulance.

40

nthony stayed behind to clean up the mess. He jolted at the blood splattered all over the whirlpool. No, not blood. It was red paint from the day before when Bethany had thrown the can through the window. In their panic, they had left the ladder under the window. That must be how Parker had gotten in.

What was a tape player doing under the toilet? It was broken, but the tape inside was intact. *Just toss it*, Anthony told himself. There were other things to worry about, serious things, like Kyle getting arrested, Parker trying to take Hannah away.

And then, of course, the ghost. Mr. Dolan had heard her too. Too much to worry about to fiddle with a tape player. But a voice deep inside him told him to check it out. He pressed PLAY.

"He tried to kill me!" Parker lisped through his swollen mouth.

Too bad I failed, Kyle thought.

"Enough!" Peter Muir said. He had driven up from Boston with Parker's lawyer, Paul Leonard. "Just be glad that Judge Potter is seeing you in his chambers before the district attorney decides on charges."

Bethany walked in, clutching Hannah. She went immediately to Kyle. "I had this crazy thought that I'd never see you again."

He hugged her, breathing in the tangy scent of her fear, wanting to wash it away with his tears and promises, and—*God forgive me, I'd drive it away with my fists if pounding Cade Parker would do any good.*

They spent an hour telling their stories to Judge Potter, who then called for a half-hour break. Peter sent out for muffins and coffee.

Kyle didn't feel much like eating, but he forced himself. It was the only way he could get Bethany to eat. When they went back into the judge's chamber, Nora was there too.

"We're going to settle this once and for all," Judge Potter said. "Dr. Hemlow will draw your blood, take it to the hospital, and have the tests run. No one leaves my office until we get the results. Then we'll discuss criminal charges."

"I'm confused," Peter Muir said. "We were told that the DNA test takes a week or more."

"We might be able to rule out one or more of the claimants based simply on blood types. It's old-fashioned, but if there are enough types represented among the four adults and Hannah, then it could work," Nora said.

"What about the Lynde girl?" Leonard asked. "Don't we need her blood type?"

"It's already on file from the shooting. O-negative," Nora said.

"Nora, you already know mine," Bethany said.

"I want it done again. So we don't have any questions. Or blood disappearing from the lab." Judge Potter glared at Parker. "Don't you agree, Mr. Parker?"

"Forget the blood test. I wanna know what you're gonna do about this!" He motioned to his broken nose and bruised face.

"He broke into my property and attacked me!" Kyle said.

"Enough," the judge said again. "We'll discuss charges after we see if we can figure out what the truth is. What do you say, Mr. Parker? Will you agree to the blood test?"

Parker looked at Kyle. "What if I just go away for a while, let things settle down here? All I'm really interested in at the moment is collecting Sable's things, getting that end of business wrapped up."

"Shut up," Leonard hissed. "This isn't what we discussed."

"So you're admitting the child isn't yours, Mr. Parker?" Muir said.

"Not at all. I'm just saying—we're running pretty hot right now. None of this helps Sable. Let me take her stuff home, get things settled there."

"But we sent you her stuff," Bethany said.

Parker's eyes narrowed. "Sable had some photos and family items that were precious to me. Some of that stuff was stored on her laptop. I don't want to lose all that in this tangle. I need closure."

He doesn't want the blood test, Kyle realized. "Tell you what, Parker. I'll give you everything in that apartment—even the furniture—if you take this blood test."

Bethany gasped, pulled him to her. "Are you insane? He just offered to go away."

"Trust me," Kyle whispered back.

"Everything she had?" Parker asked. "Regardless of how the blood test comes out?"

"Yes. Everything."

"Fine," Parker said.

"It's finally agreed, then?" Judge Potter asked.

Peter Muir asked, "Is this really how you want to proceed, Kyle?"

"Yes."

"Bethany?"

She squeezed Kyle's hand. "Yes."

"Okay, Dr. Hemlow," Potter said. Nora opened her medical bag.

Kyle's stomach rolled. Should he have taken Parker's offer to go away quietly? By insisting on the blood test, Kyle had been going on a hunch.

Or maybe, Lord, maybe I'm finally going on faith.

Anthony had no words, so he sang. Rock and roll. Rhythm and blues. Show tunes. Ballads. Opera. Hymns. Nothing seemed to work.

She's like an old person, almost dead, Anthony thought. But that didn't feel right—too hopeless. Maybe more like a newborn baby, just not alert yet. Maybe he could sing some of that lullaby that Bethany sang to Hannah.

> *When you're tucked in bed and all your prayers are said,*
> *and you wait with joy for a brand-new day,*
> *Close your eyes and sleep, dream of wishes sweet,*

Because I will love you forever and I'll be here, with you,
for always.

Sable's nurse, Marj, stepped in but didn't say a word. She just did what she had to, then left. Sable lay in her limbo. Nothing was going to change. He had tried to pray and even forgive. But nothing seemed to matter.

It was crazy of Anthony, driving all that way. She was not going to wake up. He stood and stretched his stiff limbs. It had been a long night, longer morning. He had to get back to North Conway before Kyle and Bethany got back from court.

"I'll come back, Sable," he whispered gently into her ear. But she slept on.

They spent the morning, then a good portion of the afternoon, waiting. Bethany draped a blanket over her shoulder. Strange, she knew, to nurse Hannah in Judge Potter's chambers. But surely no one would dare to take a child from its mother's breast.

Lord God, I will do anything not to lose Hannah. Anything!

Judge Potter entered and went straight to his desk. Nora walked in behind him.

Bethany knew immediately. Nora's face remained impassive, but the light in her eyes was joyous to the point of triumph. Kyle bit the inside of his cheeks, trying not to smile. Bethany could see he knew it, too—Hannah was theirs, through and through.

Thank You, Lord. Anything, I promised. Just tell me what!

Cade Parker showed no surprise as Judge Potter spoke.

"Dr. Hemlow has explained to me, based on the blood tests, that neither Ms. Lynde nor Mr. Parker could be related in any way to Hannah Dolan. The blood tests do indicate that Mr. and Mrs. Dolan are likely the baby's parents. To put this matter totally to rest, I'll order the DNA test on Hannah to confirm this. Meanwhile, the child will continue in the Dolans' custody."

Parker looked at his feet, saying nothing.

His lawyer, Paul Leonard, was red-faced. "I'd like an explanation. First, you give us this bull about using DNA to confirm paternity; now you're saying you did it with just a blood test?"

"If I may, your honor?" Peter said.

Potter nodded.

"I'll like to remind Mr. Leonard, and inform the court, that Mr. Parker himself insisted on the DNA test. Apparently these allegations could have been settled days ago, had Mr. Parker then agreed to a preliminary screening. As it is, I am eager to hear Dr. Hemlow's explanation of these results."

Nora finally allowed herself a smile. "Hannah's blood type is AB positive. Which means her parents would have to be A, AB, or B, and one of them would also have to be rH positive, since that factor is the dominant gene. Mrs. Dolan's blood type is B negative. Mr. Dolan is A positive. Which puts them in the possible blood types that can combine to produce an AB-positive child."

"What about my clients?" Leonard snarled. "This is all mumbo jumbo."

"We already knew Ms. Lynde's blood type. O negative. Mr. Parker has suggested that perhaps Kyle Dolan impregnated Ms. Lynde," Nora said.

"How cruel," Bethany snapped.

Judge Potter nodded sympathetically.

"There are two possible offspring combinations of an A positive and O negative parent. The child would have to be either A or O. With Sable Lynde's blood type being O, there's no way possible that Mr. Dolan and Ms. Lynde could produce an AB offspring. Of course, those of us who know the Dolans also know that it would be impossible that he impregnated Ms. Lynde."

"Forget Dolan. What about my client?" Leonard said. "What's his blood type?"

"This is interesting," Nora said. "Mr. Parker is also O negative."

"So? O is common, right? The universal donor?" Leonard said.

"Shut up," Parker whispered.

"Yes. O positive is very common. O negative is fairly rare. Two

O negative parents would have to produce an O negative baby. There is no other possible outcome from their offspring, because both O and rH negative are on recessive genes, meaning that no other genotype, like A or B, can possibly be present in their genetic makeup."

"So Sable was mistaken when she came to me. Or maybe she wanted some insurance," Parker said. "Honest mistake. I'm just another fool suckered by her. Where's the crime in that?"

Bethany wanted to wipe the grin off his face. All Cade Parker put them through, and he thought this was some kind of lark?

"That's the thing," Judge Potter said. "I don't think it was an honest mistake."

"Sable said she wanted a baby. I did my best to oblige. So sue me," Parker said.

"Would you swear to that under oath?" Judge Potter asked. "That you and Ms. Lynde had sexual intercourse last summer?"

"Of course."

Potter put on a poker face. "Dr. Hemlow? If you'd continue, please?"

Nora took a deep breath. "O negative is rare enough that I had some questions about the interesting coincidence of Mr. Parker and Ms. Lynde having the same blood type. So I called the folks who are doing the DNA work. Even though the baby's blood had been—" Nora cleared her throat as she glared at Parker—"misplaced, they still had started on the rest of the group. And they had some preliminary results. It appears there was a great similarity in Mr. Parker's and Ms. Lynde's DNA." She looked Cade Parker in the eye. "There's a name for sexual relations between siblings, Mr. Parker. Do you know what it is?"

"What are you talking about?" Leonard said. "Siblings? What is going on here?"

All eyes turned to Cade Parker. "So okay! She's my sister!" Parker yelled.

"What?" Leonard's eyes bulged out. "Who's your sister?"

"Who do you think, nose wipe? Sable Lynde is my sister! Are you all happy now?" Parker shouted. "Not my girlfriend or wife or lover. We have the same blood type because we had the same freakin' parents."

"I see it now," Peter said. "You assumed the baby was Sable's. You figured her DNA would be similar enough to yours to put some question in the Dolans' minds, and they'd pay for you to go away."

"I never wanted money!" Parker shouted. "I just wanted Sable's stuff!"

Leonard dropped his face into his hands. The back of his neck was crimson.

"So Mr. Parker knew there was no chance whatsoever that he could be the father," Peter said pointedly to the judge. "Yet he harassed the Dolans beyond the point of cruelty."

Judge Potter motioned to the court officer, who had been standing quietly against the wall. "Take Mr. Parker into custody. I believe the district attorney will be charging him with extortion."

"Extortion!" Parker let loose a sharp curse as the officer cuffed him.

Bethany ignored the ruckus. She leaned into Kyle. Hannah was between them, nursing peacefully. Nora smiled across the room at them. Leonard was shouting something, Peter trying not to grin. Judge Potter just shook his head and sighed.

It all ran off Bethany like clouds in the sky, blown apart by the wind.

"Thank God," Kyle said.

"Yes. Thank God," Bethany said.

41

So Cade Parker screwed up and got himself thrown into jail. Cade was the sugar in Hailey's coffee, the shine on her silver. Nice to have, but she could live without him. With the cops coming around, digging up his dirt, she had to make sure that no muck splashed back on her. She wasn't worried. Cade wouldn't be going anywhere, since she had no intention of paying his bail.

Sooner or later, he would try to plead out of the charges in exchange for her conviction. She was too smart to sit around and wait for that. Hailey would have to go underground for a while. Besides, someone needed to baby-sit Sable's money, spring it loose.

Her guy at Rensselaer Polytech promised to try again to break the bank's code. She'd had to offer him a commission. Ten percent, but so what? She could live with 90 percent of a million—especially since she didn't have to share it with Cade.

"You're grinning like a leprechaun," Bethany said.

"Of course I am. And here's my wee little pot o' gold." Kyle blew kisses into Hannah's belly. The baby giggled and grabbed his hair.

Bethany's cell phone rang. She flipped it open. "Anthony, wait 'til you—what? Say that again." She looked at Kyle, her eyes blinking furiously. "Oh, my."

No, Kyle thought. *No more surprises.* "What is it?"

Bethany closed the phone. "Anthony wants us home right away. He's found the ghost."

—∞∞—

"Don't play it again," Bethany said. "I can't bear it."

"That's what you heard, right?" Anthony asked.

Bethany nodded.

"Me too," he said.

"I wrote that lullaby and recorded it for Hannah. Sable was supposed to play it over and over so the baby would learn to recognize my voice."

"Sounds like she recorded her voice over yours," Kyle said.

"Why would she do that?" Bethany asked.

"She was delusional toward the end, with the toxemia," Kyle said.

"I can get the singing," Anthony said. "But what's the rest about? That little-girl voice—that mama stuff?"

Bethany grabbed the tape from the player. "I don't care. I'm just glad she's gone."

"Bethany, don't!" Anthony cried.

Too late. She had shredded the tape.

"There's still another mystery to be solved," Kyle said. "Who was playing the tape?"

"I didn't even think of that," Bethany said.

"I found these under the desk." Anthony pulled out a wad of candy wrappers.

"Is that why Sable's sugar was so high?" Kyle said. "She was hiding candy?"

"Not Sable," Anthony said. "Some other goblin."

—∞∞—

A few candy wrappers left in the apartment, and all of a sudden, Jacob was in the hot seat, with his mom, Anthony, and Kyle and Bethany Dolan all staring him down. That loser Parker—if he had kept to his own street, Jacob would still be driving the bus. But they had found him out, and Joan was talking about Alaska again. Her brother was in the army up there, a big, mean drill sergeant. Long nights, long winters. Cold but definitely not *cool*.

Jacob started crying. *Oh, yeah, you're workin' it now*, Laurel would say. *That's it, play the room, J.*

"What now?" his mother snapped. "You, sorry? Think we'll believe that?"

Jacob sniffed, wiped back the tears. "No. I'm not sorry at all. Someone had to do it."

"Do what?" Mr. Dolan asked.

"Someone had to show respect to Laurel."

Stunned looks all around.

"First of all, that tramp's name is Sable, not Laurel. Second, Mr. Dolan pays for the best care possible," his mother finally said.

"You think that's enough?" Jacob widened his eyes, scanning each face.

His mother glared back, angry. Kyle fidgeted. Bethany looked thoughtful. Anthony was whacked. Even the baby stared at Jacob. The kid knew Laurel better than anyone. She had spent nine months inside her. Too bad she couldn't talk and help him out here.

"You don't ask me what I think; you just do what you want. Like take me off my street." Not a scam now—the hurt was coming from inside Jacob's chest. "Like I wanna live up here in this stupid North Conway? Mountains lookin' like they're gonna fall on me any minute. Kids dissin' me like I was some snake with two heads. Anthony goes off to that snotty school of his and everyone loves him because he sings and smiles at 'em. No one respectin' what I might want. 'Cept Laurel. You're all thinkin' she's some kind of low-life scum criminal, but at least she cared about me." The tears poured out now.

"Jacob, she did some pretty horrible things," Mr. Dolan said.

"You the one to throw stones, Mr. Dolan?"

Mr. Dolan looked puzzled, then jerked his head back.

That time served in Sunday school paid off for Jacob. *Let him who doesn't cross the line be the first one with the stone in his hand . . .*

Jacob was out of his chair, pacing. "You all used her up, then tossed her away like she was nothin'. High-and-mighty Anthony gives me money to get lost so he can hook up with her. Mama, you draggin' me off to church, but I don't see you forgivin' Laurel for nothin.' Mr. Dolan, puttin' the big money on so they could use her to make a baby."

"That's enough! You are way over the line, young man," his mother snapped.

"No, Joan. Let him speak," Bethany said. "We need to hear this."

"You, Mrs. Dolan. All those games you laid on her."

"I'd like to understand, Jacob. Please, help me." Her dark eyes studied him.

"Posin' like she was part of the family. You made her exercise and eat all those salads like she was some kind of prize cow. She knew it was all for the baby. Not for her."

"Is that what you think we did?" Bethany asked, her voice watery. "Used her and forgot her?"

"Well, that's how it checks out. Which is why I took to goin' up to the apartment, sometimes listenin' to that tape I found. Puttin' some thought on her once in a while. You all made her out to be some kind of monster. But there was a person there."

He stopped his pacing, stared through the Dolans like they were smeared glass. "You just never bothered to know her," Jacob finally said. "For all your jawin' about love and that stuff, you just never did."

Steel-gray clouds gathered over Mount Washington. "Rain's coming," Bethany said.

The first poke of lightning flickered in the west, followed by a rumble of thunder. "Still way off," Kyle said.

She opened the back door to the Mercedes and put Hannah into her car seat.

"That was tough, huh?" Kyle said, backing out of the driveway. "I'm just glad it's over."

"Is it, Kyle?" Bethany arms prickled with goose bumps. She rolled up her car window.

"Of course it is. Now that we know there were bizarre but rational explanations for the lights and voices, we can just relax."

Bethany wasn't so sure. Jacob banging around in the apartment, playing that tape, explained some things. But the tracings of MAMA couldn't be explained away so easily. And there was still the crying baby. She had heard it long before she even knew Sable or Jacob. The thunder cracked; lightning streaked across the sky. Kyle flipped on the wipers and drove on, singing silly songs for Hannah.

Bethany sat in silence, staring into the storm.

42

It was the rottenest job ever.

Anthony had left the task of cleaning out the gutters until almost too late. He was still living at the Dolans', doing double duty as handyman and nanny on weekends. School had started a month before, but he had procrastinated in getting that job done.

He dug in the hoe, scooping chunks of rotted leaves, raising a deadly stink. Snakes couldn't get up there, could they? Anthony wished he'd remembered his CD player. Maestro had him working on the "Flower Song" from *Carmen*. The range was okay, but the breathing was tricky. If the dudes on the corner in Forge Hill knew he was singing opera, they'd—no, he couldn't even think about what they'd do.

He hummed, making his own music. And then he heard it—a baby crying. Had to be Hannah, he thought. But no, he could see Hannah in the backyard with Bethany. His heart hammered.

Bethany looked up at him, her face stricken. She had heard it too. "I'll get Kyle," she called.

The baby wailed again. Anthony got off the ladder as fast as he could without breaking his neck.

Kyle could not believe what he was hearing. But there he was, in Hannah's nursery, listening to a cry seeping from the walls. As Bethany had been saying all along, the cry could be heard best in the nursery and outside, under the nursery window. It did indeed sound like a baby.

He knocked on the wall. The wail rose. He followed the sound toward the corner of the room where the outer wall joined the wall between his office and this room. "Yes!"

"What? Did you find it?" Anthony called from the hall.

"Maybe. Come on outside."

Down in the yard, Bethany had the same question.

"We'll see," was all Kyle would say as he slid the ladder into the space under the eave. He climbed up, steadied himself on the corner of the roof, and swung up onto the ledge. Bracing himself, he threw one arm over the top of the eave. "Anthony, bring me up the hoe."

Anthony passed it up. Kyle hooked the hoe into the latticework on the front of the eave and yanked. The phantom baby wailed, an unearthly, hair-raising howl.

"Careful," Bethany said.

Hannah spotted Kyle up on the roof. "Da-da," she babbled.

Kyle leaned back, using the hoe as a lever to exert pressure. The lattice shifted. "Anthony, get down. Bethany, stand back in case this falls."

Kyle pulled harder. The lattice broke, tumbling to the ground. A flash of fur struck out at Kyle. He startled but held fast as a yellow-eyed creature snarled at him.

"There's your ghost," he said, scurrying down the ladder.

"What is it?" Bethany said.

"Feral cats. Looks like three or four in there, at least. I'd bet anything that a female climbed the tree, made her way into the attic through the eave. Then she took shelter in the warm spot next to the chimney, liked it so much she had her babies here, and they've been living there since. I imagine they dug deep into the wallboard, especially in the winter, which is why they're so loud in the nursery. Probably yakking at the squirrels each time you heard them."

"I feel so stupid," Bethany said.

"Don't. You heard crying, all right—just wasn't a human. These adult cats can really screech. I'll call the animal shelter and see how to move these critters down into the barn where they can be useful."

"So it is over, isn't it?" Anthony said. "The tape was Sable; the crying was the cats. The lights and stuff that moved was my stupid brother."

"Looks that way." Kyle swung Hannah up to his shoulders. "Who wants ice cream?"

Hannah kicked. "Da-da!"

That was good enough for all of them.

Kyle and Bethany walked hand in hand along the Saco River. Hannah, strapped into her baby carrier, surveyed the world from her father's back. It was Columbus Day weekend, and the foliage in the Mount Washington Valley was at its peak. The forests were brilliant with color—flaming yellows, shiny reds, vibrant golds. The sky was clear and endless, making the mountains seem small in comparison.

"She's pushing up again," Kyle said.

"She just wants to see over your head."

"Can't blame her. Beautiful day, huh?"

Bethany hooked her arm through his. "They're all beautiful."

Hannah screeched with joy as a mountain biker pedaled by.

"Good grief," Kyle said. "It's bad enough I have to worry about braces and boyfriends. But now she wants to take up extreme sports?"

"I think she'll need to learn to walk first," Bethany said, laughing.

Hannah had reached her six-month birthday two days before. She rolled over, sat up, and showed signs of crawling. She played peekaboo with her mother and kissy-face with her father.

And oh, how she loves, thought Bethany. *Thank You, Lord, that You've filled our hearts at last.*

They were meeting Pastor Woodward in an hour to discuss Hannah's dedication. Bethany and Kyle had wanted something small, but Anthony had something else in mind.

"I wrote some music and sent it to Stan Todd," he had told her in August. "The kids in the chorale have been practicing it all September."

Bethany had felt a twinge of guilt. She had thrown herself back into the Forge Hill Chorale, only to let Cade Parker bump her out again. They had neglected too many of their commitments. Big things, like the chorale. Vital things, like their friendship with Nora and David. Other things—Dol-Pak buzzed along, still growing and doing well, but they'd spent little time with Kyle's employees. Now that they'd decided to live in North Conway, she thought, they'd have to try harder to be in touch with his people, as well as the company's customers.

Bethany pulled Kyle into her. "What's up, Doc?"

He kissed her cheek. "Hemlines. Not that I mind. What's up, Doc?"

"The curtain at the Met. Season starts this weekend. What's up?"

"You're too good at this. Hmm. I know what's up—the price of gas. Doc?"

"Your pal, Roger Clemens. Up for the Hall of Fame. See, I do read the sports page. Ball's in your glove, Doc."

"What's up? How 'bout—the combined ERA of the Sox bullpen?" Kyle groaned.

"I asked what was *up*, not what was astronomical."

"Don't remind me. It's a miracle we made the play-offs. Not that we lasted long."

She took his hand. "Come on, let's sit for a while."

They sat Hannah between them on the grass. The river flowed by, rippling with reflected golds and reds. They watched in silence for a few minutes. Even Hannah was transfixed.

"Okay, now tell me what's really up," Kyle said. "You've been brewing something for days now."

Bethany closed her eyes. "I made a promise to God."

Kyle laughed. "You think you're the only one? As Jacob would say, 'Whoa, Mama.' The bargains I've been making. Like 'God, if You just do this for me, I'll walk through Boston Common in sack-cloth—better yet, a Yankees shirt—in the middle of December.'"

They laughed. Hannah looked up at them, then went back to her cracker.

"Seriously. The Lord knows what's in our hearts. If you've made some bargain—"

"I promised—with my whole heart—that if the blood tests showed

Hannah to be ours, that I would do anything the Lord wanted." She leaned against him. "I'm afraid of what that *anything* will be."

Kyle picked up Hannah and blew raspberries on her belly. She put her mouth to his cheek and tried to blow them back.

"I promised 'anything' too," he said.

"Really?"

"Of course. A thousand times. But think of this, Bethany. It's not like God is the nasty repo man, going to collect on a bad debt."

"I know. Of course, I know. But I'm afraid. I hope . . . "

"What, Beenie?"

"I've been ducking God so much in the past couple of years. I hope I'm still welcome."

He put his face in her hair. "Of course you are."

A kayaker passed by in the water. Hannah kicked and laughed. Bethany took her hand and helped her wave. The kayaker splashed a hello with his paddle, sending Hannah into giggles. The baby had come into her own—dark-brown eyes, golden hair, Bethany's long fingers, Kyle's sunny personality.

"You know what we haven't done yet, Beenie?"

"What?"

He placed Hannah's little hands in Bethany's hand, then laid his hand over theirs. "We've never prayed as a family." He closed his eyes and put his chin on Hannah's head.

Bethany let her eyes roam for a moment, taking in the startling blue of the afternoon sky.

"I love You, Lord," Kyle began.

Bethany closed her eyes. "I love You, Lord."

43

"Kyle. Kyle!" Bethany shook him awake.

"What?"

"Listen."

"What?" He pushed up in the bed, trying to focus through sleep-blurred eyes. Her hand on his shoulder was like ice, even though they were under the quilt.

"Listen."

Swish . . .

"Just the wind in the trees," he mumbled.

"No. It's something . . . inside."

Kyle sat up and swung his feet over the edge of the bed. He rubbed his eyes. The clock read *Midnight*.

Not 12:00. *Midnight*.

"What the heck—Beenie, does that clock do that?"

She looked over to his side of the bed. "No. Kyle . . . "

"Wait." He counted to sixty, slowly. Bethany fidgeted behind him. The clock continued to read *Midnight*. Tiny red letters, blazing out of a deep background.

Swish . . .

"There it is again," Bethany whispered.

"I'm dreaming."

Bethany wrapped her arms around him from the back. "Kyle, it's no dream. I swear. I'm here with you, and I hear it too."

Swish . . .

"Hannah."

"I'll get her," Kyle said.

The clock still read Midnight.

Kyle had been gone too long.

"Kyle!" Bethany called again. Why hadn't he brought Hannah in to her?

Swish . . .

Closer now. Too close.

Kyle had told her to stay put, that he'd bring Hannah right back. How long had it been? Easily five minutes. She glanced at the clock. Midnight.

She jumped out of bed and ran for the door.

Something wrapped around her ankle.

The hall was endless, stretching out forever.

Hannah's door was one down from the master bedroom. Kyle's feet moved over the oak floor, gaining ground. But when he looked up, Hannah's room wasn't any closer.

His heart banged against his chest, ready to break through his ribs.

"This has to be a dream!" His voice echoed down the hall and back at him, saying, No dream.

Something moved at the top of the stairs. A hulking shadow.

Swish . . .

It crossed the hall, trailing darkness. Pausing at the nursery door. The shape of a man, and yet the head was misshapen and the limbs seemed to writhe like snakes. It turned its eyes to Kyle. Black things, endless sockets that sucked light in and spewed darkness out.

Then he smiled—

Kyle wanted to shove the creature down the stairs, but his feet were frozen to the spot. "What do you want with us?" he cried out.

The only light in that vast darkness was the razor edge of too many teeth. Then a tongue, long and slick, flicking fast.

Kyle stumbled backward. He hadn't meant to retreat, but he had seen down that throat. He was a hundred feet away. *Oh God, my Hannah . . .*

He ran with all his might, each step moving him not one inch closer.

Bethany couldn't move.

The hand held her fast. Not a hand, she knew, though she hardly dared to imagine what it could be. Its frigid touch numbed her leg, and yet she could feel the fingers inching up her calf.

"Kyle!" she whispered, not daring to startle it. What could it want?

Sweetness.

"What?" she gasped.

You heard me.

She had to get to Hannah, even if it meant cutting off her own leg to free herself. She dug her fingers in but couldn't seem to get hold of the creature's skin. Her fingers just went deeper and deeper into what felt like vomit.

Bethany jerked sideways, trying to dislodge him, but he held fast, tipping her to the floor. As she went down, he wrapped icy arms around her body. The numbness sweeping over her was worse than any pain she had ever encountered.

"What do you want?" she cried.

To be satisfied.

He leered at her, a creature that longed to be a man, a hideous mound of snapping teeth and seeking tongue.

She punched him. He recoiled. She punched him again. Ready for her this time, the creature swallowed her arm, sucking her into an embrace.

No! Lord God, no! Dear Jesus, save me!

The last sight Bethany saw as she was pulled into darkness was the clock.

It read: *Forever.*

—⊶⊷—

Kyle's breath had left him hours ago. He ran on heart and fear, close enough to Hannah's door to brush it with his fingertips, but not close enough to go in.

Not close enough to stop *it* from going in. The creature turned its smile back to Kyle, staring with a raw hunger he could not even fathom.

"What do you want?" Kyle bellowed with what little air he had left.

Sweetness.

"No!" Kyle howled.

The creature smiled at him, then pushed through the nursery door.

44

éthany and Kyle awoke in the darkness, locked in a frantic
embrace and crying out with terror.

Kyle put his hand over Bethany's mouth. She calmed as she realized it was him. "Thank God. Oh, thank You, Lord!"

More screaming from down the hall. Hannah.

Kyle was up, Bethany with him. They rushed into the nursery and
found her sitting up in her crib.

"Hannah-banana," Kyle said as he picked her up. Her cries quieted as she snuggled into his chest. Bethany hugged her from the
back, covering her head with kisses.

They took her back to their bed and put her between them. Kyle
took Bethany's hand. They locked fingers, their hands on Hannah's
chest as she drifted back to sleep.

When the baby was breathing slowly and steadily, deep in sleep,
Kyle spoke. "I had a nightmare."

"Me too," Bethany said.

"Tell me," he said.

"I can't," she said, her face contorting with tears.

"*He* was there, wasn't he?" Kyle asked.

He felt her stiffen, then tremble. "You saw him? Or it, or whatever the thing was?"

"Yes," he whispered.

"It was just a dream, Kyle. Wasn't it?"

"A dream we had together."

Bethany shook her head and wiped her face with her hand. "Tell me it was bound to happen, after all we've been through. That it's my fears and anxieties splashing back on you."

"No. It was more than that," Kyle said.

"No. Please, it can't be."

"The horror of it—of *him*—went into me so deep."

Hannah stirred in her sleep. Kyle pressed his lips to her cheek, loving the feel of her fresh skin.

"But we're okay now," Bethany said.

"Yes." He smiled and fingered a strand of her hair.

They huddled together in the dark, listening to Hannah breathe. After a few minutes, Kyle realized he'd been listening to his own breathing, to the click of the baseboards as the heat came on, to the occasional car out on the road.

Listening to life. Life as it should be.

"It was just a bad dream," he said suddenly.

"Promise?"

"Promise. Let's get some sleep."

"Kyle, the baby's wet. I've got to change her."

"She's finally settled in. Let her sleep."

"She gets those rashes. That Irish skin she got from you."

"Okay. Let me get a diaper. Maybe if we change her without putting the lights on, she won't wake up."

Bethany swung out of bed. "I'll get it. You stay here. Watch her." She got up and left the room.

Kyle rolled over, looking for his water bottle. The clock read: *Forever.*

Kyle grabbed Hannah and leaped out of bed.

From down the hall, Bethany screamed.

And kept screaming.

Anthony just couldn't believe what he was seeing.

He had heard Bethany scream, then Kyle yelling from upstairs. He ran out into the hall and clicked on the light, then stopped cold at what he saw in the hall between the guest suite and the kitchen.

The wall was filled with writing. Repeating letters, over and over. Blood-red scrawls.

As Anthony ran up the back stairs, the letters continued, traced on the walls, even up onto the ceiling. He found the Dolans in the nursery, where Bethany cried as though the world were ending. *Which it might just be*, Anthony thought. Hannah started up, reacting to her mother. Kyle was curt, saying, "This has to end."

Anthony went into the nursery. The writing was there too. Over the crib, the letters were so dark red, they looked as if they had been burned into the wall. It looked like M, and were those A's? MAMA-MAMAMAMA, over and over.

"Can you see it, too, Anthony?" Bethany said, sobbing. "She thinks our baby is hers."

"Hannah's not hers. She's ours! If I have to go to that nursing home and wring her neck—" Kyle stopped, realizing what he was saying.

"It's everywhere," Anthony said. "Not just in here."

Kyle stormed out of the room. "Stay here."

"No! Don't leave us," Bethany cried.

"Anthony will stay with you," Kyle shouted from down the hall.

"I don't get it," Anthony said. "Who did this? Is there someone in the house? We gotta call the cops—"

"What can the cops do against this? Anthony, don't you see? It's Sable," Bethany said. "A walking nightmare, a ghost, a demon, whatever. Tormenting us."

Kyle walked back in, half-dressed. He shoved a camera into Anthony's hands. "Take pictures. Do it now. The letters are fading. Hurry up, so we can prove what we're seeing."

The letters were lighter now, but still visible. Anthony opened the lens and clicked away.

"Get Hannah's diaper bag," Kyle told Bethany.

"Why? What are—"

"Just get it. Please."

She opened the closet and pulled out the bag.

"Come with me. You, too, Anthony. Keep shooting pictures."

Kyle took Bethany's arm and steered her out of the nursery. The baby wailed, looking frantically from her mother to her father.

Anthony followed them down the stairs. There was a chill in the air, though he could hear the hot water moving through the baseboard. Even the foyer was covered in that scrawl, fading then as if someone had tried to whitewash it.

Outside, the moon was a blur behind the clouds. The security lights went on as they walked to the garage, illuminating the side of the barn. Its bright-red walls were scrawled with faded-gray letters.

Kyle backed the car out. "Get in."

"No car seat—" Bethany started.

"Get in back; hold her tight. We're going to Joan's place. She's closest."

Bethany got in back with Hannah. Anthony climbed in the front. The front window steamed up almost immediately. Letters appeared in the mist.

Bethany started to cry.

"Don't," Kyle said, starting the defroster.

The heat came up, dissipating the mist on the window. They drove in silence. The two miles to Conway seemed like an eternity. Anthony called his mother from the car.

When they pulled into the driveway, his mother ran down the porch, frantic. "What's wrong?"

Jacob appeared behind her, looking confused.

Kyle got them all out of the car. Hannah had fallen asleep. "Watch over them for me, Joan. Anthony will explain." He headed back to the driveway.

"Where are you going?" Bethany said.

He turned and faced them. "To put an end to this, once and for all." Kyle Dolan drove away, disappearing into the darkest hour of the night.

45

*H*e had made her like this. A void.

It was better this way. Lose all and gain nothing.

Sweetne—

Something rippled in the nothing. A flash of golden wonderland.
If only she dared open her eyes to see it.

Kyle gripped the steering wheel so tight his fingers went numb. He
refused to think. Refused to feel. Refused to fear. He absolutely refused
to forgive.

If Sable Lynde thought she could somehow take Hannah from
them, she was mistaken. If she thought she could haunt them, she
was wrong.

Dead wrong.

The whole thing had unfolded like a movie. Except no movie had
ever given Jacob the creeps this bad. Joan paced like a cat gone
crazy. Anthony sat still, staring at his fingers. Bethany looked as
though she were in her own coma. The only time she moved was
when the baby, sleeping on the sofa, moved.

Anthony had told Jacob and his mom the whole thing, except
the dreams. Bethany had to tell that part. She broke down before
she could finish, but they heard enough. *Some seriously whacked stuff
here, for sure,* Jacob thought.

Joan thought they'd all gone nuts until Anthony downloaded

the pictures from the camera. They didn't wait for the printer, just looked at them on the computer screen. There was writing everywhere, in the house, on all the walls. Even on the outside of the barn. Everywhere, the word was the same. MAMA.

The creepiest picture was the one Anthony had shot accidentally when he was getting into the car. The camera had gone off, pointed at the sky. There was a shadow across the moon, shaped like an M. Anthony didn't speak for a long time after seeing that.

They sat like that for several minutes. Jacob's head was jumbled, trying to make sense of it. "How can she be a ghost?" he finally said. "Laurel is still alive."

Bethany sat up suddenly. Her eyes flickered, as though someone had turned on a light that was too bright.

"What is it?" Joan asked, taking her hand.

"Joan, I need your car."

"Baby, you aren't even dressed for going out."

Bethany's sharp laugh made Jacob shiver. "Doesn't matter for where I'm going."

She bent down and kissed Hannah. She looked at his mother, then Anthony. "No matter what, don't let her out of your sight."

Jacob followed her to the door and watched as she peeled out of the driveway.

"What an ungodly noise," Joan muttered.

Jacob shivered, then shut the door. *Ungodly. She got that right.*

The front door was unlocked. It shouldn't have been, two hours before dawn, but there it was. As Kyle walked through the lobby, there was no guard to stop him. *This was meant to be.*

Kyle found the stairs easily. He had sought them out when they came for the blood draw. No way would he get in an elevator with that scum Parker. The man had gotten what he deserved, awaiting trial for extortion and multiple parole violations. He wouldn't be out for a long time.

Sable, on the other hand, continued to be a danger. This would simply be an act in defense of his family. If God wouldn't hem the surrogate in, then Kyle would have to.

Swish . . .

Kyle heard *him* as he climbed the stairs.

He mustered the courage to check the corners, the stairwell, even under the risers. Nothing. Of course he wouldn't *see* the creature. He bred in nightmares, had followed him there only because his mistress called *him* to attend to Kyle.

Kyle would send him to the same pit Sable came from.

———— ✬ ————

Bethany had to stop Kyle. If Sable Lynde had that much power from her coma, what power would she have after he killed her?

Too fast. Joan's car skidded on the pavement and slid onto the shoulder.

She had to slow down, Bethany thought, as she backed the car out. Branches and brush ripped at the side of the car. She'd owe Joan a new paint job when it was all over.

What did any of it matter? She punched down the accelerator. She had to get there in time, had to stop Kyle from killing Sable. That was what the girl wanted—to force them to push her to where she could drink, open throated, at the fountain of wickedness.

She drove on, the minutes weighing on her like eons. Finally, the sign for Hale Acute Care came into sight. Bethany slowed, took the turn, and drove up to the front entrance.

She jumped out of the car, ran for the front door, and pushed through. No one was around to stop her as she got into the elevator.

The world might see Kyle as the villain. Going after a pretty young girl—a helpless, pretty young girl—in a coma. But the world couldn't see the truth, couldn't see a girl so *hard* that her coma was sufficient to give nightmares a live birth.

Dying would only spawn something more unthinkable.

The elevator door opened onto the fourth floor. Bethany couldn't move.

Swish . . .

———∞∞∞———

Sable had faded to almost nothing.

Her skin was so pale that Kyle could see the blood flowing in her hands. She had no breath except what the ventilator delivered. Her hair was thin, her scalp white underneath.

Her power came from the unseen, of course. She had been like that in life, inhabiting some cyberworld of fantasy and violence. Was that where she dwelled even then? Had she tapped somehow into that hidden world of electrical impulses? Kyle understood only the basics of computer logic, but he knew it came down to *on* or *off*, *yes* or *no*, *1* or *0*.

The true nature of life. *God* or *Not*. Sable obviously had chosen *Not*. It would be his task to help her complete that choice. But how?

A pillow over the face wouldn't do it, Kyle knew. She breathed through the tracheotomy in her neck. What if he just unplugged her? Alarms would go off. He could pull the tube from her throat. But the alarm would sound when it didn't encounter any resistance.

It was filthy work, thinking of how to murder a human being.

What if he took the tube from her throat and pressed it to his mouth? That way the machine would continue to work. That would be perfect irony—killing her by breathing her air. Simple, yet elegant. When it was over, he could simply put the tube back to her throat. No one would even know. Not that it mattered. But it would make things easier for Bethany if the fuss were kept to a minimum.

Kyle wrapped his hand around the tube.

———∞∞∞———

Bethany was frozen in the elevator, unable to move. As if she'd been encased in ice.

I've been waiting for you.

She breathed in darkness. Her next breath would be her last and she would be caught there forever. *Don't leave me here, Jesus. I am Yours. Send me an angel. Oh, please, it's too cold here alone.*

Kyle staggered back from the bed and fell to his knees. *Lord God, can You ever forgive me?*

46

arj Owens's day started four hours too early. Julia had called in the middle of the night for reinforcements.

"It's weird," she had told Marj on the phone. "They're all restless to the point of rowdy—pulling out tubes, triggering alarms. The only quiet one is your favorite."

Marj had splashed water on her face, pulled on her scrubs, and driven over. Her favorite. The Bergin girl, now aka Sable Lynde.

The elevator opened. A wild-eyed woman stood in the corner. Julia had said the patients were batty tonight. Maybe family members were too. Marj held the door open.

"Are you getting out here?"

The woman took a step forward, looked out into the lobby, then stepped back into the corner of the elevator. Marj let the door close.

"Where to?" she asked, her finger poised over the floor buttons.

"Laurel's room."

Marj pressed the button for the fourth floor. "You're aware that we don't allow visitors outside of the posted hours?"

"I can't wait."

Marj recognized her from that group that had come in for the DNA tests. This was the woman who had custody of the baby that Laurel had borne. The woman who had shot Laurel. "Mrs. Dolan, right?"

"Yes."

"Remember me? Marj Owens. I help take care of Laurel."

The door opened. Bethany stepped into the hall, blinking hard at the fluorescent lights. Marj debated calling security. But there was something about the woman that seemed to require a loving touch, not an official one.

"Let's go see Laurel," she said.

⸻◦⸻

Bethany finally spotted Kyle in the corner, on his knees. She and Marj helped him into a chair.

"Mr. Dolan. Are you all right?"

He couldn't talk, just nodded.

"Can I do something for you?" Marj asked.

His eyes opened wide. Raw fear, Bethany realized.

"What?"

Sable looked the same—lying there, motionless except for her chest rising with each click of the ventilator. Kyle was staring at its monitor screen.

"Well. Isn't that strange?" Marj said.

"Strange? It's insane," Bethany said. "Horrific. How can you just stand there and—"

"Mrs. Dolan. I've seen too much in this place—sometimes tragic, sometimes miraculous—to ever be shocked by anything." The nurse bent over the monitor. "M. A. M . . . Why, it says *Mama.*"

"She's telling us that our baby is hers." Kyle clutched Bethany's fingers so hard she thought he'd snap them.

Anger flared in Bethany. "She's not the mother. I am!"

Marj stroked Sable's forehead. "Mrs. Dolan, I wonder if you're misinterpreting this."

"You can see it yourself. She's claiming to be the mother!"

Marj rubbed Sable's hand. "She's so young. Too young to be here alone. Have you thought that, perhaps, she's calling for *her* mama?"

⸻◦⸻

"I couldn't do it," Kyle said.

"Hush." Bethany combed his hair with her fingers, wanting somehow to restore order. Marj had unlocked the solarium so they could be alone.

"I've been praying, asking God to forgive me."

"For what? We're the ones she's tormenting," Bethany said.

"To forgive me for wanting to kill her. To forgive me for not having the guts to kill her. I don't know which failure—which sin—is worse." He dropped his head, running his hands through the hair that Bethany had just straightened. "So cowardly I'd go after a woman in a coma. So cowardly I can't do what needs doing to protect my family."

Bethany wrapped her arms around his neck. "Kyle Dolan, you are many things. But cowardly is not one of them."

Bethany stared out the window, watching as the sky lightened to a soft gray, then a pearly pink. What more did God want from them? They had tried to share their faith with Sable, but she would have none of it. But what had they really shared with her? The right words, maybe. Backed by their own expectations, and their consuming desire to have a child.

What about Sable's desperation? What was she running away from?

Swish . . .

What was that hideous thing that she and Kyle had seen in their nightmares? Was Sable bound in her coma with *him*? What if Marj Owens was right? What if these horrible scrawls were a cry for help?

"Kyle. What if it's not about us at all?" Bethany said.

"What do you mean?"

"I don't know. I really don't know. But I think we need to find out."

47

ethany gazed at the cup of tea before her, which she had barely touched. Joan had taken Hannah for a long walk. It was a warm, almost springlike day—unusual for November. Kyle paced the kitchen while Patrick Drinas studied the photos Anthony had printed out.

Patrick had driven up from Boston to see the writing for himself. The only place where a remnant of the scrawls remained was over Hannah's crib, and that was fading fast.

"It's definitely an M. And an A," he said.

"So, you see—it's supernatural after all," Bethany said. There was no triumph in her voice. "Now do you believe in ghosts?"

"I believe in God," Patrick said.

"So what are you saying? That God sends out ghosts to do His dirty work now?" Kyle's anger bubbled up through his exhaustion.

"I'm saying that God has control. Always. And He'll use whatever means He thinks necessary to get our attention."

"Scrawls of MAMA everywhere?" Kyle said, trying not to snap at Patrick.

"It's possible. Do you remember who Belshazzar was?" Patrick asked.

Kyle shook his head.

"From the book of Daniel?" Patrick prompted.

"The handwriting on the wall," Bethany said.

"God had something to say that Belshazzar needed to hear."

"Judgment." Kyle remembered the account now. "God pronounced judgment on Belshazzar. That's what the words on the wall meant. Is that what's happening here? Are we under judgment?"

Patrick smiled. "You are under grace. Start with the premise—the absolute certainty—that you are held fast in Christ. Then ask what God needs you to know."

"I've been thinking for months that someone is tormenting us. The horrible dreams. The ghostly appearances," Bethany said.

"Most of which have been explained," Patrick said. "If we let that all settle out, what is left?"

Darkness. Kyle could see it, even with his eyes open. The only sound that *swish*. The only signpost, a clock reading *Forever*. "A girl in a coma. But I don't know where to go with that."

"I talked to Dr. Chasse," Patrick said. "There is no medical reason for Ms. Lynde to remain in that coma. Her brain injury was recoverable, her EEG is almost normal."

"So why doesn't she wake up?" Bethany said.

"Exactly," Patrick said.

"Exactly what?" Kyle wanted to get in a hot bath, watch a basketball game, lie out in the sunshine, do anything but dwell on this madness any longer.

"Exactly the question we should have asked six months ago," Bethany said, her voice rising with excitement. "But we never thought to, not once."

"And before that?" Patrick prompted. "Before she was in the coma, what did you ask about her?"

"We asked who she was," Kyle said.

"No, we demanded," Bethany said. "We demanded, accused, threatened. And we feared. I was so afraid of what her deception meant to us, I never stopped to think of her. Why she needed to lie. What she was hiding from."

Her growing excitement alarmed Kyle. He had to slow Bethany down, redirect the conversation. "Patrick, why us? If God wanted something done for her, why use us? We'd had enough pain already."

"What else did you have enough of?" Patrick asked quietly.

"Blessing," Bethany whispered. "Blessing and privilege."

She looked at Kyle. Waiting.

Kyle walked to the window. The big oak still held its leaves, now brown and dry. They'd hang on until the first blizzard ripped them away. Is that what had happened to him and Bethany? Had they been ripped from their anchor? Kyle's fingers had slipped, even let go.

But God's hand held fast. Kyle felt it surge back then, in every pore of his aching body—the certainty of his life and his faith. "Blessing and privilege and love," he finally said. "With grace to spare."

"But we never drew on it," Bethany added. "We were too hurting, too scared." She stood with him now, holding his hand.

"Tell me something," Patrick said. "Before this all started— before the implantation—what did you pray for in regard to Sable?"

"The expected stuff," Bethany said. "A successful implantation. Health and more health. Each step of the way, each month, that the pregnancy would continue. Then, when we knew about the deception, we prayed for safety. Protection for us, for Hannah."

Kyle closed his eyes. What had he prayed? "Use this girl to make us a family. And, something like, welcome her into our home."

"And that the Lord would bless her as she was blessing us," Bethany said.

Patrick was with them now, placing a hand on each of their shoulders. "God sometimes answers our prayers with far more abundance than we would expect. And He always casts a larger net of grace than we can even imagine."

Bethany squeezed Kyle's hand. "So it's not about us."

"It's never to be about us," he said. "But we forgot that."

<hr />

Marj Owens had prayed for someone to claim responsibility for Laurel. She just didn't expect that someone to be the Dolans. So she still could be surprised, after all these years. *Thank You, as always, kind Father.*

Marj watched as the Dolans spoke to Sable. Kyle sat on one side of the girl, Bethany on the other, holding Sable's hands.

"Sable, it's Bethany. I wanted to tell you how sorry I am. For what happened to you. For how we let you down. And . . . for how we hurt you. How I hurt you. I hope you'll forgive me." She paused, put her cheek to Sable's hand. "I want to understand. I want to help. But most important, I forgive you. You can depend on that forgiveness. You are safe with us, Sable."

She looked up at her husband, nodded.

"Hey, pal. It's Kyle. You've been asleep awhile now. Missed the end of the season. It was a good one. The Red Sox made the play-offs. Only then, not so good. They blew it in the seventh game. I'd tell you who won the Series, but I'm afraid you'd never want to wake up. And the thing is, Sable, I *want* you to wake up. This isn't you. You're the girl who laughs at my stupid jokes, who's smarter than anyone I know. The girl who can talk computers and baseball and Jacob-speak. He misses you, talks about you all the time.

"I know we've had some tough times. We goofed up over and over. But, with God's grace, we keep going. We want you to come back, keep going with us. We want to help you get better. I forgive you. I want a chance to ask you—wide awake—to forgive me. Please come back, Sable. It's safe here. I promise."

They sat for a long time like that. Marj went in and out, attending to other patients. After a couple of hours, she had to turn Sable.

"May I help?" Bethany asked.

"You sure?"

She nodded.

"Okay. We keep a half sheet under the patient to make this easier. I'll pull the sheet towards me while you put your hand on her shoulder and hip, and turn her towards you. Okay?"

"What about the tube? It won't come out, will it?"

"No, it won't. It's taped pretty tightly," Marj said. "Ready?"

Bethany nodded. She put her hands where Marj had indicated.

"Okay, on three. One-two-three."

Marj pulled, and Bethany rolled. Sable was now on her side, facing the door.

"She doesn't react, even to this." Bethany's eyes teared up.

Her husband went to her, put his arm around her. They both looked across the bed at Marj.

She smiled. "She will. Have faith."

If I say, "Surely the darkness will hide me

And the light become night around me,"

even the darkness will not be dark to you;

The night will shine like the day,

For darkness is as light to you.

(PSALM 139:11-12)

48

*C*ade Parker seemed surprised to see them. Shocked, in fact. *Why wouldn't he be?* Bethany thought. They had put him there.

Stafford looked more like a community center than a prison. The visitors' area was like a vast living room, filled with chairs, sofas, tables, even games and a television. A glass slider opened up to a large deck. Beyond was a small yard with playground equipment and picnic tables. Beyond that was the chain link and barbed wire.

Kyle stood and offered his hand to the man.

Parker hesitated, then shook it. "Surprised to see you two here."

"We're surprised to be here," Kyle said.

Parker's face darkened. "Sable! Is she—!"

"No change," Kyle said. "Which is why we're here."

They took seats around a metal table. Parker turned his chair to face Bethany, smiling with an attention just short of flirtation. *This is his modus operandi,* Bethany realized. *He works the closest woman, gets her to do whatever he wants. Poor Jenny Hemlow never had a chance.*

"You want me to sign something, don't you?" Parker asked. "I've been wondering when you were going to transfer her to the state. That nursing home must be costing you a bundle."

"No. We're not letting go of her," Kyle said.

"Just the opposite. We want to help her wake up," Bethany said impatiently. Now that they had made the decision—now that God had led them to this path—she wanted to move quickly. If the dream they had shared was any indication of what Sable endured, and if the writings on the wall were a plea for help, then they had to act.

"Her doctor thinks there's a psychological barrier that prevents her complete recovery," Kyle said. "We can't address that because we know nothing about her."

"She lied, stole, and cheated. And she did it all far better than her big brother ever could," Parker said. "What else do you need to know?"

"Why did she do all that?"

Parker shrugged. "Gotta do something with her time, I suppose."

Kyle's fingers tightened on Bethany's. She rubbed the back of his hand with her thumb, silently calming him.

"We don't even know how old she is," Bethany said.

Parker laughed. "How old do you think she is?"

"She told us she was twenty-three. But I wonder if she's even older. She certainly knew how to handle herself. It takes a lot of savvy to steal an identity as she did."

"She is—was—very smart. Been on her own for a few years now," Parker said. "Which is amazing, considering she was just eighteen when you got her pregnant."

Bethany gasped. "Eighteen? Then how did she get in a situation where she could pull this off? And what was she hiding from?"

Parker stretched and yawned. "That's none of your business."

"Please. We want to help her," Bethany said. "Surely you'd want that."

"What's your stake in this?"

"No stake," Kyle said. "Except to get her out of that coma and help her get on with her life."

"You think I'm some kind of sucker, Dolan? You'll get her behind bars so fast, her poor little head will spin. She's better off where she is." Parker stood, laughing. "I know what you really want. You'd think with all your money, you wouldn't care . . . "

"I'm not following you," Kyle said.

"I'm not buying this do-gooding act of yours. You're after the money, aren't you?" Parker's laughter had disappeared. "Listen, Dolan. I'm her brother—anything that Sable has belongs to me."

He headed for the door.

"Wait!" Kyle jumped up, tried to grab his arm.

"No physical contact," the guard barked.

"Please, Mr. Parker. Help us help her," Bethany called after him.

Cade Parker cursed at them and walked back into his prison.

∝∞∝

Hailey Slonik was ready to chew someone's face off. Problem was, she had no one to put the bite on. The guy from Rensselaer was long gone, panicked after the FBI came sniffing around. Cade was behind bars, Sable, a vegetable.

Hailey had pawned most of their belongings, but no way was she giving up the computer—she needed it to baby-sit that million bucks. She lay on the bedroom floor, digging under the bed. There was a mess of junk under there, must be something else she could sell. Her hand brushed against hard plastic.

The video game player. When she had booked out of Sable's apartment, she'd left the tape recorder—worthless piece of junk—but she stuffed the player into her jacket as she climbed down that ladder. She should have felt bad about leaving Cade like that, but a strategic retreat made the most sense. Even if she had gotten into the mix, Dolan was so hopping mad, he would have taken her out too.

The game player was an expensive one, she realized, that might be worth enough bread to get her by for few more days, maybe enough time to work a new angle on the account. Wasn't there supposed to be a joystick to this thing? Maybe it was inside. She popped it open, found a game cartridge and a piece of paper, folded up. Some stupid e-mail to some stupid kid.

She smiled as she realized what she was reading.

. . . need to look for it with everything that's in you, man. I tried to build something special for myself, but I should have known it wasn't gonna work out for me. Never has. But if I can't have it, I want you to. 'Cuz you the money, man. In every way.

It was all coming clear. Hailey needed to find this little *man* of Sable's. Find him and shake him good.

49

*N*ot the best neighborhood for a kid to grow up in, Kyle thought. He was glad that Harry Stevens had come with them, and very glad that Hannah had not. The baby was back at the hotel with Kate Hemlow, who had strict orders to stay in the room until they returned.

Harry had used his contacts with the Boston police to reach out to the Albany PD. Parker's juvenile record yielded the name of his mother—Angela Lynde, deceased seven years before. Parker was seventeen when it happened, still going under his own name of Cade Lynde. He was already in Youth Services Detention for sweet-talking an old woman out of a thousand dollars.

The other child became a ward of the state. Youth Services refused any other information, other than to confirm that her name was indeed Sable.

"All I got definite was the address where they were living when the woman was killed," Harry said apologetically.

Not much to go on, but Kyle prayed it would be enough. Harry had arranged for the owner of the house to meet them here.

"The house isn't as bad as some of the others," Bethany said as they stood on the sidewalk. The Latham house was a triple-decker, badly in need of a paint job. But the fence that marked off the tiny lawn was bright white. There was a wreath on the front door and wind chimes on the porch.

<hr/>

Minutes later they were in the third-floor apartment, drinking hot chocolate with Lisa Latham, a middle-aged woman with deep smile lines and bright-red hair.

"Mother is in an assisted-living facility. She won't let me sell the house. And I can't imagine who'd want it. I keep waiting for the yuppies to move in, gentrify the place." She shrugged.

Bethany took out the picture of Sable that they had taken the last Christmas. Her hair was shiny, her face full and pink cheeked.

"That's Angie's kid?" Lisa asked.

"We believe so," Bethany said.

Lisa began to cry.

Hailey liked everything about Bernard DuBois. His deep voice, with that rasp in the back of his throat, was a real turn-on. Jet-black hair with silver wings, slicked back. A boxer's build that she'd fit into nicely.

"I'm not sure what you want," Bernard said.

"Resources. I could hire a PI, I suppose, but I'd prefer a partner. Someone who knows how to find people, and what to do when they find 'em."

"What's the stake? And what's my cut?"

Hailey smiled. This would be big, even for him. "A million bucks in one account, a couple hundred thousand spread out among others. I don't have all the necessary access codes and passwords to get at it. I know of someone who has them, but I don't know his name or how to find him. You find him, get the information, and I'll cut you in for a third."

He didn't move a muscle. Didn't have to—she could smell it. Yeah, he was in. And why not? She and Bernard DuBois would make a good team.

Cade would be ripping mad, but she didn't give a fig about that. Let him and Sable rot, for all she cared. They were doing a good job of it already—Cade in his prison and Sable in her coma.

They could stay there forever, for all Hailey cared.

—∞—

Lisa took Kyle and Bethany to the back hall on the first floor. "Angie had this apartment here, on the right. I can't let you in—it's occupied. Guy's really mean, too, but at least he pays on time. This door goes outside. Not much of a yard, not anymore. You put out a chair, it's gone in ten minutes. Safer to stay in."

"Is this it?" Bethany put her hand on the only other door in the hall. It was cold in the hall, surely too cold for a child.

"That's it. We were in Okinawa when it happened. Just had our first kid." Lisa frowned. "She's at school right now, second grade. If anything like that ever happened to her, we'd just . . . " She left off, shaking her head.

Bethany touched her arm. "I know. We have a little girl too."

"They interviewed a lot of guys—Angie had an army of 'em coming in here for a while. But they never caught him." Lisa moved close to Bethany and lowered her voice. "Could still be out there, for all we know."

"What sort of mother allows men in and out like that?" Kyle said.

"It's not what you think. Angie loved her kids. The times I was home—before this all went bad—I could see that. Cade, the little heartbreaker, could talk the frosting off a cake. Sable was so pretty and real smart. Not a charmer like her brother, though. Quiet. Always had her head in a science or math book.

"I remember Angie singing to the little girl. Real nice voice, until the booze ate it away. A good heart. But too friendly, if you know what I mean. She liked to have a good time, that one. Which is how this closet thing came about. Angie knew all that partying wasn't the best for the little girl, there being only one bedroom in the apartment. Old house, thin walls—everyone hears everything. Ma said the closet was actually Sable's idea."

Bethany willed herself to look inside. It was a generous space, with plasterboard walls and a worn vinyl floor. Two snow shovels and a rake leaned in the corner.

266

"It's just a closet," Kyle said. "I'm not following the significance here."

"It was supposed to be a—what do you call it? A utility closet. For a washer and dryer, and storing stuff. Ma found the little girl in there one time, sitting on a bucket, trying to read. Ma's heart almost broke for the kid. So she moved all the cleaning stuff to the basement and told Sable it could be her little hideaway. When the partying got too—intense—in the apartment, Sable would come out here."

Kyle stepped inside. "There's a crawl space at the back."

Bethany looked over his shoulder. Along the back wall there was a small enclosure, no higher than two feet, no longer than six.

Kyle pulled out a hatch, revealing two pipes that ran along the floor at the back of the space. "Must be where the plumbing was supposed to go," he said.

Bethany stepped in with him. She could hear Lisa speaking behind her.

"The cops figured that some guy went after Angie in the apartment. That's where the blood trail started. Maybe Sable heard all the noise, the screaming, and got into the crawl space to hide. Or maybe the guy went after her too. Who really knows?

"They figure Angie came looking for her, or maybe the woman just needed a place to hide. She was bleeding, her stomach cut pretty bad. Maybe she thought Sable could help her. Or, like Ma said, maybe Angie just wanted to say good-bye. Anyway, she got into the closet, collapsed, and eventually died. Probably took a few hours, they said."

"Why didn't Sable go for help?" Kyle asked.

"She couldn't," Bethany mumbled. The blood would have felt hot at first. Like Sable's blood had been right after the gun went off. But it would have gone cool too quickly, cool with that metallic smell that got deep into your nose, so strong you tasted it with every breath.

"Bethany? Come on, let's get out of here." Kyle guided her out of the closet.

"Don't you see? Her mother fell against the door to the crawl space.

Sable was inside, hiding. She must have been terrified. Absolutely—"
Bethany broke into a sob.

"Okay, okay," Kyle said, pulling her into his arms.

"No, it's not okay!" she said, yanking away from him. "Her mother's
body blocked the crawl space. Sable couldn't move the hatch, not
with that weight on it. I can't—it's unbearable—the blood just flowing across the floor, seeping into her hiding place. Sable lying in there,
terrified. Lying in her mother's blood. Listening to her mother die."

Bethany could hear that little voice. *Sing to me, Mama, so I'll
know you're still there.*

Kyle's eyes were wide now. "How long did she have to lie in there
like that?"

"Three days," Lisa Latham said. "Lying in her ma's blood the
whole time."

"Three days in the darkness," Bethany said. "Three days that have
turned into a lifetime."

50

*T*hat night, with Kyle's arms wrapped around her, Bethany prayed one simple prayer.

Show me, Lord. She began to dream . . .

Mama's latest fellow smelled like beer cans and old pizza. He had come every night for a week now. His teeth were crooked and stuck out over his lower lip when he smiled.

Nights they stayed in were closet nights for Sable. It was quieter out there in the back hall. She loved Mama, but she hated that smacking sound the men made when they kissed her. Like they would swallow her whole. Mama knew the closet was a good thing. Sable had her books and her blanket and a flashlight—all she needed to keep her happy.

Crooked Teeth had come in that night with a bag from Ling Pao's. He and Mama settled in front of the television. "Hey, kid. Want some?" he had asked Sable.

She shook her head no. She had had cornflakes for supper, with orange juice because there wasn't any milk. Sable whispered something about going out back for a while. Mama knew that meant the closet and didn't even blink when she headed out through the kitchen. Sable had her hand to the back door, about to open it, when it banged open. She almost jumped out of her shoes.

A big man stormed in, bigger even than that gorilla guy who ran the gas station. Big Man didn't even look her way, just stormed into the living room as if he owned the place. Sable smelled him as he went past. Sweat, liquor, lots of cigarettes. The scent of her whole life, it seemed.

She hated it.

She could hear Crooked Teeth trying to get the Big Man to leave. "Hey, man. Take a number and come back later."

"I had an appointment. Ain't that true, Angie?"

"Give me a minute." Mama came out to the kitchen then, cursing under her breath as she lit a cigarette. Big Man followed her out, fists clenched, face red. Sable made herself as small as she could, trying to press into the wall behind the stove.

"Hey, cowboy, I am so sorry," Mama said. "I got my nights screwed up. Can you give me a few minutes, let me get rid of dog face in there?"

Big Man grabbed Mama's arm. "I can ditch him a whole lot faster than you."

"Please, babe. No trouble. I can make him—what? What are you looking at?"

Sable. He was looking at Sable.

"Come out of there, where I can see you," Big Man said.

"Let her be. She's just a little girl."

Big Man inched closer. "She's big enough for me."

Mama pulled at his jacket. "Hey. Come on, let's you and me party."

The Big Man smacked Mama clear across the kitchen. Crooked Teeth came in, looking confused. One glance at Big Man and he backed out the door—hands up in surrender.

Big Man moved in on Sable. "You and me gonna have a little party. You like parties, don't you, sweetness?"

She was stuck to the spot. Willing her stomach to freeze so she didn't get sick. Begging her feet to thaw so she could run.

He wrapped his hand around her neck and pulled her to him. Her skin shrank from his touch. Wanting to turn inside itself. "Mama," she whispered.

Mama was up now, leaning against the kitchen table. Just staring.

"Mama."

"Come to Papa, little sweetness." He pressed against her, all salt and smoke. She couldn't breathe. Didn't want to breathe, didn't see any way out . . . except . . . on the stove . . .

A knife. A big knife that Mama had used to cut through a whole chicken.

She reached out. Too far away. Big Man pushed her against the wall.

"Get off her," Mama yelled.

She saw Mama's hand, taking the knife.

"I said, get off her!" Mama yelled.

Big Man jerked up and away from Sable. Mama must have grabbed him. She slipped sideways, looking for the back door. Something banged behind her, but she was afraid to look. She was already in the hall when Mama screamed.

Then Mama screamed again, a sound that drove through Sable's bones. "Mama!" she cried, turning back.

"Run, Sable. Hide!"

She yanked open the door to the hall closet and slipped inside.

Someone followed her out.

Big Man wasn't done with her. He didn't know about the crawl space. No one knew, except Cade. She slipped in, pulling the little door tight behind her.

The closet door opened. Sable held her breath. There was heavy breathing. Then, a thud. Something warm oozed into the crawl space.

Who would save her now?

Swish . . .

Bethany awoke with a start. Where was she? Yes, the hotel. Kyle rolled over and stared at her, that look of love that she had known for twenty years.

"Hey," he said.

"We can't give up," she said. "We have to do whatever it takes."

"I know," he said.

"I love you, Kyle."

"I love you, Beenie."

Hannah rolled over in the porta-crib. She looked around, confusion in her face. She had opened her mouth, about to cry, when Kyle picked her up. "Da-da," she cooed.

"I love you, too, pumpkin face," he said. He took her to their bed and put her between them.

Hannah put her tiny fingers to Bethany's cheek. "Mama."

"Yes, Mama is here." Bethany cradled Hannah and began to sing.

51

We've tried this before," Dr. McDonald was saying, "so don't get your hopes up."

"It's going to work this time," Bethany said. "I know it is."

Marj Owens stood at the doctor's side. Kyle sat in the corner, praying. A haze of frost lined the window. Winter, only a month away on the calendar, had already gripped that part of Maine.

Bethany took Sable's hand. "If you can breathe on your own, you can come home with us. Please, Sable. We want you to come home. Try to do it this time. Please."

Dr. McDonald looked at Marj. "Ready?"

She nodded, the Ambu-bag in her hand in case Sable needed them to breathe for her.

Dr. McDonald pulled the plug on the respirator. Then Marj stepped in and put the mask over Sable's mouth.

"Give her five puffs," the doctor said. "Remind her how it's done."

Marj squeezed the bag five times, then pulled it away from Sable's face.

Bethany linked her fingers through Kyle's. He kept his head bowed, eyes closed. They had decided he'd pray, she would encourage, through this process.

Sable's chest didn't move.

"Five more," Dr. McDonald said.

"Come on, Sable," Bethany said. "You can do it."

Come on, Lord, Kyle prayed. *Breathe life into this child.*

Marj puffed again, then stood back. Sable's chest didn't move.

"Don't give up," Bethany said. "Not yet."

"Five more, please."

Marj repeated the process, then stepped back. Something gurgled in the back of Sable's throat. Then she took a long breath.

"Praise God," Bethany said.

"Indeed," Marj said, grinning.

⸻

Joan wanted to know what Jacob wanted for his birthday.

She had offered to buy him a new CD player, let him take karate, maybe even try to learn to play the drums. When he told her what he wanted, she upped the stakes: skis or a snowboard. But he hung in there.

"I want a PlayBox," he said.

The game player had disappeared from the apartment when Cade Parker broke in. Jacob needed his own game player. And he got it, three weeks before Christmas. Joan had run out of excuses. Jacob had gotten his grades way up, stayed in Boy Scouts, and stopped running his mouth off about having to go to Sunday school.

Now all he needed was to master the highest level of Winter Slaughter. It was taking some time because he had to wait until his mother was in bed before he could play. Maybe he'd be a millionaire by New Year's. Not that Joan would let him touch the money. But Anthony's name was on the accounts as his guardian, Sable had written in her last e-mail. Jacob would propose a little deal. College for Anthony, freedom for Jacob.

He owed it to Sable to pull it off. She expected big things of him, and he didn't want to disappoint her. She'd already be disappointed enough if she woke up and found out he was going to Sunday school.

⸻

Bethany had known it would be hard, but she hadn't realized how hard.

Between changing diapers and mixing formula, bathing and walking and getting down for naps and up for active periods, she was exhausted. That was just Sable's care.

Then there was Hannah, needing to be parented and loved and nurtured.

Lord, use this girl to make me a mother, Bethany had prayed on the day that Sable had been implanted with the embryo. God was answering that prayer abundantly, as Patrick had promised. Caring for Hannah was a joy. Hannah grew and laughed and loved. Caring for Sable was a step of faith and a daily exercise in unconditional love. Sable slept on, as if anything they did for her didn't matter.

They had taken Sable to the farmhouse the day after Thanksgiving. Marj Owens and Joan Martinez had become full-time employees to assist in her care. There were daily visits from the physical therapist, weekly checkups by Dr. McDonald, and an occasional visit from Dr. Chasse to check on Sable's neurological status. *Unchanged* was fast becoming a curse word for Bethany.

She and Kyle spent time every day with Sable, talking to her, singing, praying, reading. Kyle watched all the Patriots and Bruins games in Sable's room, complaining and cheering as if Sable were doing it with him. Bethany allowed her one hour a day of her beloved talk shows each afternoon and put on old movies or played music the rest of the time. She took Hannah into the room every day before lunch so they could watch a Veggie Tales tape together. Hannah giggled and clapped with Bethany during the silly songs.

Sable slept on, responding to nothing.

Bethany was in Sable's room with Marj, learning how to clean her feeding tube. It had snowed six inches earlier in the day, but the night sky was clear. The full moon made the snow-covered yard as bright as day.

Kyle walked in with a bag of potato chips.

"Hannah asleep?" Bethany asked.

"Changed, rocked, and now off in that golden wonderland of hers," Kyle said.

"You just lost three pounds. You are not eating those chips, Dolan."

"Oh, these aren't for me. They're for Sable."

"No way you're putting those in her mouth," Marj said. "She'll choke."

"I know, I know. I thought I'd just tempt her a bit." He broke a chip under Sable's nose. Then he popped it in his own mouth and chewed loudly next to her ear. "Yummy."

"This is just an excuse to eat junk food and not get yelled at," Bethany said, laughing.

"Hear that, Sable? Maybe she's right. You'd better wake up before I eat 'em all." Kyle touched a chip to her tongue.

"Her eyes," Bethany cried. "Look."

Sable's eyelids fluttered.

"Hmm, she might be reacting," Marj said. "Kyle, take the chip away. We don't want her to swallow it."

"Come on, Sable," Bethany said. "You can have the whole bag. Just wake up."

Kyle sat down on the bed and put his hand around Sable's arm. "It's almost Christmas. We need you to help with the tree."

Nothing.

"Did we just imagine her eyes flickering like that?" he asked.

"No," Marj said. "It wasn't much, but it was something."

Potato chips, Bethany thought. *She responds more to junk food than to our promises that we want to help her get better. What will it take to wake her up and show her we can be trusted? Lord God, show us what to do.*

Santa Claus. Armed with chain saw in one hand and a machete in the other. And how did the ultimate bad dude of Winter Slaughter get in to do his bloody ugly work, then escape before he got caught? The chimney, of course.

Playing up this high in the game had made Jacob sick. Sick to his stomach while he played, sick in his dreams afterwards. He didn't know why—he was the coolest man he knew, getting up that high. Most kids he knew weren't even allowed to play this game, let alone master it.

So why did he feel like something scraped off the rim of a toilet? Not evil or wicked. Dirty, like all the blood in the game had been sprayed onto him and dried there. The night before, after playing the game almost to the end, he took a shower. Then he got Joan's antibacterial soap out—the stuff she made them use when they had colds—and scrubbed his hands. He thought he was clean then, after all that scrubbing. But he went to bed and couldn't sleep. He just kept seeing the slaughter. Hearts ripped out. Heads chopped off, rolling along the floor, screaming. Limbs in a pile. Blood spurting, splattering, flowing everywhere.

When he had his own crib, maybe he'd skip on the video games. Somehow, they weren't all that cool anymore. In fact, they were mighty whacked.

52

You're either brilliant or batty, Kyle told himself as he gassed up the snowmobile.

Downright insane, Bethany had said when he pulled into the yard on the biggest snowmobile either of them had ever seen. It took three days, but he installed a trailer hitch, then made a tow harness for the sleigh he had bought off old Will Lucey.

"We could just go to town and buy a tree," Bethany said.

"Hey, this is your family tradition, cutting down the tree on Christmas Eve."

"Hannah doesn't need a tree. She only cares about the lights," Bethany said.

"We're getting Hannah a tree, and we're getting Sable one. Marj cleared it with Dr. McDonald, made sure there wouldn't be anything that would compromise her breathing."

Bethany kissed him. "That's sweet, Kyle, but she won't know even know it's there."

"But I will. So we're going to do what we always do," Kyle said. "Go out in the woods and cut down the biggest and best ones we can find. And we're going as a family."

Hailey smiled at Bernard as he drove. He reached out, tweaked her thigh, then left his hand there. Right where she wanted it.

Bernard's contacts had come up with a name. Sean Richards. A quick series of e-mails, with Hailey posing online as a fourteen-year-old girl, had ferreted out the real user of the account. Some kid

278

named Jacob Martinez. After that it was really easy, with only one Martinez listed in the North Conway directory.

And there they were, on their way to New Hampshire.

Bernard had decided to wait until Christmas Eve to try to make the contact. All defenses would be down then. Apply the right pressure, and the little man would tell them everything they needed to know. Bernard would make sure of that.

Ho ho ho, Hailey thought.

Hannah loved the wind in her hair so much that she kept yanking off her knitted cap.

"Stop that, Hannah. You'll get a cold and miss Christmas," Bethany warned.

Hannah just laughed. Every minute or so, Anthony would turn and wave at her, sending her into another fit of giggles. They had given Marj the day off. Joan and Jacob would be over later for Christmas Eve dinner. At the moment, Bethany and Kyle were left on their own to wrestle Sable into her body support, then into the sleigh.

Kyle sat next to Sable, chatting away. "Look, there's that old birch. The one you stripped a piece of bark from and wrote the pirate's note to Jacob on. Remember that?" And a few minutes later: "There's the turnoff to Thor's Falls. If you wake up, I could take you up to the cascades on the snowmobile. How cool would that be?"

He kept up the chatter the whole time as the snowmobile chugged through the woods. Bethany loved him for his persistence and his optimism.

After about forty-five minutes, Kyle signaled Anthony to stop. "There's a stand of spruces in there, over that little stream. That's where Sable and I got the tree last year."

It seemed like eons ago, Bethany thought. The Christmas before, Sable had been five months pregnant. She was still Laurel Bergin, a sweet, smart girl headed for U.Conn. Medical School. Now, instead of loving the bright and cheerful Laurel Bergin, they were praying that God would help them love Sable Lynde. Praying that He would use them to pull her out of this inexplicable darkness where she slept, day and night.

Was *he* in there with Sable, that horrible creature with the sucking mouth and stinging tongue? Bethany already knew the answer. Of course he was. Otherwise, God wouldn't have allowed both her and Kyle to see those creatures in that living nightmare. Who was he? The Big Man that Bethany had seen in her dream, the one who killed Sable's mother? Some demonic creature that had come rushing in afterward? Or some deep-seated psychosis that took form when Sable's mind snapped?

What was Sable doing now in that darkness? Was she running down the hall, as Kyle had been, never getting to the end? Or was she like Bethany, sucked into the deep shadows, the chill paralyzing her?

The thought of it—the memory of what God had allowed them to experience—made Bethany shudder. Every day, it prompted her to hold on to all those she loved. *We're holding on to Sable,* she thought. *I only hope we're strong enough to see her through.*

How perfect was this? Joan had left him alone in the Dolans' farmhouse. Jacob had the clues now: a bell and a chimney. Inside the bell would be all the numbers he needed to get to Sable's money. He knew the bell wasn't in the apartment—there was no chimney in the barn, and the apartment was heated with electric heat. It had to be hidden in or near one of the chimneys in the farmhouse, and suddenly, he was there all by himself.

God must want him to have this money, right? Why else would it all have happened so perfectly? The Dolans were out with Anthony in the woods, trying to find a Christmas tree. Good thing they took Sable with them. Jacob hated to think that way, but the truth was, she creeped him out.

A little while before, Joan had arrived to start the turkey for that night's feast. She had made Jacob go with her. Even though he had Boy Scout badges now, she still didn't trust him on his own at home.

He sacked out in the family room, trying to figure out how he could search the chimneys without Joan knowing.

Then she yelped from the kitchen. The whipping cream had spoiled.

"Can't have chocolate cream pie without whipped cream," she said. She made phone calls and finally found a place over the border in Maine that was still open.

She walked into the family room. "Get up. We're going for a ride."

Jacob pretended he was asleep, making his face like one of the angels over the fireplace.

After a moment, his mom pressed her lips to his cheek. "I love you, little pup," she whispered.

Jacob lay still until he heard her car backing out of the driveway. She'd be gone at least an hour, he thought, maybe more, because she'd have to get gas for the car too.

He sat up, wondering where it was coming from, the spooky feeling about looking into all the fireplaces. He got to thinking back to that scene in Winter Slaughter, where Santa jumped out of the fireplace and killed a whole family opening presents.

But it was just a game, right? This was real life. Sure, Forge Hill had some nasty things go down, but this was North Conway. Stuff like that couldn't happen here.

53

All that was left was to let go. Of what, she couldn't fathom, except that it was not *him*.

In one lifetime, it might have been hope. But that was one lifetime too many ago. No hope here.

Say bye-bye and come to Papa, sweetness.

Good—

She started to—

—let—

⊶⊷

"We can't cut Sable's tree until she approves." Kyle could tell by the glance that Bethany and Anthony shared that they thought he was going overboard. But he had one ally, and he sealed that bond with a wink. Hannah scrunched her face, trying to wink back. "See! Hannah-banana agrees."

"So, how exactly do we get Sable to approve a tree?" Bethany asked.

"We'll walk her over there."

"Kyle. She's not ambulatory," Bethany said.

"She will be if we help," Kyle said. "Right, Anthony?"

"Whatever you say." Anthony just looked at his boots. This was still difficult for him, Kyle realized. The young man had feelings for the girl that went deep.

They had already cut the tree for the family room, another stunner of a spruce. It'd be a race to get it decorated before church, but with Joan volunteering to help with dinner, they should get it done. Kyle had found a perfectly formed white pine with long, soft needles for Sable. They'd put white lights on it, and maybe a star.

If Sable approved. He unbuckled her straps and let her fall into his arms.

"Kyle, please don't get a hernia," Bethany warned.

"I won't," he promised, though he wasn't entirely sure he wouldn't. At home they had all the lifting aids, plus Marj or Joan, who were trained in this kind of care.

"Okay, Sable. Anthony and I are going to take you for a walk." Kyle draped her arm over his shoulder, wrapped his free arm around her waist, and motioned for Anthony to do the same. She was dead weight between them.

O Christmas tree, O Christmas tree, Anthony sang as they moved forward.

Bethany joined in the music as she followed along, Hannah in her arms. They crossed the small stream that trickled clear and cold under delicate ice bridges. The sky was still a soft blue, but the sun was below the tree line.

Kyle had checked his watch—still more than an hour until sundown. They were well within the margin of safety. "Here it is," he said. "Isn't it perfect?"

"Thought Sable was supposed to make that decision." Bitterness tinged Anthony's voice.

Kyle mentally kicked himself. This was the first time that Sable had been in Anthony's arms since that horrible time he accused the boy of being a rapist. Sable had kept silent that afternoon. She was silent now, ironically, tragically silent. Had her betrayals and deceptions somehow caught up to her?

Kyle put his mouth to her ear. "I forgive you. God forgives you. Believe that. Please."

Silence.

"I'll take her now, Anthony."

Kyle lifted Sable into his arms like a baby. What had he prayed? *Father, use this girl to make us a family.* Kyle had expected God to put Hannah in his arms as a baby, not that girl. But there she was.

"You're safe with us, baby," he whispered.

He put her close enough so the pine branches grazed her face. "Smell it, Sable? Fresh pine always reminds me of Christmas. Take a deep breath. Smell how clean winter is. How crisp the snow is."

Had her nostrils flared, just for a moment?

"Imagine this tree with the lights, Sable. You can lie in bed and squint your eyes so the white blurs into the green. You'll think it's all a dream because it's hazy and magical. But it's not, Sable. The tree is real. We're real, and what we're telling you is true. We want you to share Christmas with us. To share our home. Please. I promise, you'll be safe with us."

Anthony turned and walked away.

"Kyle. This is a great tree," Bethany said. "Why don't we cut it, then get going?"

"No, never mind. It was a stupid idea. Probably good to get Sable out once in a while, let her breathe fresh air. But the rest of it . . . stupid of me to think . . . never mind."

Kyle carried Sable back to the sleigh by himself. Anthony sat on the snowmobile, staring into the woods. Bethany covered Sable with the thermal blanket, then passed the straps to Kyle so he could buckle her in.

Bethany gasped.

"What?"

"Look." She lifted Sable's gloved hand from under the blanket. Her fingers were twisted around a small pine branch.

Kyle grinned. "You and Anthony finish up. I've got a tree to cut."

It drummed at her like thunder.

Letgogogogogogogo . . .

Let—

Go—

Let there be—

Nothing—

Forever—

And ever—

Then.

That tiny hole opened, a flicker in the void. That which was not her and certainly not *him*.

NO! He screamed and wailed and clawed and chewed and spit and strangled and—

Maybe. Maybe yes.

———ↁↁↁ———

Things were working out perfectly. They tracked down the house, then followed the Martinez woman and her kid as they drove across town. When the woman pulled into this driveway, Hailey knew exactly where they were. The Dolans' country estate.

Rich scum had it all, by the looks of things. When Hailey had gone here with Cade, it was dark. Now there was still enough light left to the day for her to take it all in—the curving driveway, the big colonial house with eaves, turrets, and a wrap-around porch. The red barn way back off the road, lots of trees and open space. All they needed was Bing Crosby, and it'd be a puking white Christmas.

Their luck got better and better—the Martinez woman drove away, leaving the kid here. Hailey called the number that she had copied weeks back from the packing slip. So much for being unlisted. No answer. Then Bernard scouted the outside of the property. There was no movement or light anywhere in either the main house or the apartment.

Bernard pulled the car into a farm stand a few hundred feet down the road from the Dolans' estate. The place was closed for the winter, but just in case a nosy cop came by, Hailey wrote a note: *Dead battery. Be back soon with jumper cables.*

"Ready?" Bernard said.

"Oh, yeah. Let's get in there and shake that little brat for all he's worth."

———ↁↁↁ———

As soon as his mother's car was out of sight, Jacob raced around the house. There were fireplaces in the family room, living room, kitchen, and Kyle's office. He checked the outside of each one, even moving things on the mantel to make sure Sable hadn't hidden the bell behind a photo or inside a vase. Nothing.

Then he got a flashlight and climbed inside each one. Nothing.

Upstairs, there were fireplaces in three bedrooms, plus the music room. He repeated the same drill. Nothing. Where next? The cellar, he supposed. Sure enough, there were small metal doors where the four chimneys came down. He opened each one carefully. Three were loaded with soot. The fourth had a mass of hay and little skeletons. Mice, he guessed.

No time to get creeped out—he had to hurry. Joan wouldn't be back for at least an hour, but he didn't know about the rest of them, out there in the woods playing jingle bells. There was only one more place to search, and that was the attic.

Jacob hurried back to the second floor and opened the door to the narrow attic stairs. He flipped a switch, and lightbulbs popped on everywhere. The Dolans' attic was almost as awesome as the rest of the house. High ceilings, windows with curtains, furniture everywhere. Trunks, bureaus, a crystal lamp, a carved wooden music stand.

The dust was like early winter snow—white and thin. Jacob would bet anything that storage was to the left, where there were footprints and drag marks. And he'd bet that the chimney he wanted was to his right, where there was a single set of footprints, going in and coming out, mostly filled in now but still visible.

He stepped his foot into the first clear footstep. It was only a little bigger than his shoe—must be Laurel's. "Sable's," he said aloud, correcting himself.

He'd seen her last week, down there on the first floor where they kept her. The hospital bed and white cabinet were the only things that made you think it wasn't an ordinary bedroom. That, and Sable lying in that bed.

"Get with it, kid," he'd whispered the last time he saw her. He'd give up the million bucks, if Sable would just come back.

The footsteps led behind a post to a chimney that ran up through the floor. He studied the bricks, but he didn't see a door like the one in the cellar.

Then he looked up. Oh, man, how simple. The silver bell hung from a blue ribbon, right over his head, so shiny it looked like a big star in the sky. *The star in the East*, Jacob suddenly thought. Now, what was that about, his head throwing up Sunday school stuff just as he was about to score?

The bell was high up—too high. He jumped, his fingers knocking the bell. It rang again and again as it swung on the ribbon.

I heard the bells on Christmas Day . . .

What the—how did that lame song get into his head? Too much church, that was for sure. When he was a millionaire, then no one could make him go. Of course, the girls in the Sunday school class would miss him. Maybe he'd stop by and show them what they were missing.

He watched the bell swing, listening to the *tang-tang* fade to *ting-a-ling*, to *tink*. Then, silence. Okay, that sucker was coming down. One big jump, one hard yank, and he'd have it.

Jacob backed up, ran, jumped, and . . . DING!

54

*T*hey made it home right before sundown.

Bethany checked her watch. Four-fifteen. *Joan should have the turkey in by now.* Hannah had to be fed, bathed, played with. And persuaded to go to bed early so they could rouse her for the late service.

She would do the same things with Sable—feed, bathe, play. But no matter how much they sang, talked, and joked with her, no matter how carefully they moved her limbs, exposed her to different touches, Sable would not be roused. Was the pine branch a sign? Or an accident?

Anthony pulled the snowmobile to a stop near the back porch. "Wonder where my mother is?"

"Probably had to run out," Kyle said. "You can never have enough stuffing, you know."

"I'll go and get Hannah settled into the playpen," Bethany told Kyle. "Then I'll help you and Anthony with Sable."

"Be quick. We'll need you to get her through the back door."

Bethany found Joan's note in the kitchen. "Whoops. That's not good news, Hannah. We might be eating Oreos for dessert tonight." She carried Hannah into the family room and set her in the playpen. "I have to hold the door open for Daddy and Anthony, so they can get Sable in. You stay right there."

Hannah got right to work, banging a toy truck with a block.

—∞∞∞—

The Dolans had given Sable the bell last Christmas. Jacob was creeped out when he read the message inside.

May God bless you, Laurel, for bringing us great joy. Kyle and Bethany

She wasn't Laurel, and she sure hadn't brought them great joy. But they had brought Sable back into their home anyway, taking care of her every day like she was a baby. How could they do that? Maybe the same way his mom kept at him, day in and out, to be good instead of being *the man*.

No, Jacob couldn't think about that. He had work to do. He had found a piece of paper hidden in the stem of the bell. He scurried down the stairs and flicked on the light in the second-floor hall so he could see it better.

J—you are beyond cool if you found this. Congrats and all that. Here's the account numbers, bank access codes, and password for each one. What you have to do—

"Hello, there." Cold metal jammed against Jacob's temple.

"Perfect timing." Another deep voice, but this one belonged to a woman.

"Wh-wh-what do you want?" Jacob's knees felt like string unraveling. The guy was hard-bodied, with the kind of muscles you get working the street instead of the gym. The woman's smile made Jacob think of a mean dog, the kind that gets its jaw on you and doesn't let go until it's chewed off your leg.

The woman got in his face. "Same thing you do. Sable's million dollars."

The guy pressed the gun harder. "You got a problem with that?"

Yeah, Jacob had a problem with that. But he could see that was the kind of dude who offed three losers before breakfast and forgot their names by lunch.

Jacob did not want to be one of those losers.

Bethany held the back door open while Kyle and Anthony carried Sable in through the porch. It was taking longer than they thought, but they had to be careful. Sable's bones were brittle from all those months asleep. Once they got her onto the back porch, Bethany unbuttoned Sable's parka and pulled it off while Kyle steadied her. Then Kyle and Anthony slowly walked her into the kitchen and down the back hall to the guest suite.

Bethany pulled the storm door shut, then the inside door. The wood around the latch was gouged. Did they do that just now, dragging Sable in? She'd have to worry about that later. She'd left Hannah alone for too long.

<hr />

Jacob lay facedown on the floor. The dog-faced woman had her foot on his back, her gun aimed at his head. The guy had disappeared downstairs but Jacob could hear here him coming back up.

"What are you doing with that thing?" the woman barked. Jacob strained, trying to see what *that thing* was, but the woman had his head pinned securely.

"We got a situation. They're all back. I figure this will buy us some insurance."

"We got the little man here. He can be our insurance."

"It'll take us a couple days to transfer the money out, then transfer again to break the trail. We're gonna have to buy ourselves some serious time," the guy said.

"Gotcha. Good solution, then."

What were they talking about? They were going to steal Jacob's million bucks, that much was sure. But if they weren't going to hold him hostage—*Oh, thank You, God, for that; maybe You are the man*—then what were they up to? What was this good solution the woman was talking about?

Jacob heard a whimper. A kitten, maybe? He strained again, pushing his face sideways to see what the man had that was a better solution than kidnapping him.

Oh, no. Not a kitten.

Hannah wasn't in her playpen.

Bethany ran out of the family room, checking up and down the front hall. The little imp must have climbed out. She was only nine months old, but the day before she had gotten up two stairs before they caught up with her.

"Hannah?" Bethany checked the dining room and living room. Back to the kitchen, even checking the pantry. Where was she? "Kyle!"

He was still in the guest suite, getting Sable to bed. He met her in the back hall. "Something up?"

"Do you have Hannah back there? I put her in the playpen and—"

His face drained of color. "No."

She pushed past him, up the back stairs.

Kyle ran upstairs behind her. "She couldn't have climbed out of the playpen. She can't even walk."

The back hall was empty. "I'll go to the front. You look in the back rooms."

"Got it."

Bethany hustled around the corner, into the front hall.

A mean-faced man held Hannah. A hefty woman pointed a gun at Jacob, who lay with his face on the floor. Without thinking, Bethany stepped over him, reaching for Hannah. "Give me my—"

Something smacked her in the eye. She tumbled backwards over Jacob, ending up on the floor next to him. She peered through a sudden rush of blood. The woman stood over her, her hand in a fist. Somewhere behind her, Bethany heard the *beep beep* of Kyle's cell phone.

"I wouldn't do that, Dolan." Still holding Hannah, the man took a gun out of his pocket and aimed it past Bethany. "Come out where I can see you."

Kyle helped her up. She pulled Jacob up with her, holding him with one hand while she pressed the other hand to her eyebrow to stop the blood.

"I've seen you before," Kyle said. "You came to the house. Bernard."

"Guilty as charged. Sorry I never thanked you for delivering my message."

The home invader, Bethany thought. What had he said to Kyle? *Next time won't be pretty.* Her stomach clenched. Was this next time?

"What do you want?" Kyle's voice was sharp, like a violin string pulled too taut.

"Cooperation," the man said.

"Give me the baby and I'll see you get anything you want," Kyle said.

"They want Sable's money," Jacob whispered.

"What?" Bethany asked.

"She has almost a million bucks. She wanted me to have it and left me a bunch of clues how to get it. I finally figured it all out. But they're trying to steal it from me."

"Shut up." Hailey raised the gun to Jacob's face. He slid behind Bethany.

The man—Bernard, Kyle had said—jiggled Hannah in his arm. The baby's gaze went to Bethany, then Kyle, but miraculously, she didn't cry out.

"Where's that kid that was with you, helping drag the girl into the house?"

"He's downstairs, in Sable's room," Kyle said.

Anthony's hearing is so acute, Bethany thought. Maybe he'd heard the noise and already called the police. But how? They had taken the phone out of the guest suite so it wouldn't disturb Sable.

"Okay, we're going down there," Bernard said. "I want to make sure he isn't going to give us any problems."

"Please let me carry my baby," Bethany said.

The man just laughed and motioned at the stairs.

They started down, Bethany and Jacob in the lead, then Kyle, followed by the woman with the gun. Bernard walked behind, with Hannah. Bethany's arms ached for her child. *Don't let this man drop her or hurt her or take her away from me, please, God.*

In the guest suite they found Sable propped in the recliner, still in her body cast. Anthony at least had had time to stick the tray in place so she wouldn't tumble out.

"That's her? The Lynde girl?" Bernard asked. "She used to be so hot . . . "

"Hey, this is an improvement," the woman said. "No more smart mouth."

Such cruelty—but what could Bethany expect from a woman who would put a gun to a young boy's head? More importantly, what could she expect from that Bernard, holding Hannah like an armful of laundry?

"Where is he, that skinny kid?" Bernard looked at Kyle.

Kyle shrugged. "Maybe he's gone outside to put the snowmobile in the garage."

"And left her hanging out of the chair like that? I doubt it." Bernard looked inside the closet, then the bathroom and sitting room. There was no sign of Anthony.

Bernard turned to the woman. "Go pack a bag for the baby. Lots of diapers. Three, maybe four days' worth."

"No!" Bethany gasped. Kyle stiffened at her side. He wouldn't let it go on much longer, she knew. But what could he do? It would be madness to go against a man with a gun.

Just as it would be madness to let them walk out of there with Hannah.

"Take the little mutt with you," Bernard said, motioning at Jacob. "Let him pack the stuff while you keep a lookout. Make it fast. I want out of here in the next three minutes."

Jacob walked slowly out of the room ahead of the woman.

"Please don't do this," Kyle said. "Let my wife take the baby. If you need a hostage of some sort, you can take me."

Hannah looked from Bethany to Kyle, then back. Her cheeks were crimson, her mouth crumpling. She was gearing up to scream.

"This little sweetheart is a whole lot more portable."

"I can't let you take her," Kyle said.

"No way you're gonna stop me, sucker."

Kyle lunged. Bernard took a quick side step, then slammed the gun against the side of Kyle's head. He fell to his knees, eyes wide in shock. Bernard hit him again.

"No!" Bethany screamed. Hannah howled, kicking frantically in Bernard's grasp.

Kyle tumbled sideways, his scalp pouring blood. Bethany pulled at him to get up, then realized it was safer to settle him against the wall. He rolled face first onto the floor. Bethany rolled him over.

"Da-da, da-da," Hannah babbled over and over. Bethany reached for her. Bernard warned her back with a wave of the gun and turned Hannah into his chest so she couldn't see.

A ragged cut slashed Kyle's forehead, and a lump was forming. Kyle moaned once, then went silent, his face a dreadful shade of gray. Bethany put her hand on his back, reassured to feel it rise and fall.

Hannah squirmed and fussed.

"Hannah. Daddy's all right. Please, be a good girl." Bethany pushed herself to smile, trying to get Hannah to keep eye contact.

"Mrs. Dolan, I don't want to hurt anyone here. But if I have to, I will. Now, listen carefully. This is how it's going to be." Bernard droned on about not calling the cops, about lying low while he and that hideous woman got their business done.

The word *days* battered inside Bethany's head. Three, maybe four endless days. How could Hannah endure being with those horrible people, separated from her parents for that long a time? She could choke or fall out of a window or just be left in her dirty diaper the whole time. Not fed. Not held. Not taken care of.

And what if it was too much trouble to return her when they didn't need her anymore?

This was all Sable's fault, this wave of trash washing out of her past. And she just sat in her chair, a lump of breathing, uncaring flesh. A biting anger rose again in Bethany. If anything happened to Hannah, how could she forgive Sable?

Hannah, our heart. Lord, help me.

Bethany looked at Sable, the child lost in darkness. The child she and Kyle had taken into their home.

Hannah our heart, Sable our child. Lord God, we are in Your hands.

The woman returned, her hand pinching Jacob's neck like a claw. She almost stumbled over Kyle. "What happened to Superman here?"

"I did him a favor. Beat the stupid out of his head."

"Okay. We're heading for the car to pack it up, me and the kid here."

"Make sure you get that seat for the baby, so we can strap her in. I'll be there in a minute—I need one more word with Mrs. Dolan."

"Want me to take the kid?"

"No. She's grown attached to me," Bernard said.

The woman laughed again, then shoved Jacob out the door ahead of her.

Bernard smiled down at Hannah and chucked her under the chin with his gun. It was the cruelest thing the man had done thus far.

Jacob was practically wetting his pants. He had never been so scared in his life. He'd seen what that guy Bernard had done to Mr. Dolan. Poor guy was collapsed on the floor, head cut open, face the color of dead leaves. Maybe Joan would come back right now, just as they crossed the yard and headed for the car. But what could she do against a gun?

Where had his stupid brother gone? He had been with the Dolans, but somehow he'd just disappeared. Then again, Anthony couldn't do anything against a gun either.

And neither could Jacob. He thought he was the man, but he was just a stupid kid. He used to daydream about taking some action, maybe down the corner. But the metal to his back was real, not a daydream. Who could save his backside now that he was really in the action, not in some video game but in real life, the part of life that was ugly and mean?

Oh, God. Please. I need You to be the man here. I sure can't be.

Bernard's gaze worked over Bethany, the line of her neck, the curve of her breasts, her hips, her legs. It was as if she stood naked before him.

"Please," she said. "Leave Hannah here. Take me instead."

Bernard licked his lips, tilted his head to the side, considering the offer.

"I beg you. I'll do anything."

"Anything?"

That's what she had promised God, wasn't it? Was this the *anything* He required?

She understood why Bernard wanted Hannah. Her presence would ensure their silence. A baby couldn't identify people and places. If he agreed to take Bethany, he'd probably have to kill her when he was done with whatever business Sable's money required. But what did it matter what Bernard did to her, if Hannah was safe?

"Absolutely. Just leave the baby here."

"Come here," he said. "Let me see what I'd be getting."

"Why don't you put the baby down? She's in the way." Making her voice like music. Playing for time.

Bernard kept his eyes locked on her as he lowered Hannah to the floor. She toppled sideways and lay near the foot of Sable's chair. *Don't react*, Bethany told herself. *The floor is carpeted; she won't have been hurt.* She heard a slurping noise, Hannah sucking on her fingers.

Music, she told herself. *Compose it; play it. Sell it.*

Bernard reached out and touched her face. It took her entire will not to recoil. An equally massive effort to lean into his touch and raise her eyes to his. He placed his palm against her throat, wrapping his fingers around her neck. He could end her life in an instant, she knew.

"A beautiful woman is like a fine wine. You may not get it often, but when you do, you drink it all up," Bernard said.

Bethany kept her head up, her eyes locked on his. What happened to her didn't matter, as long as Hannah was safe. Hannah and Kyle. *And please, God, Sable too.*

⸻⸙⸻

Light now, pouring in from the edges.

Light and voices.

You can't get away.

He was out there too. But so was . . .

. . . was . . .

. . . hope?

Maybe.

Maybe yes.

⸻⸙⸻

Bernard slid his hand down her throat, exploring the line of her collarbone. Farther down now, one hand cupping her breast. "Nice. Very nice." The other hand still clutching his gun.

Bethany's skin shrieked in protest, nerve endings beating out a protest that his hand was where it had no right to be. *Feel the music, not the fear,* Bethany told herself. *Feel the faith, not the doubt.*

She heard a clunk as he let the gun drop onto the tray of Sable's chair. Using both hands, Bernard pulled her closer and put his lips to hers, using his tongue to probe open her mouth. Bethany wanted to bite it off, spit it out. Instead, she let him kiss her while her hand drifted out, seeking out the gun.

Bernard broke it off suddenly, laughing as he pushed her away. "I'd love to swallow you whole, but my friend out there would castrate me." Bernard picked up Hannah. "Say good-bye to Mama."

The gun sat, a foot away, on Sable's tray.

"No," Bethany begged. "Please, no. I beg you, take me. I'll do whatever, give you whatever, just take me. Don't take my baby. Please."

"Ma ma ma ma," Hannah wailed at the top of her lungs.

⸻⸙⸻

Mamamamamama—

Forget Mama. Come to Papa, sweetness.

No!

CHILD.

Shadows burst into flames, flames into ash, a mighty wind, blowing *him* into the nothing he is.

She breathes. She hopes. She hears.

She sees.

Light now, blinding, golden, a wonderland.

MY CHILD.

Yes?

MY CHILD, COME OUT!

⸻

Hannah knew now that she was being taken, and she fought with every inch of her tiny body, crying over and over, "Ma Ma Ma . . . "

Bethany started forward.

"You know how fast I could snap this little snot's neck?"

Lord God, Bethany prayed.

"I'm not putting up with this, no way." Bernard slapped his hand over Hannah's mouth.

"Mama!"

Startled, Bernard let the baby slip from his arms. Bethany grabbed her before she hit the floor.

"Mamamamama." Not Hannah. A wild cry, almost insane in its sudden joy. Sable, eyes suddenly, astonishingly wide, crying *Mama*, over and over.

Bernard lunged for the gun. Sable's arm shot out straight, as if she were gripped by a seizure, knocking the gun off the tray. Bethany kicked it under the bed. Bernard shifted toward the bed, then changed direction, going back for Hannah.

Bethany shoved Hannah into the chair with Sable, then blocked them with her body. She raised her fists—ridiculous, she knew, but she'd do anything to stop this man.

Bernard grabbed her wrist and jammed it backward, sending pain shooting up her arm. She drove her shoulder into him, and he staggered backward.

The bathroom door opened, banging the back of Bernard's head.

Anthony charged out, swinging a paint bucket, slamming it against the man's head. Anthony swung again, getting in another blow before the bucket popped open and red paint splashed everywhere.

Bernard fell to his knees. Anthony jumped on him and pressed his knee to the man's throat. Bernard instinctively turned his shoulders, but Bethany stomped his arm before he could grab Anthony. She jumped onto Bernard's legs, helping Anthony pin him.

Sirens rose from outside. A cyclone of sounds spun Bethany—Bernard's cursing, Anthony's panting, Hannah's wailing, the sirens, closer now. Over it all, that impossible, bizarre, miraculous voice.

Sable crying, "Mama."

55

W hat happened?" Kyle asked.

"Hush. We'll talk about it tomorrow." Bethany tucked the quilt under his shoulders.

The painkillers had finally kicked in, and his trembling—as much from adrenaline as discomfort—was subsiding. Kyle should have stayed overnight at the hospital, but even Nora didn't put up much of a fight when he had insisted on coming back home.

The night had seemed like an eternity and a flash. *Thank You, God, for Anthony,* Bethany prayed. *And thank You, blessed Lord, for Sable.*

Anthony had heard the intruders, slipped out the bathroom window, and called the police from Kyle's car phone. He went back to help, grabbing a bucket of paint from the garage to use as a weapon. Once they subdued Bernard, Bethany and Anthony sat on him until the police burst in.

Later, the police told Bethany that they had found Jacob on the side of the road, sitting with his head in his hands.

"Don't cry, son," the policeman had said.

"You blind, man? I ain't crying," Jacob had yelled. "I'm praying!"

No one knew the cruel woman's name or where she had disappeared to.

Joan Martinez arrived home with the whipping cream, astonished to see all the cruisers, then terrified by the ambulance. She made sure her sons were fine, then assumed care of Hannah, not leaving her side for a second while Bethany went to the hospital with Kyle. Jacob sat with his mother and talked nonstop, Joan later told Bethany.

Harry Stevens raced up from Boston and stalked the property for hours to ensure that no more intruders were lurking.

Anthony got Sable into bed. She didn't speak another word, but her eyes locked on his, so clear, Anthony said, that he knew they saw better days coming. He held her hand and sang her to sleep.

Bethany couldn't sleep. Somehow, the adrenaline that had purged her body of fear had pumped her with a tremendous energy.

Kyle had thrown the quilt off, as she knew he would. She felt his skin, made sure he was warm enough, then kissed him and left him to sleep.

In the nursery, Hannah slept soundlessly. Bethany put her lips to the baby's cheek, breathing in her innocence.

Joan slept in the guest room. Bethany could hear Anthony in his room, humming in his sleep. She didn't find Jacob until she got to Sable's room. He was asleep in the cardiac chair, his head down on the tray.

Bethany was about to turn Sable, but before she could pull the sheet, Sable slowly turned herself, going from her back onto her side. Then she brought her arms up to her face—the same prayerlike pose Bethany had just seen Hannah in.

Bethany's skin tingled and her muscles burned. *Not adrenaline*, now, she knew. She was coming alive. Coming alive after being so frightened and so angry and so far from God for so long. She wanted to run up to Thor's Falls and shout with the wind and water coming off the mountain. Or bang on the piano until the music forced the sun to come up early because it just had to burst into song with her. Or climb the highest mountain, lift her arms up to heaven, and then climb a higher mountain and lift her arms again.

I've got time, she told herself. *I will do it all in its time. In God's time.*

She went to the porch, slipped on her boots, and went outside. There was one thing that had to be done tonight.

It didn't take long.

When Bethany finished, she made one last round of her home—kissing Kyle, kissing Hannah, blessing Joan, blessing Anthony, hugging Jacob who still was head down but peaceful in the cardiac chair.

Then she slipped into bed with Sable. Bethany put her arm over the girl's shoulder, kissed her cheek, then sang herself to sleep.

I will bring a light to your darkest night.
Because I will love you forever and I'll be here, with you, for always.

The wind blew on, a gust of laughter and music and joy.

Every corner clean, every darkness bright.

No hiding now. No need to.

For how long?

FOR ALWAYS, CHILD.

"Ma-mum-morn-morning."

Bethany opened her eyes. Sable smiled, only half of her face able to get there, but exquisitely beautiful just the same.

"Good morning to you. Though it's still the middle of the night." Bethany brushed the hair off Sable's cheek. "Sleep well?"

Sable closed her eyes. "B-b-bad," she finally said. "Till . . . you . . . up . . . me . . . waked . . . "

"Until I woke you?"

It took great effort, but Sable nodded. "You . . . called . . . child, come out."

Child, come out.

Bethany had been called like that, too, in the middle of a storm of music and self-doubt and loneliness. "Someone greater than I called you, Sable," she said. "But I'm so glad you came out. So glad you came home."

"F-f-for . . . " The struggle to find words was exhausting Sable.

"For always?" Bethany prompted.

"Yes."

Bethany tightened her arms around Sable. "Yes. For always."

Her head dropped against Bethany's shoulder. Within a minute, her breathing slowed and she slept. Bethany got up, made one more set of rounds of kissing and blessing, then went back to Sable's room.

She flipped the light switch on. The tree that she had decorated an hour earlier glittered with white sparkles. Bethany left the lights on—she wanted them to be the first thing Sable saw when she woke up again.

As it turned out, the lights were the second thing that Sable saw. The first thing she opened her eyes to was Bethany, asleep next to her on the bed.

Holding her hand as if she'd never let it go.

When I awake,

I am still with you.

(PSALM 139:18)

FOR ALWAYS
(Hannah's Lullaby)

When the birds of spring come alive to sing
in their golden wonderland,
I will dance with you under skies of blue.
Because I will love you forever and I'll be here, with you,
For always.

And when geese fly by in the autumn sky
gliding above the earth in her lunar glow,
I will bring a light to your darkest night.
Because I will love you forever and I'll be here, with you,
For always.

When you're tucked in bed and all your prayers are said,
and you wait with joy for a brand-new day,
close your eyes and sleep, dream of wishes sweet
Because I will love you forever and I'll be here, with you,
For always.

Words and music by Victoria James © 2003
Victoriajamesmusic.com

ACKNOWLEDGMENTS

Many thanks to Janice McDonald Freeman for a quiet place to write and medical advice; to Mary Potter for lending her granddaughters; to Beth Confrancisco for a steadying hand; to Marjorie Overhiser for information on psychological disorders; to the Rev. David Rinas for guidance on pastoral counseling; to my pastor, the Rev. Richard Woodward, for faithful encouragement; to Victoria James for writing Hannah's Lullaby; and to Debi Bailey, Kate Bergquist, David Daniel, Judith Loose, Beverly McCoy, Joan Pena, Robert Sanchez, and Patricia Thorpe for enduring all the early efforts and not losing faith. Much gratitude to a loving and generous Lord who has blessed me with an inspirational, patient, and wise editor in Jenny Baumgartner, and with an agent who knows my writing better than I do in Lee Hough.

ABOUT THE AUTHOR

𝒦athryn Mackel is the acclaimed author of *Can of Worms* and other novels for middle readers published by Putnam, Avon, and HarperCollins. She is a produced screenwriter, having worked for Disney, Fox, and Showtime and was on the screenwriting team for *Left Behind: The Movie*, Frank Peretti's *Hangman's Curse*, and Bill Myers's *Wally McDoogle: My Life as a Smashed Burrito*. She serves as an instructor and member of the editorial board of the Jerry B. Jenkins Christian Writers Guild. Her second novel with WestBow Press will be available everywhere March 2005.

HEAR "FOR ALWAYS," HANNAH'S LULLABY,

AND SEE THE VIDEO TRAILER FOR

The Surrogate AT

WWW.WESTBOWPRESS.COM.